DIANA PALMER

WYOMING HOMECOMING

HQN

ISBN-13: 978-1-335-52909-1

Wyoming Homecoming

HQN
22 Adelaide St. West, 41st Floor
Toronto, Ontario M5H 4E3, Canada
www.Harlequin.com

Printed in U.S.A.

To Dr. Mark McCracken, who saw me safely through COVID pneumonia at the Northeast Georgia Medical Center in Gainesville, GA, last year. Thank you so much!

WYOMING
HOMECOMING

CHAPTER ONE

The funeral home was crowded. Charlie Butler was well-known in Catelow, Wyoming, and he owned a considerable amount of property outside the city limits, in greater Carne County. In fact, his land adjoined a small ranch that Cody Banks had purchased the year before. He'd been reluctant to leave his rented home in the city limits, but he was tired of people. Cody wanted room to breathe. Most of all, he wanted a refuge from his job.

He loved being sheriff of the county. This was his second term, and no serious opponents had jumped up to run against him in the last election. Apparently he was doing a good enough job to satisfy his critics as well as the handful of people he called friends.

He was alone, standing apart from the crowd in his uniform. He'd come to pay his respects. His late wife, Deborah, had been distantly related to Butler by marriage. So he was sort of family. He'd been fond of the old man. He'd stopped by to see him often and made sure he had heat and groceries and whatever he needed while he fought the long battle with cancer that finally claimed him. Cody had a deputy in a squad car standing by to lead the funeral procession to the cemetery, after the service.

He glanced toward the closed casket where a woman was standing with a little girl. He knew them. He winced. It had been a long time. Almost six years ago. He'd stood in the parking lot at the Denver hospital where his beloved wife, a doctor, had just died, and accused the woman and the child of killing her. The child had been sick with a virus that was deadly to a handful of people, his wife included. It hadn't been until days later that he'd learned the woman and child had been at a funeral home to arrange services for her brother and sister-in-law, who'd been killed in an accident. His wife, Deborah, a distant cousin to the deceased woman, had gone to the funeral home to see them and express her sorrow. It was there that she'd contracted the fatal virus, and not from the woman or child, but from a funeral attendant who later also died of exposure to it.

Cody had been out of his mind with grief. They'd only been married for two years, much of it spent apart while his wife pursued her career as a neurologist in Denver, at a famous hospital. She'd commuted and only managed to get home one or two days a month, sometimes not even that much. It had been largely a long-distance relationship, but Cody had loved her so much. Too much. He thought his life was over when she died. But he picked himself up, thanks to his cousin, Bart Riddle, a local rancher, and he'd gone on. It had been hard. He hadn't been thinking clearly, then. He'd lashed out at the most innocent people. The woman and child, standing by the casket.

When he'd walked in the door, both of them had looked hunted. The woman had taken the little girl by the hand and walked her back to the restroom. By the time they returned, Cody was at the other end of the room talking to one of the city council members. They watched him, almost fearfully. It disturbed him to see how badly he'd wounded them, so badly that they wouldn't come near him all these years later. He wanted to apologize, to explain. He couldn't even get close enough to do that.

She was elegant, he thought. Not beautiful. Not really pretty, but she had a pretty figure and a creamy complexion. Her long, silvery-blond hair fell to her waist in back, neatly styled. Her eyes were a pale, almost silver gray. She was dressed in a suit, very conservative. Well, she worked for attorneys in Denver, he recalled, probably she had to dress to maintain the dignity of her office. She was a paralegal. He'd often wondered why she didn't go on to law school. But his cousin, Bart Riddle, had said that there was no money for the training. And besides that, she was reluctant to leave her little niece Lucinda in someone else's care at night. She loved the child dearly, because of the fact that the little girl was the last family she had on earth and the last link she had with her late brother.

It had touched him, what Bart said. He had cousins, at least, although his parents were long dead. Abigail Brennan had nobody; just little Lucinda, who was nine now. Technically, he supposed, he and Abigail were related by marriage. Debby's sister-in-law's second marriage, after her husband's death, was to Abigail's brother Lawrence, and both Lawrence and Mary had been killed in a wreck just days before his wife Deborah died. Mary had been Debby's former sister-in-law, which was why Debby had gone to the funeral home in the first place.

"Why is the casket closed?" Cody asked his cousin Bart, who'd just joined him near the potted plant at the other end of the big viewing room.

"He died of cancer," Bart reminded him. "He said he didn't want a bunch of yahoos staring down at him in his casket, so he put in his will that he wanted it closed." He frowned. "Why are you standing over here all by yourself?"

Cody sighed. "Because when I walked over to Abigail to apologize for what I said to her six years ago, she took the little girl by the hand and almost ran to the restroom."

Bart, who knew the background of these people very well, just nodded. "Shame," he said quietly. "I mean, she and the child have nobody now. Her brother raised her, you know. Their parents died together in a car crash when she was still in school. Ironic, that her brother and his wife died together in a similar manner. Charlie, there," he indicated the casket with a nod of his head, "was the last living relative she had, besides Lucy." He laughed softly. "And he wasn't much of that, either. She sent him cards on his birthday and at Christmas. Would have come to see him, but he didn't want the kid around." He indicated Lucinda, who was pretty, with the same silvery-blond hair as her aunt. "He never liked children. It's a shame. She's a nice child, from all accounts. Polite and sweet and doesn't talk back."

"I know a lot of nice, sweet people who get on the internet and become Frankenstein's monster with a keyboard at their fingertips," Cody mused.

"And isn't that the truth?"

"What's Abigail going to do with Charlie's place?" he asked.

"No idea. She works in Denver. That's an impossibly long commute."

"It's a good ranch. Clean water, lots of pasture, and I think he still had a pretty decent herd of Black Angus cattle, despite the downturn in the economy."

Bart was staring at him. "What if she came to work here? J.C. Calhoun's wife, Colie, is pregnant with their second child and she really wants to stay home with her kids. God knows Calhoun makes enough, working on Ren Colter's ranch as his head of security. That means her job will be up for grabs, and there aren't that many paralegals in a town the size of Catelow."

Cody winced. "I don't think she wants to be any closer to me than Denver," he said quietly. "I wish I could take back all the things I said to her that day. I scared her. I scared the little girl, too," he added sadly. "I love kids. It hurts me, remembering how they both backed away from me and ran for her car." His eyes closed. "Dear God, the things we do that come back to haunt us."

Bart laid a hand on his shoulder. "We can't change the past," he said. "We can only deal with what we have right now."

Cody's eyes opened, dark and somber. "I reckon." His face was hard. "Six years," he said. "And I still mourn her. I blamed everybody except myself. If I'd insisted, she might have come back here to live and got a job at our community hospital."

Bart didn't remind his friend that Deborah had been aggressively ambitious. She wanted to be the best in her field, and that was only possible working at a big hospital, where such opportunities were available. He knew, as Cody never seemed to, that Deborah was never the sort of woman who'd want to cook and clean and have babies. She'd even told Cody, when they first married, that children were out of the question for the immediate future. Cody hadn't seemed to mind. He was obsessed with Deborah, so much in love that if she'd said she wanted to go to the moon, Cody would have been looking at ways to build a spaceship. Obsessive love like that seemed to Bart to be destructive. There was an old saying about relationships, he mused, that one kissed while the other turned the cheek. Cody was in love. Deborah was affectionate, but her true love was her work, not her husband. In the two years they'd been married, they'd spent far more time apart than together. Cody saw what he wanted to see.

"I'm going to say hello to Abby," Bart said, hesitating.

"Go ahead," Cody replied. "I'll be standing here, holding up the wall."

Bart's eyebrows lifted in a silent question.

"If I start over there, she'll find a way to get out of the room," Cody replied quietly. "It's all right. I won't be here much longer. I was fond of Charlie and I wanted to pay my respects. I didn't come to terrorize the women and children."

The last remark sounded bitter, Bart thought as he walked toward Abigail. Cody didn't realize that he was just as intimidating to men as he was to Abby and Lucinda. He did a hard job and it had made him hard. He wasn't the easygoing, friendly man who'd attracted Deborah during a visit eight years ago. The Cody of today would have sent Deborah in search of a man who was more easily controlled. He laughed to himself. He wondered if Cody realized how much he'd changed since he'd been sheriff. He truly doubted it.

Abigail was saying goodbye to an elderly woman who'd gone to school with Charlie.

The old woman smiled at her and held on to her hand. "You should come back home," she said, smiling down at Lucinda as well. "Small towns are the best place to raise a child. And besides, Colie's pregnant and she's going to resign from her job at the attorney's office. They'll need a paralegal." Her eyebrows lifted. "Charlie has a nice ranch, with a house he'd just renovated, and there's kittens in the barn."

"Oh, boy, Aunt Abby. Kittens!" Lucinda exclaimed, and her whole little face lit up.

Across the room, Cody saw that delight on the child's face and felt a weight on his shoulders like a concrete slab. He'd wanted children so badly. But Deborah had said they had years to think about kids. She didn't really like them. Cody did. But he loved Deborah enough to sacrifice his own hungers. Now, looking at Lucinda's joy, bright and shining, he felt the hunger again, deeper and stronger.

"You look well," Bart told Abby, smiling as he hugged her gently. "How do you like Denver?"

She made a face. "I hate it. Lucinda's in a school she doesn't like, and we live in a poky little apartment on the top floor with a drunk next door and a drummer on the next floor." She leaned toward him. "He likes to practice at two in the morning!" She laughed.

Cody saw that laughter in her face and felt as if he was smothering to death in a misery of his own making. He turned and went out the door. It hurt, to see the woman and child so happy, when they looked at him as if he'd committed all seven deadly sins and was bent on retribution.

Abby watched him go and she relaxed. "Why was he here?" she asked bluntly.

"He and Charlie were friends as well as third cousins," Bart told her. "They played chess together. Cody got tired of town living, so he bought Dan Harlow's place, the ranch that adjoins Charlie's property."

She looked hunted all over again.

"Don't," Bart said gently. "He's sorry for what he said to you and Lucy," he added. "He said he'd give anything to take it back."

She averted her eyes. She didn't have to tell Bart about her past, he knew. Everybody in Catelow knew everybody's business. It was a big, sprawling family, and there were no secrets in it. Abby's father had been a hopeless drunk. He'd gambled away everything her mother had, and there had been a good deal of money when they'd married. He'd turned to strong drink when his luck at the gaming tables turned, and he'd been brutal. Abby and her mother wore concealing garments so that the bruises wouldn't show. It was almost a relief when the old man died, but he took Abby's mother with him. Her older brother, Lawrence, had come to get her and take her to live with him and Mary. They both loved her dearly, and she'd been grateful for a home, even if it was in Denver.

Abby got a job with Lawrence's firm as an administrative assistant just out of high school and immediately enrolled in night classes to get her paralegal training. Abby hated having Lawrence responsible for that training. As intelligent as Abby was, she couldn't qualify for any scholarships that would have paid her way. Private schools were expensive. She hadn't even had her parents' home after their deaths. It was mortgaged to the hilt. Lawrence, her brother, had sold it when he took Abby to live with him and his wife Mary.

She loved her brother and Mary, but she felt she was a burden on them, with Mary pregnant and a bedroom needed to convert to a nursery. They protested; they loved her and she was welcome, they emphasized. But she was determined to go, to make room for the baby they'd anticipated for so long. So, she moved into a small apartment. Lucinda was born soon afterward. Abby had loved her from the start, finding excuses to visit, so that she could hold the little girl. She was as fascinated with her as her doting parents.

Then had come the car crash and the agony of the funeral. Deborah had come to pay her respects to her first cousin, Mary, and contracted the fatal virus from one of the attendants, who also died of it. Deborah had been admitted to the hospital with a high fever and Abby had gone from the funeral home where Lawrence and Mary were together in a viewing room to the hospital to see about Deborah.

Cody had come across them in the parking lot, after being told by an aide that Deborah had gone to the funeral home and caught the virus from somebody there. He'd assumed it was the little girl, because she was feverish and sick. Abby had stopped by the emergency room to let a resident look at Lucy and give her something for the complications that had presented themselves. She'd given up the idea of visiting Deborah, with Lucy so sick, and had actually been on her way to the car to take Lucy to Lawrence's apartment where a friend would take care of the little girl while Abby came back to see Deborah.

That was when Cody had encountered them in the parking lot and raged at them out of his grief.

Abby shivered, just at the memory of his unbridled rage. She was afraid of men anyway. That experience had put a nail in the coffin of her desire to ever get married. First her father, then Cody. Men frightened her in a rage, and she'd rarely seen her father any other way. She'd stay single and raise Lucy and never get involved with a man, she decided.

"Hey, it's okay, he's gone outside," Bart said softly, noting Abby's expression.

She swallowed. "You think you can get over things. But sometimes, you just can't."

"Are you okay, Aunt Abby?" Lucy asked softly, catching one of her aunt's hands in her own. She had Lawrence's eyes, pale blue and piercing, and full of compassion.

Abby smiled in spite of herself. "I'm okay, honey," she replied. "Really."

Lucy sighed. "I'm hungry."

Abby realized then that they hadn't even had breakfast. There was still the funeral service and the graveside ceremony to get through. "It will be just a little while, okay?" she asked.

Lucy smiled up at her. "Okay," she said.

She was an easy child, eager to please, loving, industrious and gentle. The school she went to in Denver was a hotbed of violence, usually contained, often not. The principal had become used to seeing Abby in her office about various problems Lucy encountered in the course of a week. The classrooms were dangerous. Abby said so. The principal just sighed. She had political considerations to weigh her down and there was very little she could do. She apologized, and sympathized, but Abby saw that nothing would ever change. Lucy was growing more frightened by the day. It was a bad neighborhood. It was also all Abby could afford. Lawrence and Mary's apartment had been leased soon after Lawrence died, and the landlord immediately filled the space with a new family, giving Abby only a few days to clean everything out, save the most valuable mementos, and find a new place to live. On her salary, she did the best she could. It wasn't enough.

She wrapped her arms around herself. "I'd love to come back here and live. Except he's here," she added bitterly.

"Abby, you won't have to see him unless you want to," he said, aware of Lucinda's rapt attention. "He knows how badly he frightened you. He won't come near you. Case in point," he added, nodding toward the door where Cody had left.

She drew in a long breath. Her pale eyes were old with sorrow. "I hate my job. I hate where we live. I hate having to practically live at the school, complaining in the principal's office about harassment, just to keep Lucy safe," she added bitterly. "The school has two separate gangs who hate each other, and violence breaks out almost every week."

"Then come home," Bart said simply. He smiled. "I'll do anything I can for both of you," he added. "It will be an absolute joy to have relatives around. Besides Cody, I mean," he added with a grimace. "And I never see him except at business meetings or when somebody dies."

She smiled at him. "You're a nice cousin, even if you're only a relative by marriage," she said.

Lucy laid her head on his shoulder with a sigh. "You're nice, Cousin Bart," she murmured.

He chuckled. "So are you, precious," he replied, dropping a kiss on her blond head.

"You should have married and had kids," Abby said gently, noting his fondness for her niece.

"I tried." He sighed. "I have no luck at all finding women who want to live on a poky ranch in a small town."

"It's not poky," she argued. "And you're one of the nicest men I know."

"With all due respect, Pockets, I'm about the only man you know."

She laughed. "I'd forgotten that you gave me that awful nickname."

"You were forever sticking things in your pockets when we were Lucy's age and in school together. It was a natural assumption," he said with a grin. "So. Coming home?"

She drew in a long breath and looked worriedly at the front door. She got glimpses of a sheriff's uniform just beyond it.

"You'll be safe here," Bart persisted. "So will Lucy. You won't find any violence in our local schools. Honest. And there are some very nice people at the law office."

"They probably have a whole list of paralegals who'll want that job once it opens up."

"Tomorrow I'll take you over there and introduce you," he said.

She looked at Lucy, who was smiling and happier even at a funeral than she'd been at their apartment in Denver. The school there was so dangerous, and getting worse by the day. A teacher had been assaulted right in her own classroom, and something even worse had happened to a young girl, just a little older than Lucy.

"Okay," she said.

Bart laughed. "Okay."

The funeral service was nice, but it brought back terrible memories. Her parents had been buried in Catelow. She'd hated and feared her father, but she'd loved her mother. She still missed her. Lawrence and Mary's funeral had been in Denver and they were buried there. She'd asked Lawrence about that once, at their parents' funeral. He'd said that he had all he ever wanted of Catelow and didn't want to return, even in a pine box. So Abby had honored that wish.

Still, the funeral brought back the sorrow and anguish of losing both Lawrence and Mary all at once. Little Lucy seemed to sense that feeling of loss. She slid her hand into Abby's and squeezed it as the congregation rose to sing "Amazing Grace." Tears rolled down Abby's cheeks, and not just for her late cousin. She wept for her whole family, almost all gone, except for the precious child beside her, holding her hand, and her cousin, Bart.

She had a tissue in the hand Lucy wasn't holding. She dabbed at her eyes. Her cousin, Charlie Butler, who'd been in such terrible pain, was surely in a better place. So were Lawrence and Mary, even her parents. But she was left to take care of Lucy and going back to Denver seemed a terrible prospect. Her cousin had left her a prosperous ranch. The attorneys had told her that, even before the reading of the will, which would come later. It was a surprise. She knew that the late Mr. Butler was also a relative by marriage to Cody Banks. It would have been more natural to leave it to him. But he hadn't. She wondered why, but chances were that she'd never find out.

Now she had to decide what she was going to do. Bart had mentioned taking her to see the lead attorney at the law firm where Colie Calhoun worked. She supposed it wouldn't hurt to at least apply for the job. If she got it, she and Lucy could live at the ranch and she could commute. She had a nice little car that got good gas mileage and she could get Lucy into the same grammar school where she'd gone herself many years ago. She knew most of the older families in the area. It would truly be like coming home.

They buried the old gentleman in the family plot, which was only three gravestones down from Abby's mother and father. After the very brief service she and Lucy went to stand over them. It seemed unreal somehow to look down on the carved name and realize that her family was buried under them.

Lucy held her hand again. "That's your mama and daddy, isn't it, Aunt Abby?" she asked softly.

Abby nodded. Her throat felt full of pincushions. "And your grandparents, my darling."

Lucy sighed. "So now I don't have grandparents at all. Mama's mother died when she was little like me, and Grandaddy died just after that. But I still have you, Aunt Abby," she said.

"And I still have you." Abby smiled down at her.

A tall man in a sheriff's uniform watched them from a distance. He could feel the sadness. Abby hadn't had an easy life, even as a child. Everybody knew her father had been brutal to his wife and daughter. It was no wonder she was wary of men. After what he'd done to her in the parking lot so long ago, she'd probably decided that all men were lunatics and she was better off without one.

His eyes went to the child holding her hand so tightly. His teeth ground together. He turned away, sickened by the memory of his own behavior. He'd have given a lot to go back and change what had happened. It was too late now.

The day after the funeral, Bart came by the motel where Abby and Lucy were staying to take her to meet the attorneys at the law firm where Colie Calhoun worked. Lucy went along, left to sit in the waiting room while her aunt discussed a possible job.

The eldest partner in the law firm, James Owens, was friendly and kind, married and with three grandchildren. He liked what he'd already heard about Abigail's paralegal abilities. Abby didn't know that Bart had asked Colie to put in a good word for Abby at the law office.

"We can always use a paralegal," Owens told her. "And

we don't have anyone with actual experience who's applied. If you want the job, we'd love to have you." He went on to mention salary and benefits. "There's also a nice rental house going spare—"

"One of my cousins just died and left me a ranch," she interrupted with a sad smile. "I hear he's got a good manager and nice help, so all I'll have to do is stand back and let them do what they do best. But I'm still going to work," she added. "I'm not a stay-at-home person. Besides, my little niece lives with me. I'll have to get her enrolled in school here." She grimaced. There was another worry, what to do with Lucy between the time school let out and Abby got home.

"Your ranch manager is Don Blalock," he told her. "His wife, Maisie, has a little girl just about Lucy's age and she'll go to the same school. I'll bet you can arrange something there. Maisie is a sweet woman."

Abby let out a sigh and smiled. "I was so worried when I came up here. Life in Denver...well, Lucy's school is dangerous, and I'm not happy where we have to live. I'm sorry to lose my cousin, but it's like a miracle that he left his place to me. It's a whole new life opening up for Lucy and me."

"You'll like living here again."

Her face tautened. She grimaced. "You know about my father...?"

He nodded. "It's a small town. We know everything. But that was long ago. Things will be very different now." He smiled. "If you want the job, we'll expect you Monday at eight thirty."

"I'll be here Monday at eight thirty. Thanks very much, Mr. Owens."

"You're most welcome. And by the way, we were handling your late cousin's legal business, including his will. We'll have the reading of it tomorrow at the ranch if that suits you. About ten in the morning?"

"That would be very nice."

"You could move in now if you wanted to," he added.

She smiled. "We'll wait for the will to be read," she said softly. "It's going to be a difficult time for the people who work for him. I want to do things by the book."

He smiled back. "Then that's fine. One of us will be out there tomorrow for the legal formalities."

Abby shook hands and went to get her niece from the waiting room. One of the administrative assistants had given her a soft drink.

She smiled at Abby. "Hi. I'm Marie, one of Colie's friends. I came to replace her best friend, Lucy, who used to work with her, but Lucy and her husband moved up to Billings. Welcome to the firm!"

"How did you know?" Abby laughed.

"I happened to be walking past Mr. Owens's office just now." She grinned. "You'll love it here. The attorneys are all nice people and great to work for."

"I'm very grateful to have found a job so quickly." She glanced down at Lucy. "We hated living in Denver."

"I have a son just about Lucy's age," came the reply. "The schools here are wonderful, and she's going to love it."

"At least I won't have to be in the principal's office begging for protection for her," Abby said on a sigh. She shook her head. "Schools have changed a lot since I was in grammar school."

"Tell me about it!"

"I'll see you Monday, then."

"See you." She grinned at them. "My Matt's having a birthday party next month. Lucy's going on the guest list, too! I bake my own cakes and make homemade ice cream."

"Oh, boy," Lucy said.

"You can come, too," Marie added, wiggling her eyebrows.

"I have a separate table for the mommies so we can all have treats while the kids do."

Abby laughed. "Now I've got to come! I love cake and ice cream."

"Me, too!" Lucy enthused.

"I'll see you Monday, then," Marie said. "Bye, Lucy. It was nice to meet you both."

"Nice to meet you, too," Abby and Lucy chorused.

She and Lucy drove out to the ranch the next morning. It was out in the country, in a stand of lodgepole pines and aspen trees, with the sharp outline of the Tetons far in the distance. The ranch was in a valley with a silvery stream running through it. Autumn was in full glorious display, and the trees were red and gold and the air just nippy enough to make a jacket comfortable. Probably there were trout in that pretty stream, Abby thought. She was an avid fisherwoman, though mainly of the cane pole and bait variety, but she wouldn't mind learning how to use a rod and reel. In fact, she and Lucy could learn together.

It was a very big ranch. It seemed a long time before they got to the main ranch house, sitting apart from a scattering of buildings. One looked like an equipment shed. The other two were, most likely, a stable and a barn. The fences were relatively new and seemed sturdy enough. The pastures were full of black cattle. Black Angus, Abby recalled.

She pulled up at the front door. The house was rustic, but elegant, basically a huge two-storied cabin, with a long, wide front porch. There was a swing and a few rocking chairs. The steps were firm. The house had been recently stained, because it was a bright dark mahogany color.

She got herself and Lucy out, a little concerned because the people who lived and worked here might not like an outsider taking over the operation.

But as she watched, the front door opened and a large, smiling woman with gray hair in a bun and a colorful apron on came out onto the porch.

"Abigail Brennan, as I live and breathe! How lovely to see you again!"

Abby let out the breath she'd been holding. "Hannah," she laughed, and ran to hug the older woman, who'd been a close friend of her mother's all those long years ago.

"And who's this?" Hannah asked, bending down as little Lucy came onto the porch, smiling.

"I'm Lucy," she said shyly.

"I'm Hannah. Welcome to the Circle B Ranch!"

CHAPTER TWO

The arrival of the visitors hadn't gone unnoticed. It was late afternoon, and some of the men were just coming in from the vast reaches of the ranch where they were checking on the cattle. The ranch foreman, Don Blalock, was one of them.

He was a tall, lanky man with a quiet demeanor and a kind smile. He tipped his hat as he came into the kitchen, where Abby was having coffee.

She got up to shake hands. "I've inherited the ranch from my great-uncle," she said in her soft voice, and she smiled. "I'm a paralegal. All I know about cattle is that they taste great in stews." She pursed her lips as he seemed torn between laughter and horror. "My plan is to sit back and let you guys do what you do. I doubt very seriously if my great-uncle was much of a hands-on person in recent months, considering how sick he was," she added. "So if we haven't had to file for bankruptcy, it's obvious that you know what you're doing. I'd like all of you to stay on."

He looked as if a great weight had been lifted off his shoulders. "Ma'am," he said quietly, "you don't know how much we're all going to appreciate that. Ranching jobs are thin on the ground right now, and this ranch, along with a few others, is pretty much the local economy. If it closed down, some of us would never find work again, especially a couple of my older hands. They're great at carpentry and odd jobs, but they'd never be able to hold down anything more demanding."

She smiled. "I'm sure there's enough to keep them busy, so that's not going to be a concern. Depending on how the economy goes, we may be able to add on some Christmas bonuses. I'm not promising," she added quickly. "But I'll do what I can."

"Thanks."

"Sit down for a minute and have coffee," Abby invited.

"I've just now brewed a new pot," Hannah commented, and she commenced to pour him a cup.

"I like cattle," Lucy piped up, smiling as she went back to eating the peanut butter sandwich Hannah was feeding her.

"I like them myself," Don said, smiling back.

"I'm going to work for Mr. Owens as a paralegal," she said, sipping coffee. "He mentioned that you and your wife Maisie have a little girl about Lucy's age, and that Maisie might be willing to let Lucy ride with them back and forth to school," she began.

"Indeed she would," he said. He gave her a long look. "And I'll warn you, if you try to offer to pay her for it, I'll pour my coffee down the sink drain and quit on the spot."

It took her a few seconds to get it and she burst out laughing. "Okay, then. Thanks."

"We live in a small community," Don commented. "So we all look out for each other."

"I remember," she replied. She sighed, pushing back the bad memories. "I'll need to go over the books with you sometime," she added. "I have no idea what sort of expenses we have or how we pay them, or who we owe…" She threw up her hands. "I can manage money very well. In fact, Lucy and I lived on next to nothing in Denver, but there are things I need to know."

"Miss Brennan, you don't have to work," he told her, tongue-in-cheek. "Mr. Butler runs a purebred herd here. Or did. It's worth a small fortune. We have herd sires that are very lucrative, and we sell off a prime crop of calves every fall."

"Oh, I do have to work," she replied with a smile. "I'm not the type of person who can just sit around. I love my job."

He looked at her with new respect. "I love mine, too. Thanks for letting me keep it. Me, and the crew."

"Tell them they have job security until I die," she promised. "And I'll try not to do it anytime soon." She sighed. "I'll miss my great-uncle," she added. "Except for Lucy he was the last living relative I had."

"Maisie and I will share ours with you," he said. "Between us we have about fifteen nieces and nephews, and any number of in-laws. It's a challenge to squeeze them all into the house when we have parties," he chuckled.

"I may take you up on that. It sounds like great fun."

"We have all sorts of gatherings in town, too," he added. "There are charity dinners, dances, and we have a terrific little skating arena of our very own. One of our residents is married to a former gold medal Olympic skater, and the rink is owned by a woman who competed and later trained Olympic skaters."

"Wow! We can bring our skates when we pack up our stuff," Lucy burst out. "I love skating!"

"So do I," Abby said. "We spent a lot of weekends on the ice. Not that we'll ever be a threat to any medal winners," she added with a grin.

Don chuckled. He finished his coffee. "If you need any help moving, the boys and I can drive down to Denver in a U-Haul and pack you up."

"You'd do that?" Abby asked, surprised, because people in big cities didn't warm up to other people, or so it seemed to her. Nobody she knew would have offered to help her move.

"Sure, we would," he said, and seemed shocked.

"In that case, how about next Saturday? And I'll buy pizzas for the whole crew!" She frowned. "Do we have a pizza joint?"

"You bet we do," he said. "And the boys love those meat-lover ones with extra cheese."

"I'll remember," she said. "Thanks, Mr. Blalock."

"Just Don." He tipped his hat. "Nice to meet you. Now I'll go tell the boys they can stop worrying."

She just smiled.

"Made his day, I'll bet," Hannah said as she warmed Abby's coffee. "They were all scared to death that some city person with dollar signs in her eyes was going to sell up the whole outfit."

"Not me. I was born here."

"Don wasn't. But Maisie was. Her mother was a Wiley."

"Goodness, not the Wileys who used to live on Long Bridge Road?"

"The very same."

"Mr. Wiley helped out at our place when we got snowed in one winter." She grimaced. "My dad was too drunk to care if we froze and starved, but Mr. Wiley came with a plow and cleared our driveway and brought us food. Mama cried. It was so kind."

"Maisie's like that, too," she said.

"I think she was in one of my classes. I didn't know her well." Abby sighed. "I didn't like to get close to people. I couldn't invite anybody home, you see, and Dad was unpredictable about other people."

"No need to explain. I remember your dad all too well," Hannah said. "But you're here now, and he isn't, and you're going to love living on a ranch. There are kittens in the barn," she added, and laughed at the way Lucy's eyes lit up.

"So we were told at the funeral home, before Bart joined us. He's such a sweet man. Why isn't he married?"

"There was this stupid woman who took him for a ride and then married somebody else," Hannah said. "Then he got mixed up with a couple of other women who tossed him over. He's gun-shy."

"I guess I would be, too." Abby grimaced. "Well, I am." She drew in a long breath, thinking about Cody Banks. "I don't want anything to do with men. My only concern now is Lucy," she said, smiling at the little girl. "I just want her to be happy."

"I'm very happy, Aunt Abby!" she replied, bright-eyed. "And I'll be ever so happy if we can just go out to the barn and look at the kittens!"

Abby sighed. "Okay, sprout. But finish your sandwich first!"

The boys came and moved them from Denver back to Catelow. It took the better part of a whole day, beginning at dawn, but after everything was in the ranch house, and old Charlie's things moved into the attic to make room for Abby's stuff, she ordered pizzas all around. They all sprawled in the living room, on the chairs and over onto the floor, eating pizza and drinking the beer Abby had bought on the way home.

It was like being part of a huge family. Abby had never felt anything like it since her brother and Mary died. She was going to love living in Catelow, she decided. She only had to come to grips with her irrational fear of Cody Banks.

Ironically, her first day on the job, Cody Banks walked in the door with a second man, wearing a nice and expensive suit.

They walked up to the receptionist, Marie. Cody didn't even look toward Abby, who had her desk next to the front window.

"We need to see Mr. Owens in reference to the Blakely case," Cody said quietly, and he smiled.

"Let me see if he's at his desk," Marie said, smiling back. She buzzed the boss and announced his visitors. She listened, said, "Yes, sir," and hung up. "He'll be right out," she told them.

She barely had time to get through the announcement before Mr. Owens was down the hall to meet the two men.

"Come on back," he told Cody, slapping him on the shoulder. "I've got my investigator on this case…"

His voice faded away as they went into his office and closed the door. Abby took a deep breath and went back to the case notes she was making. Ridiculous, she told herself, to be so intimidated after six years. He was just a man, after all, not some raging monster. She remembered him that long-ago night, yelling and cursing her. It was her father all over again, a man out of control, big and dangerous. She took another deep breath and forced herself to concentrate.

They were in the office for several minutes before they came back out. Mr. Owens shook hands with both of them, assured them that he'd given them all the information he had, and walked them to the front door.

Abby kept her head down. She didn't even look up when Cody went out.

The kittens in the barn were white with blue eyes. Lucy was mesmerized by them. She sat in the loose hay with two of them in her lap, stroking them and laughing when they purred.

"Oh, Aunt Abby, it's just heaven to live here," she said with a big smile. "I hated where we were."

"So did I, baby," Abby replied, sinking down beside her. They were both wearing jeans and cotton blouses and light jackets, because it was early autumn. Soon, the birches and cottonwoods would don their bright colors and leaves would fall and crunch underfoot. She sighed. "I don't think I've been this happy in a very long time."

"We can stay, can't we?" Lucy asked worriedly. "I mean, that mean man won't come here?"

Abby forced a smile. "He's the sheriff, sweetheart. I'm sure he has better things to do than visit people who don't...well, who don't want him around."

Lucy relaxed. She nodded and went on petting the kittens.

"It was a long time ago," Abby said absently. "His wife had just died, only days after your parents did," she added very gently. "He was hurting and sad and..."

"But we didn't do anything," Lucy protested.

"I know that. But he didn't."

Lucy was quiet for a minute or two. "I didn't act like that when Mommy and Daddy...well, after they were gone."

"Neither did I. But people react differently." She moved closer. "We've both blown it up in our minds until we think of the sheriff as a monster. But he protects people. That's his job, and he must be good at it, because he's starting his second term in office. And he was a deputy sheriff for years before he became sheriff." She glanced out the barn at the pasture where cattle were grazing behind an electrified fence. "Marie, where I work, said that he hates men who hurt women, that he'll go to any lengths to send them to jail. She said Cody's father got drunk and beat him and his mother."

"Oh." Lucy was thoughtful. "That's sad." She noticed the look on her aunt's face. "Did your daddy do that to you, Aunt Abby?"

She bit her lip. "Yes. To me and your father and your grand-mother. He was vicious when he drank."

"Is that why it scared you when the sheriff was yelling at us?"

Abby took a breath. "Maybe it is. I don't know." She looked at Lucy. "Since we have to live here, we have to try to get along with other people. The sheriff has no reason to come out here, after all. We probably won't see very much of him."

Lucy nodded. "That's good." She looked up. "Does he have any kids?"

"No. His wife was a doctor," she replied. "She was concentrating on her profession." She picked at a loose thread on the hem of her jeans. "She lived in Denver most of the time."

"Didn't she miss him?"

"Look," Abby said. "He's playing with your shoelaces!" She laughed and indicated one of the kittens.

The distraction worked. Abby had a lot on her mind. She didn't want to add the sheriff's issues to them.

They brought the playing kitten into the house to live, after a quick trip to the vet for bloodwork and vaccinations. He was male and sweet and funny, and he commandeered Lucy's bed the first night he was in residence, ignoring the nice cat bed they'd bought him, along with other necessary accessories.

Abby started to protest, but when she saw the sleeping child smile as the kitten clawed its way under the covers and onto her shoulder, she gave up. They'd named the kitten Patrick, for reasons neither of them could quite explain, except Lucy said that he looked like a Patrick. They'd both laughed over that. It was a new thing, to laugh. They'd lived in poverty and misery and grief for so long. Moving to the ranch was like living a dream. Abby prayed that it would last.

As the days went by, work became more familiar. She learned the names of all the office workers in the legal practice and where to get the best food. She took Lucy to little

Matt's birthday party and met several local mothers. She liked them all. Lucy enjoyed herself, too.

Abby also went to check out the skating rink. It was delightful to note that they not only rented skates, they sold them as well. It was a sideline the owner told her that had become quite lucrative. Abby decided then and there to fit them both with skates that had toe stops, not the hockey boots that were familiar to beginners. That was also the sort that Abby and Lucy owned. Lucy had loved skating on the rink in Denver and she was very good on the ice. So was Abby. It seemed a great many people in Catelow, and outer regions of Carne County, spent time at the skating arena. In fact, while she was there, she met a couple who'd come down from Billings to skate at the rink and have lessons from the Olympic medalist who taught there. Maybe, Abby thought, if the ranch prospered, she might enroll Lucy in a skating class. There hadn't been nearly enough money for lessons in Denver.

The ranch did, indeed, run itself, thanks to Don Blalock, who was a magician when it came to keeping the operation going. Abby made time in the evenings to sit with him at the computer and go over the books and learn how the sales team worked. She hadn't even known that there was one. Don explained that it was a specialized thing and needed people who knew what they were doing. Besides, he added with a grin, it kept the ranch solvent. That being said, their salaries were worth paying.

There were so many things that had to be done even on a daily basis that it blew Abby's mind. Just keeping the tack up to date and the animals checked and fed was a nightmare of tasks. Soon it would be winter, and the ranch was already being prepared for the cold weather that would result in making things complicated. As she learned about her great-uncle's enormous spread, she was even more grateful for Don.

Maisie took Lucy to and from school. The little girl loved her new school, especially when she realized that she didn't have to be afraid to go into a classroom. The teachers were very good and conscientious, and they had a principal who backed them up if there were disciplinary issues. It was a well-run school, with small classes and good teachers, many of whom were born and raised in Catelow. Abby was grateful that her niece fitted in so well.

Things had been going so well that Abby hadn't had a single worry. Then, one afternoon late, Hannah called to tell her that Lucy had gone out to see the other kitten and the mother cat in the barn and had vanished into thin air.

"I'm just so sorry!" Hannah said, almost in tears. "I was making a cake and I didn't think she could get into any trouble just going out to see the mama cat and the other kitten. In fact, I had one of the cowboys keeping an eye on her, but there was an emergency and he had to leave. It's my fault...!"

"You stop that," Abby said, and hugged the older woman despite her own very real fears. Rural areas like this had bears and coyotes and all sorts of other predators. Also, it was Saturday and there were hunters in the woods, and Lucy wasn't wearing bright clothing. It was a nightmare in embryo.

"I'm going out to look for her," Abby said. "I've got my cell phone. I can call for help if I have to. I'm just going to get my boots on and a heavier coat."

"I'm sorry I had to get you away from work..."

"I was working overtime for Mr. Owens on a case," she replied with a smile. "I'd only just finished my research when you called. Now don't worry!"

"Should we call somebody? The sheriff..." She bit her lip, having remembered too late about the difficulties that would involve.

"Not just yet," Abby said.

"Okay then."

★ ★ ★

Abby got into warm clothing and her boots, stuffed her thick hair into a knitted cap, put on her leather gloves, and went to the barn. She had one of the men saddle a gentle horse for her, because it had been a while since she'd ridden one. A horse could go places that a car couldn't and it was easier to see tracks on the ground at the slow pace. Don organized several of the cowboys into a search party, dividing up the ranch so that they covered more ground.

It had started to snow earlier that afternoon, something that was not that unusual for autumn in Wyoming. It was just a few flurries, but that was a blessing, because Abby could see little footprints in the light snow on the ground.

She followed them into the woods, wondering why in the world the child had gone that way. The ranch sat in a valley, with a stream running through it, and just beyond was a forest thick with fir trees and birch and cottonwood trees. There was a big hill far on the other side. The woods were forbidding. There was a lot of undergrowth to get through. Abby wished she'd brought a pair of hedge-cutters with her, and that she was wearing chaps, because the going was tough. She'd ridden into an area that was thick with thorny wild berry vines—very nice in the summer, she expected, because they could pick berries and make pies and jams with them. But at the moment, they were a problem she didn't need. And all the while she worried about Lucy. Did she have her thick coat on, was she frightened, why had she gone into the woods? Abby bit back her fear and soldiered on.

Cody Banks was off duty. It was a quiet Saturday anyway, and he was enjoying the peace on the ranch he'd bought a few months ago. He loved the solitude. Mostly, he loved living in a house with no memories of Debby, his late wife. He'd lived in the past too long already, so that mourning her had become a way of life. Here, in the solitude of acres and acres of grazing land and forest, he could lose himself in nature.

Beside him was the beautiful Siberian husky that Debby had left for him with a nurse in Denver the week she died. He loved the animal dearly. It was almost six years old now, and still as active and happy as it had been as a puppy. He spoiled the dog, buying it treats, letting it sleep on the end of his bed. It was like the child he and Debby had never had. He'd wanted children very much, but Debby had been working her way up the ladder in medicine and she hadn't really been interested in children or homemaking. He'd known that when he married her, of course, and he'd loved her with his whole heart, so it hadn't mattered. But now, left alone at the age of thirty-six, with nobody much left in his family except for cousins, he was feeling the loneliness just a little too much. If it hadn't been for his Anyu, his husky, he would have been alone in the world. He reached down and patted her with a big, gloved hand. She looked up at him with bright blue eyes in a laughing face surrounded by white fur with deep gray mixed in. Her name, Anyu, was an Inuit word for "snow." It had been taught him when he was first elected sheriff, by a temporary deputy with that heritage.

He was wearing boots and his shepherd coat and his silver-belly Stetson. It felt odd to be out of uniform, because that's what he wore most of the time. On the ranch, however, it wasn't necessary.

He'd gone down a logging trail on property that adjoined his and the land of his great-uncle who'd just died when he heard a sound. He was lonely and thoughts of Debby and the life they'd had haunted him. He'd walked for several minutes when he stopped abruptly and scowled. That wasn't an animal cry. It sounded like a child.

He shouted. There was an answering cry not too far away. He started toward it, through the underbrush. It was very thick. He took out his hunting knife from its leather sheath on his belt and cut some of the underbrush out of the way, mostly thick thorny berry bushes that bore fruit in the summer in great abundance.

When he got through, he found a small child caught in a veritable web of berry bushes with thorns.

"I can't get loose," she said, her eyes brimming with tears, her lower lip trembling. "Can you get me out, mister?"

"Of course I can. Hold on a sec. You hurt anywhere?" he asked gently.

"I'm just scratched," she said, drawing in a sobbing breath. "It didn't look so thick when I got into it. I was crawling after Myra, she got through, but I got stuck."

"Myra?" he asked absently as he cut away the undergrowth and gingerly separated the thorns from the little girl's down jacket.

"She's our cat. She had two kittens. A big old dog scared her and she ran away, so I had to go after her. But it was such a long way…"

He smiled. "Myra's probably sitting back home waiting for you," he said. "Cats are crafty about getting in and out of places."

There was a long howl. "Over here, honey," he called.

Anyu came bounding across the pasture, stopping at his soft command when she got to the bushes. She leaned forward, sniffing the child.

"Oh, what a pretty dog!" the child exclaimed. "And it's got blue eyes! Is it yours?"

He nodded, still concentrating on freeing her. "Her name's Anyu. She's six years old."

"She's a husky, isn't she?" the child asked. "She's beautiful! I wish we could have a dog. But at least we have a cat. He lives inside the house with us and sleeps on my bed with me."

"I don't mind cats, but I love Anyu. She's a lot of company."

"Do you got any little kids?" she asked, because he seemed very nice.

His face closed up. "Just Anyu," he said after a minute. "There. See if you can walk toward me. But go slow, so you don't rip your jacket."

"Okay." She moved a little bit at a time until she was finally out of the thorny bushes. "Thanks, mister."

"You're very welcome."

She looked up at him. It was a very long way up. "Are you a cowboy?" she asked.

He chuckled softly. "Sort of. I guess."

"We got lots of them at home. They're all very nice. Can I pet your dog?"

"Sure. Let her smell your hand first, though. She's wary of people she doesn't know."

"Okay." She held her hand out. The husky moved forward cautiously and sniffed. Then she laughed, panting, looking up at the little girl with her bright blue eyes.

The child laughed with joy. "I never saw a dog with blue eyes before!" she said, excited.

"Who are you and where do you live?" he asked.

"I'm Lucy. I live over there." She pointed to the general direction she'd come from. "It's a ranch. I live with my aunt Abby."

His expression was strange. "We'd better get you home," he said after a minute.

"You didn't tell me your name," she persisted.

He grimaced. "That's probably not a good idea. Not just yet. I might need to…oh, hell." He ground his teeth together as a woman approached them on horseback. She reined in just in front of them and dismounted, throwing the reins over the horse's head so they trailed the ground.

"Lucy!" She ran to the child and picked her up, hugging

her, fighting tears. "Oh, Lucy, where have you been? I've been looking forever…!"

"I got stuck in the thorny bushes," Lucy explained. "Myra got scared and ran away and I came to look for her. He got me loose," she added, smiling at the tall man in the low-seated Stetson with the taut face. "His dog is so pretty! She's a husky and her name is Anyu."

Abby swallowed, hard, and tried not to show the discomfort she felt. "Thank you," she said, and meant it. "I was so frightened. She's never done this before."

"You're welcome."

"Did your dog hurt her paw?" Lucy asked. "Look. She's limping a little."

He frowned and looked down. Sure enough, Anyu was favoring her right paw. "Maybe she got a thorn in it," he said, kneeling down. "She runs like a maniac when I let her out of the house." He checked the paw, seeing no thorns, but Anyu whimpered when he took her big paw in his hand.

"I hope she's okay. She's very sweet. She let me pet her, Aunt Abby," she added, unaware of the tension between the man and the woman. "I wish we could have a dog," she sighed.

"Is she all right?" Abby asked, watching the tender way he handled the dog. It was a far cry from the man she'd seen at the hospital so many years ago.

"I think so. I'll run her by the vet and let him have a look. It could be a stone bruise." He stood up and turned his attention back to the others.

"Thanks," Abby repeated, lost for words. "I was at the office. I don't usually work Saturdays, but Mr. Owens needed some research for a brief he's writing. Hannah only looked away long enough to get her cake in the oven and Lucy was just, just gone."

"We had a little girl run away from home last year, following a rabbit." He grimaced. "That didn't end quite this well. She was half-dead from exposure and dehydration by the time we found her. The whole sheriff's posse turned out to search for her, along with the police, the firemen..." He paused, forcing a smile. "It's a close-knit community. We watch out for each other."

Abby drew in a breath. "It's not quite like that in Denver," she said.

"I don't like Denver," Lucy piped up. "I like it here a lot!"

"We'd better go home," Abby said. She pulled Lucy closer and moved back to the horse.

"You get on," Cody Banks said quietly. "I'll hand Lucy up to you."

She mounted and let him position the child in front of her.

"Go carefully," he said, standing back. "The snow will make the trail slick if it sticks more than this, and it probably will."

She nodded. She forced a smile.

"No more wandering off chasing cats, young lady," he said, but he smiled.

"I won't," Lucy said. "Bye. Bye, Anyu," she added, smiling at the dog.

They rode away. Cody was standing where they left him, his big hand on his dog's head.

"That was ever so nice a man," Lucy said. "He cut me out of the thorny bushes. I crawled under them after Myra, but when I stood up, I couldn't get loose. There was a lot of bushes. His dog was pretty! Who was he, Aunt Abby?"

Abby hesitated to say. She'd just had a look at a totally different Cody Banks than the one she was certain she knew.

"Aunt Abby?" Lucy persisted.

"That was our sheriff," Abby said finally. "Cody Banks."

CHAPTER THREE

Lucy looked up at her aunt with a surprised expression. "That was our sheriff?" she asked. "But he was so nice! He got me loose and let me pet his dog!"

"People change, peanut," she said, using the old familiar nickname that her brother had given to his and Mary's only child. She smiled. "Maybe our sheriff has changed also."

"His dog was really pretty," Lucy said. "And she had blue eyes!"

"She's a Siberian husky," Abby said absently. "I think a lot of them have blue eyes."

"Oh, not like Anyu's," Lucy countered. "They were as bright as the sky on a clear cold day."

Abby smiled at the expression. Cody Banks had surprised her, too, with his tenderness toward the child and his lack of aggression. The man who'd frightened the woman and the child all that many years ago faded in their memories with this new one of a man who rescued little children and loved his dog. She could only imagine how much he'd loved Debby. She'd never really been in love, although she thought she had, once. That had ended badly. Of course, she'd had crushes on

movie stars. But she was wary of men. Her father's brutal behavior even in memory was enough to keep her single. Her
mother had said once that he was a wonderful person before alcohol got such a hold on him. So how did you know
what a man would be like behind closed doors? You didn't.
So Abby did her job and kept to herself. She had Lucy, too,
who gave new meaning and happiness to a formerly lonely
life. She missed her brother and Mary, but Lucy was an ongoing blessing.

In all her life, Abby had only had one moderately serious
boyfriend, when she was a senior in high school, and he'd just
dated her because his father was looking for a job in Abby's
brother's law firm, and he hoped he'd get his brother on the
inside track by hanging around with Abby. It had been like
a shot of cold water when she found that out, because she'd
fancied herself really in love with the boy. It hadn't helped
when he dumped her, and added quite a few personal insults
about the way she looked and dressed and acted, emphasiz-
ing her refusal to sleep with him. She'd only been eighteen at
the time, and she had low esteem anyway because of the way
she and Lawrence had been brought up. Their furiously, frequently drunk father had done that to them. She tried not to
think back, but sometimes memories intruded on daily life.
Her memories of men were either frightening or sad. She kept
to herself. Now that she had the responsibility for Lucy, if
she even found a man who wanted to marry her, he'd probably be put off by the child. But Abby loved Lucy and she'd
never agree to putting her up for adoption. Even the thought
of it was distasteful. Lucy was her own flesh and blood, her
late brother's only child. The fictional man would have to be
willing to take on Lucy as well as Abby. So it was probably
a good thing that Abby didn't have much interest in men.

She thought about the new image of Cody Banks she'd
had. He hadn't been frightening at all. He'd been so kind to

Lucy, so gentle with her. Probably he was always like that with children. Someone had told her that he was godfather to several children in the community and he never forgot birthdays or Christmas. The shouting, grieving man of six years ago seemed to have been consumed by this new, patient and kind one.

To be fair, he'd loved Deborah obsessively. People said he was never the same when she decided to work for a big teaching hospital in Denver and only came home infrequently. It was as if Cody was an afterthought in her life, while she was his whole world.

She couldn't even imagine being loved like that; to have a man care so much about her that nothing else in life mattered. And sadly, the only thing that had mattered in life to Deborah was being a doctor. To be fair, it was a noble profession, and Deborah was good with people. She was a good doctor and she was on her way to being a well-known one in medical circles, especially when she began to specialize in neurosurgery. But all that work was gone in a flash when she died. Cody was left alone.

In fact, he was totally alone now, after the death of Charlie Butler, whose ranch his great-niece by marriage, Abby, had inherited. Cody was only related to Charlie by marriage and although they were fond of each other, it was Abby who inherited the ranch. She hadn't questioned that legacy before, but now she did. Cody had a ranch of his own, of which some little bit adjoined the land that Abby had inherited. Why had Charlie passed over Cody and given his estate to Abby? It was a question she wished she'd asked while Charlie was still alive. While fond of her, he'd showed no great affection for her and he was frank about not liking Lucy underfoot when his kinfolk visited him. He didn't like children, which might explain why he never married.

"I don't guess we could get a dog?" Lucy asked wistfully, bringing Abby out of her thoughts.

"We might just do that, a little later on," Abby said without actually promising anything. She smiled. "But let's wait until we're properly settled first, okay?"

Lucy grinned. "Okay!" She cocked her head. "Could we get a husky dog like the sheriff has?"

Abby felt her pulse leap. Odd reaction, she thought. "And we'll see about that as well."

Lucy hugged her aunt's legs. "I love you, Aunt Abby."

Abby laughed and picked her up. "I love you, too, peanut!"

Cody Banks was disturbed by the fact that he hadn't noticed Anyu's limp. The child had seen it at once. Nice child, he thought as he drove to the vet with Anyu in the passenger seat of his SUV. She had a sweet smile and pretty manners. Her aunt loved her, that was apparent. He'd wanted children a lot, but Deborah wanted a career more. He cared so much for her. He'd have given her anything she wanted, even her work as a doctor, without complaining that he only saw her rarely, and usually only for a day or two at a time. He went on with his job, and tried not to worry that if she'd loved him as much as he loved her, she might have settled for a job at the local hospital and not wanted to work a state away down in Denver. But she'd been ambitious, and there were no children to feel neglect, so he'd said nothing.

It had been lonely without her. Perhaps that was why he'd bought the ranch. He loved animals. He had a few head of cattle, in a growing herd, and chickens that laid him fresh eggs. There was a full-time cowboy, a brother to Abby's foreman Don Blalock, and a couple of part-timers who helped tag and brand new additions to his herd. Of course, if he ever had a lot of cattle, nearby ranchers would all turn out to help with branding and vaccinations and the other odds and ends that cattle ranching required. It was a nice little community, Catelow, and full of kindhearted people. Cody couldn't really imagine living anywhere else.

He'd wondered once why Debby never asked him down to Denver to her apartment. She always had some excuse about being on call or having to go to meetings or see private patients. Funny that he hadn't noticed it while they were married. Probably though it was just as she'd said, she worked so hard that she didn't have time for visits, even from the husband who loved her.

He pulled up in front of the vet's office and took Anyu in. The receptionist asked him to have a seat and almost at once, a vet tech came out to lead them into a room.

"The doctor will be right in," she said with a grin.

"Thanks."

The tech stopped to pet Anyu and admire her pretty blue eyes before she went out, leaving Cody and Anyu in the neat treatment room with pictures of dog and cat breeds in colorful posters on the walls.

He was halfway through the sporting dog group when Dr. Shriver came in. He was a tall man, taciturn with people but loving with animals.

He nodded at Cody and looked at the chart. "She's limping, you said."

"Yes. I didn't notice until…well, someone else said she was favoring her right leg." He made a face. "I should have seen it."

"Often we don't see things that outsiders do," Shriver said. "Let's have a look." He bent and lifted Anyu onto the examination table. When he manipulated her paw, she whined and drew it back.

"Could be a broken toe," Dr. Shriver murmured to himself. He looked up. "We'll need to do X-rays and some lab work. Can you leave her with us?"

"Sure. I've got a full day ahead," Cody said, shaking his head. "We have whole days when there's nothing more urgent than a traffic stop or a fight to break up. And then we have others when there needs to be about twenty more men than I've got. We had a bank robbery yesterday, for God's sake!"

"I heard about that on the radio." Shriver shook his head. "And people think we never have such problems in small towns."

"Crime doesn't have a permanent address," Cody said dryly. "You'll call me, when you know something?"

"Of course. But it may be a couple of days before we have the results of the other tests. We'll take good care of her, if you can leave her."

"I guess I can do that." He hugged the laughing dog. "You be a good girl," he added. She just looked at him with her sparkling beautiful blue eyes, as if to assure him that she would.

He went back to work. There was an odd case on the books that he was working on. A man from back East had befriended Charlie Butler, who'd left his ranch to Abigail Brennan. The man, Horace Whatley by name, had signed on as a foreman, citing impressive and extensive references from some of the biggest ranches in Texas. Charlie had been diagnosed with cancer by then and he was in a lot of pain. He took Horace on as an employee mostly on faith. The young man was easygoing and mixed well with the other cowboys. He was especially kind to Charlie, eager to help out in any way he could, in gratitude for his job.

But odd things started happening after a few weeks. Horace was given work as the assistant to the cattle foreman, a position of some responsibility. The cattle foreman himself, Dick Blakely, had a heart attack and had to resign his job. It was offered to Horace as the assistant, and he jumped at the chance of promotion. Charlie gave him the job and explained its responsibilities. Horace was certain that he could cope.

Cowboys as a rule didn't like to rat out their comrades. They worked in close proximity, and pretty much knew each others' business. They didn't carry tales. But it became apparent to Don Blalock, who was the overall ranch foreman, that the cattle foreman wasn't doing his job at all. His rigid feeding schedule for the livestock was ignored while Horace went to a separate vendor and ordered new equipment and new feed for the cattle he was maintaining. The vendor was known to Don, who refused to do business with him. He was unscrupulous and sold inferior product. On a ranch such as this one, with specialized livestock, that could spell disaster with the breeding program. So Don went to Charlie and laid it out for him.

Subsequently, Charlie called Horace into his office and read him the riot act. He had no authority to do what he'd done, and he'd far overstepped his authority. Horace argued that he had some really good ideas to try out and that he knew Mr. Butler would be pleased with the results. Charlie read him chapter and verse about the vendor he was dealing with, and questioned just how much experience Horace had as a cattle foreman.

Horace produced his references again and restated his desire to experiment with the feeding program. Charlie told him that if he persisted, he'd be looking for another job. Horace subsided, but not without complaint.

Sick and frankly upset by his new employee, Charlie called in Don Blalock and had him phone all the people Horace listed as references.

It was enlightening. None of the people who recommended him had ever met him, and a couple of them were hot under the collar that someone had so badly referenced them in what sounded like an illegal and liable business. Don Blalock had assured them that nobody on the ranch would ever talk about it to anyone except the people actually involved.

Armed with the information, he went back to Charlie, who was shocked at the new man's impertinence and his ability to lie.

He had Horace come back into the office, where he told Don Blalock to tell the man what his investigation had uncovered.

Horace had been momentarily speechless, and his face had gone sad and resigned when Don added that a couple of the ranchers he'd alluded to as references were talking about legal action. Horace admitted then that he'd exaggerated his abilities, but he was willing to learn, if Mr. Butler would just give him a chance to make amends. He loved animals. He'd try very hard to do what he was told.

At which point, Don asked him if he'd ever been on a ranch before in his life. The answer had both men blinking. No, Horace said, but he'd watched lots of old TV Westerns and live ranch shows on YouTube, and he'd even played video games that had cattle to manage, so he was sure he knew how to manage cattle.

Charlie gathered his scattered wits and told the man he needed a lot more background than that for the job he was assuming. He offered him work as a regular cowhand, but Horace was reluctant. He didn't think he was strong enough for physical labor. Actually, it was the truth. The young man was a bit overweight and not in excellent physical condition.

He seemed shocked when Charlie told him that managers on his ranch worked their way up from cowboys. There was no on-the-job training for it, except being a cowboy and learning the job from the ground up. He advised Horace to go back to his video games and gave him a week's severance pay.

Horace told him he was missing a chance to make his ranch truly great. He gave the men a sad shake of his head as he left.

Charlie and Don thought that was the end of it. But it wasn't. Horace went around town telling people that he was the cattle foreman at the Circle B and that he was going to be showing Mr. Butler's pedigree bulls at the big upcoming convention in Denver.

That was the last straw. Charlie called his attorney and had him inform the erstwhile former employee that there were severe penalties for people who told deliberate lies about other people. Horace just smiled at the man. Charlie had hired him, he insisted. It was all just a misunderstanding. The attorney, who had no sense of humor and a bad temper to boot, told the little man what he could expect if he didn't shut his mouth.

Horace had stopped making that claim, but he was still in town, still insisting that he had some great ideas about how to improve pedigree herds, and that he was going to find work doing that very soon.

Charlie and his attorney thought the man had mental health issues. It hadn't been checked out, because Charlie died soon after and nobody knew where Horace had gone. Now the poor, demented soul was hinting again that he was going to be working on the Circle B Ranch very soon.

That would put Abigail and Lucy on the firing line, if the man tried to get a job there. Don Blalock would warn her, Cody was sure, but it would be easier to tell her himself. Or have Don do it.

He decided to do some more checking on the misguided Mr. Whatley. He started making telephone calls.

One local man knew Whatley: Bart Riddle, Cody's distant cousin.

"What can you tell me about him?" Cody asked over the phone.

"He's got problems," Bart said simply. "I'm sorry Charlie didn't see through him. If he'd been himself, and not so sick from the chemotherapy, he'd have spotted that lie right off the bat. I certainly did. I checked his damned references and discovered he didn't have any."

"Charlie discovered that as well, finally," he replied. "Do you know where Whatley's from?"

"Sadly, I do," he replied. "He belongs to the Whatleys of Miami. The family is filthy rich and their aim, apparently, is to keep their troublesome relative as far away from them as they possibly can. His parents are long dead, but there's a sister who can't stand the thought of having to be responsible for him. She gives him an obscene allowance and lets him follow his delusions around the world. The last one, I heard, was that he was a famous chef who'd worked for billionaires as a cook on their yachts. So this fancy restaurant in New York hired him."

"And?" Cody was mesmerized.

"He burned down the kitchen his first night on the job," Bart replied. "Then he saw an episode of that old TV series *High Chaparral* and came out here to help run a ranch."

"Good Lord," Cody said with feeling. "Does he have some kind of mental illness?"

"Severe, but he's no longer under treatment and has, in fact, gone to court to make sure he isn't medicated against his will," Bart added. "Damned shame. I actually talked to his sister. She said that when he's taking his meds, he's the sweetest, kindest man you'd ever meet. Off them, he's an accident looking for a place to happen. He has delusions, and they're getting worse. And we're stuck with him for the present, it seems, because he likes it here. A lot."

"Well, damn," Cody muttered. "That, on top of Anyu, is enough to depress even a strong man."

"What's wrong with Anyu?" Bart asked, because he knew what the dog meant to Cody.

"She was limping. I didn't even notice, but that little niece of Abigail's saw it and pointed it out to me. I took Anyu to the vet. I haven't heard back about the test results yet."

"Probably a thorn in her paw or some simple thing like that," Bart said bracingly. He paused. "How did you meet the child?"

"She'd gone after a mother cat who was spooked into the woods. She got stuck in a berry thicket by all the thorns and couldn't get loose. I found her when Anyu and I went for a walk."

"Well!" That was interesting. Bart knew how afraid Abby and Lucy had been of him. "I'll bet Abby was frantic. She loves that child."

He laughed softly. "Yes, she does. She looked ready to drop when she rode up to us." He sighed. "I didn't think a city girl like her would know what to do with a horse."

"She used to ride in rodeos when she first moved to Denver to live with her brother," Bart reminded him. "She was good, too. She has a way with horses. With most animals. They love her."

"I noticed that." He sighed. "Well, I'll get back to my paperwork. If you hear anything more about our vicarious cowhand, let me know, will you?"

"Sure thing. Maybe he'll get hooked on science fiction and go down to NASA to teach them a better way of building spaceships."

Cody chuckled. "They've got Elon Musk as a partner, with Starship priming to be an interplanetary spaceship. What a guy!"

"He's a phenomenon, all right."

"I'll talk to you soon."

"So long."

It had been a long day at the office for Abby. Nothing went wrong, but her work was tedious. She had to double-check all the references in law that she cited for Mr. Owens so that he could hold his own in court. It was a good job, and she enjoyed it. But it was a whole new life, here where she was born. It took a little getting used to, after living in a city the size of Denver.

When she got home, Lucy was already there. The little girl jumped up from in front of the television and ran to hug her.

"I'm so glad you're home," Lucy sighed, looking up at her aunt with a beaming smile. "It's so nice here, Aunt Abby," she added. "I've got so many friends, and we get to live on the ranch with real cowboys!"

Abby laughed. "Well, yes, I suppose we do. Suppose we go try out the ice rink tomorrow?" she asked. "It's Saturday."

"Oh, could we!"

"Yes, we could. We both need some relaxation after work and school for a whole week. We'll go after breakfast, how's that?"

"That's just fine!"

The rink had a lot of people on it, even at this early hour. Abby and Lucy tied on their skates and walked gingerly onto the ice, holding hands.

"Now, don't let go because I'm very nervous and I might fall!" Abby said with a grin.

Lucy laughed. "Okay. I promise I'll take good care of you, so you don't slip on the ice!"

They turned and melted into the crowd, skating slowly at first, and then faster as music came out of the walls. It was a nice touch, soothing music, not loud or with words. Mostly classical pieces, and very suited to the kind of skating Abby loved.

Abby had wanted to be a champion figure skater when she was young, but the ice rink here in Catelow had no instructors back then, and Denver was a long way off. Besides, Abby's father would never have let her escape his domination. She wasn't allowed out of the yard except on weekends when he was too drunk to care that her mother took her skating. Once she got home from school, on weekdays, it was like being a prisoner. She couldn't even have a friend over to play with her. By the time her father died and she went to live in Denver with Lawrence, she'd lost her interest in figure skating except for watching the competition at the Olympics. Skating here brought back those lost dreams.

Her expression was broody. Lucy squeezed her hand. "You have to be happy here," she chided. "We have everything. We even have cats!"

Abby burst out laughing. "So that's the secret of life, is it? Cats?"

"Cats," Lucy agreed smugly, and grinned up at her.

Abby smiled from ear to ear. "I don't know what I'd do without you, Lucy. You make the world bright and new, every day."

"Thanks."

"And here I thought the secret to life was 42."

Lucy gaped at her.

"It was in a book. And a movie. The world is owned by white mice and the secret of life is 42." She laughed with her whole heart. "See, there was this terrific writer called Douglas Adams, and he wrote a book called *The Hitchhiker's Guide to the Galaxy...*"

By the time she finished giving her niece the bare bones of the story, Lucy was entranced and asking if they couldn't find the movie and rent it online.

"You bet we can," Abby said. "In fact, we'll watch it after supper tonight, how about that?"

"That sounds just great!"

★ ★ ★

Despite frequent calls about his dog, Cody wasn't given any of the test results. He was asked to wait until the vet had all the information at hand.

It took several days. It was the following week when Dr. Shriver called him at work and asked him to come by the office as soon as he could.

Cody burned rubber getting to the animal hospital.

Dr. Shriver was in the waiting room when he walked in. The vet motioned him down the hall into his office and closed the door.

"Have a seat," he said.

Cody sat.

The vet drew in a long breath. This was one thing about his practice that he truly hated. "Your dog has cancer," he said after a minute.

Cody felt his very heart ripping inside him. Anyu was all he had in the world. He ground his teeth together. "How bad? And can we treat it?"

"Very bad," was the reply. "It metastasized. It's in her internal organs as well as the bones."

Cody just sat there, looking at him, uncomprehending. "But you can treat it…"

Dr. Shriver leaned forward, his hands locked together on the desk. "Do you want the truth or sugarcoating?"

Cody took a long breath. "The truth."

"I can do chemo and radiation. We have the facilities for it. The cost will be in the thousands of dollars. And at the end of it, Anyu will still die, but it will mean coming in often for treatment. Besides that, there's the issue of pain."

Thousands. Of course he'd pay it. He had savings he hadn't spent. He'd do anything to prolong her life. Anything!

Dr. Shriver saw that in his lean face. "Sheriff Banks," he said quietly, "she's in pain. A great deal of it. Animals hide that from other animals in the wild. They hide it from humans as well. So by the time we find it, many times it's too late to stop it. And even then, it can metastasize in such a little amount of time."

"If it were your dog, that you loved, what would you do?" Cody asked tightly.

"I'd take her home and let her live out the rest of her life the way she wanted to," came the quiet reply. "I wouldn't put her through the treatment, which will only prolong her life, not save it."

Cody looked at him. "How long?"

"Maybe six months. Maybe a great deal less."

There was a pause. "How will I know, when she needs to come back here…"

Shriver got up and put a hand on the lawman's shoulder. "You'll know."

Cody got up, too, feeling older than his years and absolutely drained of life. "Six months. Well, I'll make it the best six months she's ever had," he said after a minute. "I'll spoil her even more rotten than I have."

Dr. Shriver smiled. "That's exactly what I'd do." His blue eyes were sad. "I lost my golden retriever about five months ago. She was fourteen years old. My sister and I passed her back and forth, but she'd been staying with me for the past year. It hurt like hell to give her up." He met Cody's eyes. "I know how it feels. I'm sorry. If there was anything that would cure her, I'd do it."

"I know that." Cody paused. "Thanks. Can I take her with me now?"

"Of course. I'll give you a couple of medicines that will help with the pain," he said. "We have our own in-house pharmacy. I'll have one of the girls fetch Anyu for you while I'm getting the drugs. If you need anything, I'll be here," he added.

Cody forced a smile. "Thanks."

★ ★ ★

He put the bag of medicines on the back seat and Anyu on the front seat beside him. She didn't look as if she had a care in the world. He hugged her, frightened of a future that would leave him totally alone. Anyu was all he had. She was everything!

But miracles happened. She might recover, he told himself. She might even go into remission. It wasn't hopeless. Maybe the tests were wrong. He ruffled Anyu's fur. He'd give her the meds, of course. But the doctor might be mistaken.

"We'll go home and eat chili and watch wrestling," he told the pretty fluffy dog. "How would you like that?"

Her blue eyes laughed at him.

He smiled. She was a constant source of joy to him. He couldn't lose her. He couldn't! Maybe he could manage the cost of the radiation and chemo. He'd think about it for a few days and decide what to do. It was a situation that required serious thought.

He took Anyu home and they settled on the sofa with his homemade chili and a soft drink, watching wrestling. It was a great way to shake off the job for a few hours, kick back and relax.

He was halfway through the second match when the phone rang. Anyu started howling. He laughed. She always did that when the phone rang.

"Sheriff Banks," he said tersely.

"Sheriff, can you come into the office?" his newest employee, a young deputy, asked.

"What's up?"

"Well, we've sort of got a, well, a murder…"

"How the hell can you sort of have a murder?" Cody demanded, furious.

"This guy came in a few minutes ago and said he'd found a body over near the Butler place, off the road in some weeds.

He says he's a detective from Miami and he'd be happy to volunteer his services to help solve the case."

"A murder. A body. An out-of-town detective who found it." Cody took a calming breath. "Okay. Where's the body? Have you brought it in yet?"

"See, that's the hitch. The detective saw the body but apparently it's been moved. He wants to help us look for it."

Cody stared at the wall. First Anyu, now this. It was getting to be a very rotten day. "Okay, I'll come into the office and we'll go from there."

"Thanks, Sheriff."

"This detective, does he seem to know his business?"

"I guess so. He sure reminds me of that TV detective Remington Steele. He's not handsome, but he dresses like the detective did. Very suave."

"I'm on my way." Cody hung up.

CHAPTER FOUR

The detective from Miami was dressed, as the young deputy had said, in very suave clothing. An expensive suit, a white silk shirt, and his hair was very much like the TV detective's. The only thing the man was missing was height. He was shorter than Cody. Of course, Cody was over six feet tall, so a lot of people couldn't match his height.

"Are you the sheriff?" the other man asked with a big smile, extending his hand. "I'm Mike Steele. From Miami."

Cody shook the hand. "Nice to meet you. I'm Sheriff Banks. Now what's this about a body?" he asked somberly.

"I found one! It was in the briars just south of the ranch house at the Butler place," he assured the other man.

"What condition was it in?" Cody asked, because the snow from the last storm had just melted, and he expected the crime scene investigator would need a sturdy body bag. And maybe a shovel.

"The body?" the other man asked. He frowned. "Well, it was wearing clothes like the cowboys do, and there was an arrow through his chest."

Cody blinked. "Excuse me?"

"I mean, a bullet hole. Yes. A bullet hole." He grinned. "Sorry. I mixed up my point of reference."

"Where was the bullet hole?"

The little man thought hard. "In his chest."

"Powder burn?"

The other man scowled. "I didn't really notice."

"Powder burns are hard to miss," Cody said, hiding a sudden suspicion about the identity of the so-called expert here. "What condition was the body in?"

"Well, it was dead," came the stark reply.

"Obviously. I mean, was it wet, dry, decomposed, dismembered...?"

The little man shuddered. "Oh, of course not! It was in one piece!"

"Great. Where is it now?"

The detective raised his eyebrows. "It's gone missing."

"You should have called us in before coming in here to report it," Cody said. He scowled. "And why didn't you call from the crime scene?"

The questions were disturbing the little man. He coughed, pausing as if he was searching desperately for a reply. "My cell phone isn't charged!" he said after a minute, triumphantly. "And it's still in my motel room, plugged in," he added. "So I couldn't take a picture at the crime scene," he finished.

"Damned shame," Cody replied. "Photos would have been a great help. But we can go out there with you and look for trace evidence."

The detective hesitated, but then he smiled. "That would be great! I remember exactly where it was."

Cody herded him out the door to his SUV and indicated the passenger door while he got in under the steering wheel.

"Where to?" he asked when his companion was seated.

"This gear is so neat!" came the reply. "All this fancy, up-to-date equipment! It's like something out of *Star Trek*!"

"Are you a fan?" Cody asked.

"Oh, yes. I used to go to every single convention. I even went on a cruise with the cast once!"

"That must have been interesting."

"It was! One of the best few days of my whole life," he added with a long sigh and a smile.

"So, where do we go?" Cody asked when they hit the main highway.

"It was beside the big gate that has the Circle B logo on it," he replied. "Just a few feet away in the grass," he added.

Cody was frowning as he drove. "Odd that one of the cowboys didn't spot him."

"Oh, it was very early this morning," the man said. "Even before they went out to work."

"How do you know what time they go to work?" Cody wanted to know.

"I have all these surveillance devices," came the smug reply.

"I hope you have a good reason to use them," Cody said. "You need a warrant for some of those."

"A warrant?" He coughed. "Oh, yes, a warrant. I set up the surveillance devices after I found the body, though."

"Quick thinking," Cody replied. He glanced at the man. "You had those in your possession already?"

"Oh, yes. I try to be prepared for anything. There," he said suddenly, pointing. "That's exactly where the body was!"

Cody pulled off the road next to the gate proclaiming to any visitor that this was the Circle B Ranch and trespassing was forbidden.

They got out of the SUV and started looking around. "There!" the detective said, pointing to a grassy spot nearby. Not a surveillance device in sight, no significant disturbance of the area, no visible tracks in the little bit of snow that had fallen earlier in the day.

Cody had just started to move closer to it when the sound

of an engine approaching distracted him. He turned in time to see Abby stop her little car in front of the gate. She and Lucy got out.

"Hi, Sheriff Banks!" Lucy said, walking up to him with a big smile.

His heart melted. "Hi, Lucy," he replied and smiled down at her. "How are you?"

"I'm good," she said. "How is Anyu?"

He ground his teeth together. "She's very sick," he replied. "If you hadn't noticed her limping, I'd never have known that she was."

"I'm so sorry," Lucy said, her soft eyes on the sheriff's face.

He was fighting despair but he forced a smile for the child. It wasn't her fault. That sweet expression made him regret bitterly the scare he'd given her so many years ago.

"I'd like to have a dog, but Aunt Abby says we don't have time right now. But she said we could get one someday. I love dogs. Your dog is so beautiful."

"Yes, she is," Cody replied. "She's all I have in the world," he added quietly, without thinking.

"Aunt Abby's all I got," the child replied, her little face sad and wise beyond her years, as if she could see right inside Cody to the pain that was almost physical. Cody was surprised at the kinship he felt with the child, as if they were somehow connected. He was already fond of her.

Abby came forward after a word with the detective and joined Cody and Lucy. "Should I call Don up to take Lucy home with them?" she asked Cody.

He was fighting strong emotions. His dog's illness was getting to him. But he thought for a minute of the trauma the child would face if they found the body somewhere close by. He looked at Abby and nodded. "That might a very good idea."

She called Don on his cell phone and explained in nebulous terms that she needed him to let Lucy stay with Maisie and his little daughter for a while.

Don rode up while she was still talking to him on the phone. He gave the detective a puzzled look, as if the detective was familiar to him somehow, but passed it off when he realized that his would-be cattle foreman that the visitor resembled wasn't dressed up that fancy and he'd pretty much forgotten what the man looked like. It had been several weeks ago.

Don chuckled. "I was patrolling. We've had a trespasser, it seems." He put up his cell phone and looked at Cody with both eyebrows raised.

"We'll talk about it later, Don," he promised. "Right now we need you to take this little one home." He looked down at Lucy and smiled. She grinned up at him.

"I can take her back with me now. Want to ride on a big horse, Lucy?" he teased.

"Oh, yes! Can I, Aunt Abby?" she added, with a pleading look at her aunt.

Abby chuckled. "Of course you can." She moved closer to lift Lucy onto the horse, but Cody was closer and quicker.

He lifted the girl easily, loving the feel of her soft little arms around his neck as he handed her up to Don, who put her in front of him in the saddle.

"Thanks, Sheriff Banks!" she said.

"You're very welcome." He thought the child was adorable. She was like the child he'd imagined he and Debby might have one day. But that dream was long dead.

"I'll take good care of her," Don said.

"I know that," Abby replied. "You be good for Maisie," she told her.

"I will, Aunt Abby."

Don tipped his hat to Abby, turned the horse, and galloped away with Lucy.

"Now," Abby said, turning to the two men. "What's this about a body?"

"That's where it was," the young man said. He'd been standing to one side with his back to Don until the foreman rode off. But now he moved forward, pointing to an indentation in the grass. He started toward it, but Cody's arm shot out and prevented him.

"It's a crime scene, until we know it's not," Cody told him. "I'll bring out my investigator and let him go over it."

"Well, how can he find anything if there's no body?" the young man asked and seemed strangely nervous.

"You'd be surprised. I have a few more questions for you," Cody added.

The young man's phone rang. He looked at the number and ground his teeth together. "I'm sorry. I have to take this." He moved away from the others.

Abby moved closer to Cody. "I suppose you noticed that the body print in the grass is just the size of your visiting detective," she said under her breath.

"That's not all I noticed," he replied.

"I'm truly sorry, about your dog," she said uneasily. "I had one of my own, once, when I lived here. I was about seven. My dad was drunk and my dog got in his way, trying to protect me and Mama…" She broke off. She couldn't talk about it, even all these years later.

"I didn't know you back then," Cody said quietly. "We kept to ourselves, too. You're not the only one with a father who got drunk and used his fists on people. It's why I became a lawman. Trying to prevent other kids from going through what I did."

"It's why I became a paralegal," she said after a minute.

"To try and salvage people who were victims of it. You don't meet happy people in law offices," she said. "You meet broken lives, broken dreams, broken people."

"Your boss, Owens, has a good practice," he remarked. "He's respected in the community, even by people he helps into prison."

She smiled. "I noticed that."

His eyes were on the detective, who was speaking rather shrilly into his phone. "You've done a good job with Lucy," he said. "She's a sweet, kind child."

"My brother was like her," she replied quietly. "I miss him every day."

"I miss my wife," he said. He drew in a breath. "We carry scars inside us that never heal."

"I know exactly what you mean."

He looked down at her, his dark eyes quiet and soft. "We've both been through the wars. I'm sorry I made things harder for you, when you'd just lost your brother and sister-in-law."

She tried to smother the memory. It was still disturbing. "I've never had feelings that ran that deep for anyone," she confessed. "Well, maybe once, but that ended badly. I had a friend, just a friend, one of the men in Lawrence's law office. He was crazy for this girl he'd met in a bar. She was really beautiful. He was crazy about her and even bought a ring because he wanted to marry her. Then he discovered that she was a paid escort. Everybody in the office felt sorry for him. One day he didn't come to work and nobody knew why. They found him in his apartment, dead of a self-inflicted gunshot wound." She shivered a little. "He really loved her, but she only saw him as a client. Poor guy!"

"Men get involved with a lot of the wrong sort of women before they find the one good one."

She nodded. "Deborah was one of the kindest people I ever met. I imagine she was a very good doctor."

"One of the best." It hurt him to talk about her. He glanced toward the detective, who was still on the phone and almost yelling now, something about not coming home and people needed to mind their own business. He hung up and stood smoldering until he realized that two other people were staring at him curiously.

"My office," he announced importantly, lifting the cell phone before he put it back in its holder on his belt. "A few hitches. Nothing serious."

"This, er, body," Sheriff Cody said. "About your height?"

The other man paused, glancing at the lawman's taciturn face. "Well, as a matter of fact, yes, he was!"

"And you have no idea where the body went?"

"No," he replied. He grinned. "But we'll have to search for it, right?"

"If we have to get all my personnel out here to search for a body we might not find, how am I going to explain the loss of time in man-hours that we spend here? Salaries have to be paid, you know, and this would amount to a lot of overtime."

"Oh, I could make a sizeable contribution, if that's all," he said airily. "Because we have to find the body."

Sheriff Banks pushed his hat back over his blond-streaked brown hair and stared down at the man, his dark eyes watchful. "I'd like to see your credentials. And I don't know your name."

"But I told you. It's Mike Steele."

"Driver's license, please."

The other man's face lost color. "Driver's license?"

"Yes. Let's see it."

He hesitated. "But I told you…"

Cody moved a step closer. He looked intimidating now. "I want to see your driver's license, Mr. Steele. Now."

There was no way out of it, the man saw. He grimaced, but he pulled out his license and handed it to Cody. He looked at it closely. "Horace Whatley," he read. He looked up. That name was familiar. Don Blalock had told him the story about his fictitious livestock foreman, laughing all the while. This was the same man. But nobody was laughing.

Cody handed back the license. "Mr. Whatley," he said coolly, "reporting a false crime is an actionable offense. It wastes time and resources. I really should arrest you and let you speak to the judge when your case comes up."

"Please don't," the little man said, his bravado dissolving. "They'll make me go home to my sister." His face fell. "She treats me like an idiot. They all treat me like an idiot. They want to dose me so strongly that I won't know my name, and put me...put me away." His pale eyes looked up into the sheriff's. "I'm not as far gone as they think I am. I just like acting out my fantasies sometimes." He sighed. "I'm independently wealthy. I can take care of myself, and I would, if they'd just let me! I've never hurt anybody in my life. I never would." He looked up again. "Please don't make them send me back to Miami."

"I gather that your sister was just speaking to you on the phone?"

He grimaced. "They called her, about when I was pretending to be a livestock foreman. She's been out of the country. They couldn't reach her until today—her attorneys, that is. I didn't mean any harm. I really do have some good ideas about livestock feed. I've read all the journals, all the expert opinions. Please don't send me home," he added again, and his expression would have melted a harder heart than Cody's. "I'll stop trying to work on ranches. Honest!"

Cody pointed at his chest. "You stop making up dead bodies," he said firmly. "You get one second chance. After that, you're back to your sister's. You got me?"

"You mean, I can stay?" he exclaimed, and fought tears.

"I'll stay out of trouble. I promise! I'll be the best citizen in town. I'll work at it real hard! I promise!" he said again.

Cody laughed softly. "Okay. But no more experimenting with cattle feed and pretending to have experience with ranching, and mostly, no more fictional dead bodies. You got that?"

"I got it!" The little man grinned at him. He glanced at Abby and flushed. "Miss Brannon, I don't guess you need any more help?"

"I wish I did," Abby said honestly. "Mr. Whatley, why don't you get a place of your own? If you have a private income, it's not a bad investment. Times are hard, and ranch properties are opening up all over the place, even here in Carne County."

"A place of my own?" His face almost glowed. "I've never had anything of my own. They give me money and push me out the door, so I won't get in the way or embarrass them. A place of my very own." He took a deep breath. "I'll do that." He smiled at both of them and almost ran for his car.

"God, what have I let myself in for?" Cody groaned. He glared at Abby. "Now see what you've done!"

"Nobody else wants him," she said softly. "He's all alone. Sort of like us." She grimaced. "I just thought he might fit in here, if he tried. And if he had a place of his own, he'd be more concerned with it than with mythical dead bodies...?"

He laughed. "Okay. I see your point." His dark eyes slid over her face. She wasn't pretty, but when she smiled, it was like sunshine. "However, if you do find a dead body, please call me and not Mr. Whatley."

She crossed her heart. "Yes, sir!"

He just grinned.

So Horace Whatley bought himself a real ranch with real cowboys, and immediately started work on remodeling it to suit his own taste.

★ ★ ★

Mr. Owens was troubled. He was an easygoing man for the most part, but for the past several days, he'd been absent-minded to a surprising degree.

"Do you know what's got Mr. Owens so worried?" Abby asked Marie while they were eating a quick lunch in the local café, in a corner booth where they wouldn't be overheard.

"He's got a nephew, Jack," Marie told her. "The boy's been in and out of reform school and his parents couldn't do anything with him. He assaulted another boy over a girlfriend and Mr. Owens was just barely able to keep him out of jail." She shook her head. "I've seen so many cases like this," she added. "Kind, sweet people with a renegade in the family who can't or won't live up to expectations. The boy had two scholarships and he tossed them away. His grandmother left him a little money, but he spent it all. He's been in trouble with the law all his life. Not his fault, you understand, it was the police harassing him, to hear his father tell it. His father spoiled him rotten right up to the day he died."

"I know the type," Abby replied. "In Denver you see all sorts of people. I worked as a receptionist in my brother's law firm before I started school to be a paralegal. We had death threats!"

Marie grinned. "We have them here, too," she said, surprising Abby. "Oh, yes. Mr. James had one a couple of weeks ago over a land case he handled. The defendant wasn't happy about the judgment."

"Wouldn't it be a perfect world if we lived in harmony with all our fellow humans?" Abby asked absently.

"How are things going at the ranch?" Marie asked.

"Just great. Lucy's so happy, not only there but at school, too. And she's got a new hero," she laughed. "You'll never guess who."

"Our sheriff."

Abby's eyebrows arched.

"He did happen to mention to a few people what a sweet and well-behaved little girl she was," Marie added. "Not to mention that Lucy noticed his husky limping when he hadn't even seen it himself."

"She's very observant," Abby said, smiling. "Like her dad. I miss him every day. I miss Mary, too. They loved Lucy so much. I just hope I can do right by her."

"You're doing a fine job from what I see." She leaned forward. "My husband works with the husband of one of the vet techs in Dr. Shriver's practice. He told my husband some sad news."

"What?" Abby asked, curious.

"Sheriff Banks's dog has cancer."

"Oh, no!" Abby said with concern.

Marie nodded, grimacing. "It's so sad. She's all he had left of his wife. Deborah left him the dog as a puppy, just before she died. He's going to go crazy when he loses her."

Abby felt the sadness like a brand. "He said she was all he had left."

"He feels that way, too. Such a pity they didn't have a child, but, then, Deborah would never have settled for just being a wife and mother in Catelow, Wyoming. She was always too big for this little town."

Marie wasn't a mean or spiteful person. The remark was unlike her.

"Sorry, I sound catty, don't I? But she wasn't the little saint that Cody makes her out to be. I have a friend who lived near her apartment in Denver." She looked up. A small group was headed for the booth next to theirs. She was quiet, all of a sudden.

On their way out the door, Marie paused. "You lived and worked in Denver. Didn't you ever see Deborah?" she asked.

Abby laughed. "I was a schoolgirl. And Lawrence didn't have anything to do with her. Mary hardly mentioned her." She frowned. "Funny, that never occurred to me before. Lawrence and I were from the same hometown that Deborah was, Catelow, but they didn't ever have her over to visit and they certainly never visited her." She paused. "I overheard them talking once. Mary said that she didn't dare drop in on Deborah. I never heard why."

"There was a really good reason for that." Marie paused. More people were coming out the door. "Goodness, look at the time," she said suddenly, having glanced at her watch. "We'll be late back, and poor Mr. Owens isn't in the best of moods lately!"

They went back to work and Deborah wasn't mentioned again.

Abby was sorry about the sheriff's dog. She wondered if there was a treatment, like there was for people.

She mentioned it to Hannah while Lucy was in her bedroom doing her homework.

"Oh, yes, they have all those treatments, but they cost thousands of dollars," Hannah said. "And when they get through with them, the poor animal does die, but after going through hell first. Being taken back and forth to people, even kind and loving people, who hook you up and stick needles in you when you're already sick and scared. That's mostly how an animal would see it, even though we know vets do their best to keep our pets alive and well. And it's not like it cures them. Maybe if they catch it early enough, on a young animal, whose people can afford it all." She sighed. "Not a choice I'd like to have to make. My old Thomas is fourteen. He's a sweet cat, but I'm not sure I'd put him through all that even if I could afford it." She glanced at Abby while she took food off the burner. "You've heard about Sheriff Banks's dog, I gather."

Abby grimaced and nodded.

"He'll go nuts," Hannah said. "Absolutely nuts. Loves that dog like a child. Takes it everywhere with him, even to work."

"I wish there was something we could do," Abby said quietly.

Hannah wiped her hands on her apron. "Not much anybody can do. Except to be there, when he really needs a friend."

Abby nodded.

The men were repairing a section of the barn, with loud banging and a few lilting remarks back and forth to each other, when a luxury SUV pulled up in the driveway. It was Saturday, and Abby wasn't expecting company.

She went out, finishing a piece of apple she'd taken from the bowlful that Hannah had peeled and cored ready to make an apple pie.

It was the Miami man, Mr. Whatley, who'd pretended to be first a livestock expert and secondly a detective. She forced herself not to smile as he climbed carefully down out of the cab, using a step that he'd obviously had added to the huge, tall vehicle.

He came up to the porch, dressed in neat jeans and boots and a Western shirt with snaps under a shearling jacket that looked two sizes too big on him. He had on a Western hat, too—a Stetson with its trademark belt buckle hatband.

"Mr. Whatley," she said, with a pleasant smile. "What can I do for you?"

He tipped his hat. "Miss Brennan, I'm just learning how to run a ranch and I need some advice."

She hesitated. "You know, Mr. Whatley, the only thing I know about running ranches is that you leave that to people who know what they're doing. I don't."

"Oh, it's not that. I have to find a kindly woman like Aunt Bee who cooked for Sheriff Taylor on *The Andy Griffith Show!*"

Abby reminded herself that letting her jaw drop wasn't helpful. She swallowed. "Well, Mr. Whatley, the best thing would be to advertise in the local paper. In the help wanted column," she added helpfully.

"Oh, no, that won't do, I might get just anybody," he said at once. "I pay really good wages," he added, "and I'll never ask for food after midnight or do anything to upset her. I promise." He smiled.

She was racking her brain for some sort of answer when Hannah came up behind her. "There's Mrs. Julia Donovan," she pointed out. "She's just widowed and about to lose her house because her husband left the house and all he had to his shiftless brother-in-law, who took over the property and told her she could have two weeks to find someplace else to live. Sweet man. How I do hope he trips over a stump and goes headfirst into a bed of stinging nettles." She smiled sweetly.

Abby was hard-pressed not to die laughing. She coughed instead.

"Is she a nice person?" Mr. Whatley asked.

Hannah grinned. "Shouldn't you ask if she could cook first?"

"Oh, I'm used to bad cooking. My sister can hardly boil water. But being nice is more important than anything else," he added very solemnly.

"Well, she cooks like an angel. And she's one of those people who are taken advantage of because they're nurturing folk."

Mr. Whatley smiled and nodded. "Just the sort of lady I'm looking for. Could you tell me how to get in touch with her?"

"I certainly can. I'll write down her telephone number for

you right now, and I'll phone her first and tell her you'd like to see her about a possible job. She's rather shy…"

The smile on Mr. Whatley's face was even bigger now. "That's nice. I'm shy myself. It's hard for me to talk to people. Not to you, Miss Brennan," he added when Hannah had gone back into the house, "or even to the sheriff. I'm by myself a lot."

"A goodly number of us are that way, Mr. Whatley," she said sympathetically.

Hannah was back with the telephone number. "Now you give me a few minutes to talk to her first, Mr. Whatley, if you don't mind."

"I don't mind at all. Thank you very much. And I hope you both have a very good day." He tipped his hat, climbed laboriously into the cab of his enormous vehicle, and went off with a wave.

"Will she suit him do you think?" Abby asked.

"I think she'll be just what the doctor ordered," Hannah said. "Her husband was a cheap, thoughtless, mean man. He gave her a meager little allowance, so that she only had enough to buy a new dress once in a blue moon. The house will probably fall down around her brother-in-law's ears the day he moves in," she added with a big grin. "And serve him right! She'll like Mr. Whatley. He'll like her, too. She's barely twenty-eight," she added.

"Probably Mr. Whatley isn't much older than that," Abby said thoughtfully.

Hannah wiggled both eyebrows.

"Hannah, you devil, you!" Abby burst out.

"Just helping nature along," she said. "Besides, it will be the saving of poor Julia Donovan. That sorry, shiftless brother-in-law of hers, giving her two weeks to find another home, not even caring that she'd never had a job because her husband refused to let her work!"

"Was he the only sibling?"

"The only one, and his dad raised him to be just like he was. He never had a chance. But Julia will have one. Bless her heart, she'll think she's landed in heaven."

Abby smiled.

Abby noticed that Mr. Owens was jumpy for the rest of the week, and his mind wasn't on statutes of law. He passed one of his cases down to another attorney in the firm, Sally Toller. He made phone calls. When he wasn't making them, he was sitting at his desk, staring at nothing and looking as if the world was sitting on his shoulders. Abby wondered if it was his nephew who was causing him such distress. He was a nice man. She hoped he could straighten things out at home.

CHAPTER FIVE

Cody had been working on the bank robbery case. It was only the second one he'd had since his tenure in office, and a puzzling one it was, too. The bandit had been wearing a full face mask of a dead president, carrying an old-time revolver in a holster. He hadn't spoken a word, just shoved a note in Miss Dorothy Hanover's face and indicated his pistol. She'd handed him the contents of her cash drawer, so upset that she'd forgotten to push the silent alarm button. Nobody had blamed her. She was in her late sixties, and it was hardly a daily event.

People in town had been worried about their savings, but the bank president had assured them that all his assets were protected. And Sheriff Banks would catch the culprit, he added with supreme confidence. Their sheriff was one of the best in Wyoming. Which made Cody walk a little taller, despite his lack of a suspect.

Ordinarily the job would have gone to the local police department, but the police chief was on a short vacation due to the birth of his first child, with his wife. It was a tiny little boy and the chief said these first few days were precious and he was going to take some time off to be with his family. The mayor had just laughed and wished him well. His next in command, Bill Harris, was taking over the chief's duties, but he was older than most of his men and pretty much beyond tracking down bank robbers, with his health issues. He was much loved, because he'd been a beat cop years ago, always walking around town. He picked up a lot of useful information that way and he got to know the people in his town. He was a bank of information that many of the other officers relied on when they were working on cases.

Cody was careful not to step on Bill's authority, but the other man was just grateful to have him on the case. Cody was known for his persistence in catching criminals and he never stopped until he solved a crime. That was a remarkable record. But then, Catelow had a very small population and everybody knew where the bad guys lived and who their relations were. It wasn't like a big city, where there were millions of people who could have committed the crime.

Cody sat down in the visitor's chair in Bill's temporary office. He took off his Stetson and sailed it into another chair. "A bank robbery. In our town." He shook his head. "I don't even remember one before these."

"Oh, I do," Bill said, grinning. He ran a hand over his bald head. "It was back in the sixties, and the perp turned out to be a sixteen-year-old boy who wanted to buy his mama a nice birthday present. She had cancer, you see, and it was just him and her, and there was no money. He tried to kill himself when he got caught but they went easy on him. He was a juvie, after all, and he had a clean record. He got first offender status and when he came of age, we wiped his record. He went on to law school and after working as a prosecuting attorney for many years, he became a circuit judge."

"His mother would have been proud of him," Cody replied.

"She was, because he turned himself in and really worked

to rehabilitate himself. People in town helped." He smiled. "It's one of the nicest things about Catelow, how forgiving and unprejudiced people are here."

"I've noticed that," Cody agreed, smiling.

"Do we have any suspects?" Bill asked.

Cody shook his head. "The mask wasn't obtained locally, because we only have one store in town that even sells masks anymore. And the weapon he used wasn't found." He shook his head. "Broad daylight, people all around, and he robs a bank and gets away. The bank teller was so shaken that she didn't hit the silent alarm. He made some pretty bad threats in the note, the witnesses said. They'll be off work for a day or two, trying to get over it." He shook his head. "He even took the note with him, so no chance to get prints or even a handwriting expert in. The teller said that when a gun is pointed at you, that barrel looks three times as big. I know what she means. I've had guns pointed at me, too."

"It sort of goes with the job."

He nodded. "My investigator's getting fingerprints. We have to do everybody in the bank, so we can sort them out." He shook his head. "It's going to be a mess. I wish the chief was here. He's a great investigator."

"So are you, Bill," Cody protested. "I miss him, too, but if I had a brand-new baby, I'd be home for a week, too."

"She's a sweet girl, his wife. Went through a lot while they were courting, but they're really happy. I'm glad for them. I still miss my wife, and she's been gone over fifteen years."

"Mine's been gone six," Cody said. His face tautened. "Her, and now Anyu…"

Bill scowled. "What about Anyu?"

Cody took a steadying breath. "She's got cancer. It's spread too far for the drastic treatments to do much beyond lengthening the pain. I won't let them put her down. I said I'd take her home and pamper her, and I have. They gave me pain meds for her." He ground his teeth. "She's all I've got left in the world," he said gruffly.

"They're like our kids, aren't they?" the other man said quietly. "I've got three. All mutts, but I'd do most anything to save them."

"I can't imagine life without her."

"You know, God never closes a window except he opens a door." He cocked his head. "You understand what I'm saying?"

Cody thought about it for a minute. "I guess I do." He sighed. "It's just so damned hard!"

"We're leaves floating down the river, Cody," Bill said softly. "We think we have control, that we can do anything. But in the end, even with free will, there are limits. We have to consider that there may really be a higher power dictating what happens to us. And if that's true, it's easier to just float than to try to paddle to the bank. And if we could do that," he said, leaning forward with a grin, "we'd miss the whole adventure of life!"

Cody burst out laughing. "You should have been a preacher, Bill."

"Yes, I should have, but I wasn't called to it." He smiled. "I guess I'm more of a chaplain here, when you get down to it. My big shoulder gets a workout. So many officers have problems of one sort or another. I just sit and let them talk."

"It helps more than you know," Cody said. "Just somebody to listen."

"You don't have anybody to do that."

"I have Anyu."

"Yes, but she doesn't answer you. I hope," Bill added quickly and with mock horror.

Cody laughed. "No. Not yet." He grabbed his hat and got up. "I'll keep you in the loop. And if you talk to the chief, tell him I'm envious. I'd have loved a child," he added wistfully.

"I read about a man fifty who just had his first child," Bill said with pursed lips. "You're not that old, son."

"I feel like it sometimes." He shrugged. "I'd never get over Debby. Anybody else would be second best. I couldn't settle for that." He went to the door. "I'll let you know if I find out anything."

"You do that."

Cody closed the door and walked back to his SUV. He forced Debby and Anyu to the back of his mind. He had a case to solve.

Hannah and Abby were getting supper started a week or so later when a truck pulled up beside the house. It was the one Don Blalock drove. He picked something up and came up the steps.

Abby was there just as he knocked on the door. She opened it and her lips fell apart. He was holding the most adorable fluffy furred little animal she'd ever seen.

"I've got an orphan who needs a home," he said with a sigh. "Found her out in the thicket while we were rounding up the pregnant cows to move to a closer pasture. She's cold and hungry."

"And say no more." Abby took the puppy from him and nuzzled her. The dog made a whimpering sound and tucked her little head into Abby's chest. "Oh, that did it," Abby said. "I'm never letting go of this puppy until I die!"

Don chuckled. "Thought you might feel that way. Lucy wanted a puppy, I remembered, and you said you'd think about it. Want to think about it some more?"

"Not on your life! This baby isn't leaving."

Hannah came over to pet the tiny thing as well. "She's adorable!" she said.

"And just what we need," Abby said. She sighed. "Well, we'll get through housebreaking somehow."

"Maisie's brother used to train dogs for the police," Don said with a grin. "Might ask him for some pointers."

"Thanks! I will!"

"I'll get his number and text it to you."

"Great! And I need to get her to the vet as soon as possible."

"I can take her for you right now, if you want me to. She'll need a checkup and her shots."

"Can you? We're in the middle of cooking supper."

"Won't take long." He took the puppy back. It curled up in his arms, too. "She's a sweetie! She'll make you a great pet."

"Thanks so much, Don!"

"No problem."

Lucy came home from school and did her homework first, wondering why Hannah and Aunt Abby looked so strange.

"You guys look funny," she said finally.

"We have a secret," Abby replied.

There was the sound of a truck pulling up outside.

"And it's coming in the door right now," she added.

Don came up the steps with the puppy in his arms. She'd been cleaned up. She was snow-white with black tips on her ears, and big, beautiful blue eyes.

"Oh, she looks like snow!" Lucy cried, jumping up and down. "Please can we keep her? Please, Aunt Abby!"

"Yes, we can, and what a sweet name you've given her. Snow it is."

"Snow," Lucy repeated as the pup was carefully lowered into her arms. The puppy licked her face and she laughed.

"She's had her shots." Don handed her the papers from the vet. "You'll have to call and tell them her name. She's just listed as Abby's dog right now," he chuckled.

"I'll do it right now," she promised. "Thanks so much, Don!"

"It was my pleasure. Dinner sure smells good," he added.

"I'll bet Maisie's waiting on me to put ours on the table. I'll
get on home."

"Thanks again!"

He threw up a hand as he went out.

Abby called the vet and gave them the dog's new name
and her credit card number, to pay for the visit and the injec-
tions. And for a night and a day and another night, nothing
got done in the house because its occupants were too busy
cuddling the puppy.

Anyu walked the property with Cody. She moved a little
slower every day, and he could tell that she had pain. He gave
her the tablets and worried. She looked up at him with laughing eyes, but her ability to walk became less and less. One day,
she couldn't get up at all. And Cody finally called the vet.

He spent Anyu's last day with her on the couch beside him.
It was a lingering, painful farewell. She was so much a part
of his life, his companion, his partner, his best friend. Anyu
was his last link with Debby. He didn't know how he was
going to manage this. He fought a hot mist in his eyes as he
stroked Anyu's soft, clean fur and stared into a dark future.

Finally, he carried her out to the SUV and put her carefully on the front seat. "We're going to go for a ride, okay?"
he asked as he got behind the wheel.

She made a faint whimpering sound and her blue eyes
looked up at him, but they didn't laugh. They were dilated
with a pain he could only imagine.

"No more pain, pretty girl," he whispered as he bent to
hug her one last time. His eyes stung. It was like giving up
Debby all over again. "How am I going to live," he whispered brokenly, "without you?"

He blinked away the moisture and put the vehicle in gear.

It was like taking a victim to the guillotine. And not just any victim. His whole life in one beautiful furry package.

Dr. Shriver met him at the door, waving away the vet tech who usually did the paperwork and ushered in the patient.

Cody had Anyu in his arms, held close. "It hurts her to walk," he said, grinding his teeth together.

"Bring her back here," the vet said.

Cody followed him into the back where the operating table was. He put Anyu down gently. She still whimpered. Everything seemed to cause her pain. He looked at the doctor, his eyes begging for a miracle.

The vet put a big hand on his shoulder. "Listen to me," he said quietly. "The pain will get worse. She won't be able to bear it. She'll have to be so drugged that she won't know you. And she'll still..." He couldn't bring himself to say the word. Behind him, one of the assistants was calming Anyu.

"There's no hope? None at all?" Cody asked, his voice choked with emotion.

"I'm so sorry. No, there's nothing, Cody," he said, drawing him out of earshot of the assistant. "I've stayed with my own animals that I had to put down. The last one was so hard on me that I had to take a few days off. Let me advise you. Don't stay and watch this. Anyu will be drugged. She won't know or care what's happening to her. We'll talk to her and soothe her." He forced a smile. "One day, you'll pass yourself, and she'll be waiting for you at the gate. That's what I think about my own pets. It's all that makes it bearable. We all go. Nothing in life is permanent. It's just a little separation."

Cody nodded. "If it was any other animal, I'd leave." He smiled through his grief. "She never quit on me. I won't quit on her."

"Okay, then."

The vet let Cody stand by the table and hold Anyu's paw.

She looked up at him one last time with those soft blue, loving eyes. And then they put her under, very gently, and her eyes closed forever.

Abby was in the local café having lunch. One of Dr. Shriver's technicians sat down at the table next to hers with another one of the vet's employees.

"That was so hard," she said to the young man. She shook her head. "Honestly, I thought we'd have to sedate Cody before it was through. Somebody should have stopped him from driving. I've never seen anyone grieve like that."

Abby's heart jumped. She sat still and listened some more.

"His wife gave him the dog, didn't she?" the woman asked.

Her coworker nodded. "It was like losing her all over again," he said.

"He shouldn't have stayed with her and watched it," the woman said heavily. "I had to have my sixteen-year-old cat put down last year, and I just couldn't bear it! I had Lily stay with him while they put him down." She sighed. "I had them cremate him. He's in an urn on my mantel."

"I've done that a time or two."

"The sheriff didn't want that done. He carried her out to his SUV after and drove her home. He said she had a favorite spot, under an apple tree. He was going to bury her there himself."

"It's a shame he doesn't have any family," the other one said.

"I know. Gosh, he doesn't need to be alone right now. Losing a pet you love is really like losing a member of your family. People grieve for animals just like they grieve for people. Especially somebody like Cody. He doesn't have anybody."

"Too true."

Abby got up, her meal half-eaten, and left a tip before she went out the door.

★ ★ ★

Cody rarely drank, but this was an occasion. A horrible occasion. He had a fifth of Jack Daniel's that he'd never opened, a Christmas present from one of his deputies. He broke the seal and poured himself a big glass of it.

He knew now, too late, that the vet had been right. He shouldn't have stayed. For the rest of his life, he'd see Anyu in her final minutes of life, hear the soft whimper, watch her paws move restlessly just briefly. He saw the life seep out of her. She lay still, like snow against the silver metal of the table. He'd managed not to break down. He carried Anyu out in his arms to the SUV, put her in, and drove her home.

He dug a big hole under the apple tree and then went to find a cloth to cover her with. He couldn't bear to see her face while he finished his chore.

The mound of earth looked somehow right, where he'd put it. Anyu would be there, close by, close to him, as long as he lived. He wasn't ordinarily a sentimental man, but he was going to put flowers on her grave.

He thought that he'd never put flowers on Debby's grave. He'd wanted to bring her back to Catelow for burial, but the funeral director was adamant about her last wishes. She'd wanted to be buried in a cemetery in Denver, near the hospital where she worked. One of her colleagues, a neurologist named Craig Stern, had sided with the funeral director. He'd known Debby, he said, and she'd told everyone where she wanted to be if she should lose her life. He'd thought it odd that she should have spoken of such a thing to a man besides her husband. The doctor looked as if he'd had too much to drink. He was almost staggering at the funeral. When the last prayer was said over Debby, in the cemetery, he'd seen tears in the doctor's eyes before he turned quickly away.

He must have been a coworker at the hospital, Cody decided, possibly the mentor who was teaching Debby new theories in neurology. The man was very well dressed and looked about five or six years older than Cody. Considering how unsettled the man was, he hoped there were no patients waiting at his hospital. He put it out of his mind. He knew very little of her work. She never spoke of the hospital or her colleagues there. It was only history now. Debby was gone forever. The light had gone out of the world.

Cody thought about that while he had another drink. His undersheriff was on duty. Cody had managed a quick explanation of his need to be off for a couple of days. Of course by now, everybody in Catelow knew about Anyu. Gossip traveled far.

He finished his drink. Was it his third or fourth? He couldn't remember. Everything looked fuzzy.

His dark eyes went to the sofa that Anyu had always shared with him. Tears stung his eyes. He didn't bother to stop them. There was nobody to see them. Nobody at all.

The sudden knock on the back door startled him. He struggled to his feet and prayed that it wasn't an emergency, because he could hardly walk. He sure as hell couldn't drive. He staggered to the door and looked out through the glass insert. He blinked.

He opened the door and Abby looked up at him and winced.

"You should go home," he said curtly. "I've been drinking. A lot."

She noticed the fumes on his breath, but he didn't seem dangerous. Anguished. Miserable. Worn. Torn.

"I'm so sorry, Cody," she said, and the sympathy was in her eyes as well as her voice.

"I stayed with her, while..."

"I stayed with our old cat at my brother's house when she

died. I would never do it again." She shook her head. "It tears the heart right out of you."

He nodded. His face showed every year of his age. His dark eyes were already bloodshot and he was wobbly. She closed the door and went back to him.

"I've got nobody now," he ground out.

She didn't even think. She put her arms around him and held him close, her head on his broad chest where the soft material of his shirt covered it. He smelled of soap and leather and cologne. It was a good smell.

He hesitated, but only for seconds. His arms went around her and tightened. His face went down against her throat, where her hair was thick and soft. She felt wetness there. Her fingers spread into his thick, blond-streaked brown hair and she rocked him in her arms. She didn't say a word. She just held him.

The comfort was unexpected. He wasn't sure he liked the feeling of helplessness that went with it, but it was nice, being held, being comforted. He couldn't remember anyone caring about him when he was hurt. Certainly not Debby, who just told him to pull himself together when he came home sick at heart and anguished because he'd had to shoot a man. He didn't kill the perpetrator, but it was a man he knew. The bullet went into his hip and shattered bone. He was transferred to Denver to have the damage repaired. Then he sued the county and the sheriff's office as well. It only added to the misery. Debby had come home for the weekend, but she left for Denver early the next morning after she had a phone call. She'd taken her cell phone into the bathroom to talk to whoever it was. Cody had been so traumatized that he was barely lucid. Debby had said that the man was obviously a criminal, he got what was coming to him. And Cody was an idiot to let himself get into such a state over a shooting that wasn't even a fatal one. She'd left Cody behind with a vague promise to come back within a month or so. She hadn't even kissed him goodbye.

And here was Abby, who'd been afraid of him, rocking him in her soft arms because he'd lost his pet. Debby wouldn't have done that. She was truly remote from any tragedy. He'd wondered sometimes what sort of doctor she was. He loved her dearly, but she was lukewarm with him, even in bed. She looked upon intimacy as her duty, but she was meticulous about taking her birth control pill every day. She didn't seem to enjoy Cody, ever. He loved being with her, because he loved her, but he knew she wasn't enjoying it. She'd mentioned once that he was too conventional and frankly boring when it came to intimacy. She let him do what he liked. But it was like making love to a pillow. He hated that memory.

It was the only really uncomfortable thing about their marriage. Well, that, and her insistence that she had to live in Denver to get her studies done. It was a long drive from Catelow. Cody offered to make the trip any time she was free, but Debby always had an excuse. She seemed to feel that Cody belonged in a small town, not in a hospital in the city.

Why hadn't he ever noticed that? She'd never wanted him near her apartment in Denver. Now he was curious. She let him come to her apartment in Denver one time, only one time, and she was with him the whole time. She was visibly relieved when he left, and she only showed him the living room.

She was always looking around even when Cody came to visit her at the hospital, as he had a few times, when the loneliness got the worst. He hadn't thought about that, either. He hadn't thought about a lot of odd things that Deborah did. Like the night she wanted to go to a friend's house for drinks. That doctor, Craig Stern, who'd been at her funeral and insisted that she'd asked to be buried in Denver if anything happened to her. Cody had been uncomfortable, but the doctor had been even more uncomfortable. Debby had stayed right beside Cody and Dr. Stern had managed to avoid him the whole time they were there. Afterward, Debby had grown quiet and withdrawn. She seemed relieved when Cody said he'd have to get back to Catelow and didn't have time to spend the night.

His mind was too busy to hold the thought in very long. Besides, the soft body pressed up against his so trustingly made him feel protective. Abby was fiercely independent, but she had a good heart.

"Come here," she said after a minute. She took his big hand and led him to the kitchen table. "Sit down. You need to eat something."

He took a deep breath. His head was swimming. "Shouldn't you be at work?" he asked quietly.

"I phoned and said I had to take the afternoon off," she said, turning to the stove. She opened the fridge. There was bacon, some eggs and butter. She pulled them out, found a skillet, and proceeded to make bacon and eggs with buttered toast. She made a pot of coffee while she was at it.

Cody sat and watched her, fascinated. It had been years since he'd watched a woman cook. Debby couldn't. She bought TV dinners and heated them up, or went to get take-out in Catelow. Abby was a woman of many talents, he was learning. She could ride a horse, work at a job, cook, and manage a huge ranch—with some help from Don Blalock—and she had a big heart. The care she took of her niece was proof of that. Now here she was, out of the blue, taking care of him. He felt better. Her very presence was comforting.

He wasn't going to say that, of course. He wasn't an overly emotional man. He was a lawman with a responsible job. Except that right now, he couldn't do his job, because he was stinking drunk.

He made a sound deep in his throat and weaved a little in his chair.

"Here you go," she said, putting everything on the table. "You'll feel better if you eat something."

"It looks good," he said.

She smiled. "Lucy and I have breakfast for lunch or supper sometimes, especially if I have to work late."

He frowned as he watched her pour coffee into two mugs. "You live on a lonely stretch of road. The ranch is two miles from the main highway. It's dangerous at night."

"I keep my doors locked," she assured him.

"If you'll let me know when you have to work late, I'll have one of my deputies follow you home."

She put cream in her coffee and tried to adjust to this new and very different friendship that was developing between them.

"You aren't afraid of me anymore?" he asked and seemed to mind.

"No," she replied softly. "Of course not." She smiled. "You're not a mean drunk."

He chuckled. "I don't get drunk, as a rule." His face tautened as he saw all over again Anyu on the silver table, lying so still and trusting as the life slowly drained out of her.

"You're thinking about it, aren't you?" she asked gently. "It's all right. She's all right. She's chasing rabbits in the snow and laughing."

He took a quick breath, fighting the moisture again. It was so damned painful. He'd be all alone now. Completely alone. He had nothing, nobody. His last link with Debby was gone forever.

"Lucy was saying last night that she wished she knew how to train a dog," Abby mentioned without looking at him.

They ate in silence for a couple of minutes. "Lucy's got a cat, doesn't she?" he asked, puzzled. His mind was still cloudy.

She nodded, finishing a swallow of hot coffee. "Yes, but Don found an abandoned puppy in the snow. He brought it to us, after he took it to the vet to be checked. It's a female. She's snow-white with blue eyes. Lucy's crazy about her. We could never have pets in Denver. She's over the moon. A kitten and a puppy, all at once. Except we don't know beans about how to take care of a puppy."

His emotions were so raw that, at first, the words went right over his head. He finished the impromptu meal and sat back with his coffee, staring at her. "Lucy's a sweet child," he said finally.

"Yes." She smiled. "She has a big heart. But she's sensitive. It was horrible for her at the school she attended in Denver. There were gangs. A teacher was assaulted. A little girl, not much older than Lucy, was dragged into a bathroom by three boys and..." She stopped. "Well, you can imagine what happened next."

"Were they found?" he asked tautly. He was outraged at the thought of what had happened in a school, where students had the right to protection from such things.

"Yes. And prosecuted. But they were all juveniles, you see. They went to detention and only remained there until they came of age. They're probably out there, stalking some other poor child."

"And the child?"

"Her parents took her to a therapist. The last I heard, she was doing very well." She sighed. "It's such a shame. It was in school, you know. Children are out of control in our society."

"You don't know the half of it," he said. "The government has its hand in everything now. Parents who discipline their children are subject to arrest if the child calls family and children's services and reports the parent. We have to have a psychologist interview children who witness traumatic events."

He managed a smile. "And anything you say will offend somebody, who may go on social media and tear you to ribbons."

"They can be prosecuted," she reminded him. "We can track down an IP number. It's not even hard." She laughed. "It's amazing how many kids think everything they say online is okay, that they're completely anonymous when they bully other kids. And they aren't."

"We had a kid last month that we arrested for harassing a student online. The victim tried to kill herself, and fortunately failed. Lawsuits were involved."

"Good," she said curtly.

He smiled. "You're a good cook."

Her face flushed a little and she laughed self-consciously. "Thanks." Her eyes lifted to his bloodshot dark ones. She studied the grief, still evident there. "When I leave, you'll be all alone here." She looked down at her coffee cup. "We have a spare room. Hannah could make up a bed for you." She looked up and met his shocked eyes. "I know, you're a big, tough guy who doesn't need a nursemaid. But you do need people around you, just overnight." She cocked her head and stared at him, smiling uncertainly.

He drew in a breath. His eyes went to the sofa and he winced, because he'd never see Anyu there again.

"Hannah's a really good cook. She's making stroganoff tonight, too."

His eyes shot back to her. "I love stroganoff."

"So?"

He managed a smile. She was a sweet woman. Maybe it wouldn't hurt to be coddled, just for one night. Besides, there was Lucy, and he was already fond of her.

"Okay," he said. He finished his coffee. "Thanks," he added gruffly.

"Oh, you don't need to thank me. I'm buttering you up."

His eyes widened. "Excuse me?"

"If we feed you up nicely and take good care of you, you'll come in with guns blazing if we ever get attacked by Martians."

It took him a few seconds to get that. He threw back his head and laughed, a genuine laugh. "You are one strange girl," he accused.

She grinned. "And I work at it, too. You aren't on call tonight?"

"I'm too drunk to be on call."

"That reminds me. Where's the whiskey bottle?"

He was still weaving a little. He grinned. "In the trash can. I drank it all."

"Oh, dear," she said, worried.

"Not to worry. I can hold my liquor."

Maybe he could, but he didn't. Barely a minute later, he was out of his chair, running for the bathroom.

Abby followed him, wetted a washcloth she found in a vanity drawer, and cleaned him up when he was finally through.

He just stood there, looking at her.

"What is it?" she asked.

"Nobody's ever looked after me like this. Not since my mother died."

"Well, there's nobody else here to do it," she said matter-of-factly. She smiled. "Here." She handed him a glass with some mouthwash in it. "I'll phone Hannah and have her make up a bed in the guest room."

"Okay." He hesitated. "Thanks."

She studied his hard, tormented face. "You'll get through this," she said softly. "It just needs time. And people around you."

He didn't answer her. He did smile.

CHAPTER SIX

Hannah was surprised at the phone call, but she went ahead and made up a bed in the guest room for Cody, mentally re-working the ingredients she was using for the stroganoff so that she had enough for a hungry man as well as for the three of them.

Lucy came in, with the puppy in her arms. "Why are you in here, Hannah?" she asked.

Hannah smiled at her. "The sheriff is coming to spend the night with us."

"He is?" she asked, surprised. "Why?"

"He lost his dog today. Your aunt says he's very sad and doesn't need to be alone."

"You mean Anyu is…" She stopped and swallowed hard. "Oh, that is very sad," she agreed. "The poor sheriff. He can hold my puppy," she added at once. "She'll help comfort him."

Hannah smiled at her. "You really are a sweet girl."

Lucy just grinned at her.

Cody hesitated at being asked to ride with someone else driving.

"Well, you have to," Abby said simply. "You obviously

can't drive and it's a long walk to my place. Besides," she added, tongue-in-cheek, "suppose one of your deputies saw you slogging along and wondered why you were weaving all over the road."

He chuckled softly. "I see your point."

"Feeling better?" she asked as they went out to her vehicle and got in.

"Much," he said. "This was kind of you, inviting me over for the night."

"I had a friend who did this for me, when I lost my brother and sister-in-law," she said. "She worked in the law office with me. I never forgot it." She glanced at his face, taut with grief. "Losing an animal you love dearly is not so much different from losing a person," she added. "They tell us now that people finally understand what a traumatic thing it is to lose a much loved pet. The grieving process is basically the same."

"I never understood it before," he said after a minute when they were underway. "Anyu was one of the few pets I ever had. It would have been impossible to have an animal when I lived at home. Now, I have all sorts of critters hanging around, besides the cattle." He laughed softly. "I've got a family of raccoons living in one of the outbuildings, and there's an owl who sits in the tree next to the house and hoots at me every evening. There's even a woodpecker."

"Do you feed birds?" she asked.

"Yes."

She grinned. "So do I. We've got bird feeders everywhere. I like birds."

"Me, too."

She stopped at the intersection and waited for the light to change. They didn't speak again, but then, it was a comfortable silence, as if they were old friends. How very odd to feel that way, she thought.

Cody was thinking the same thing. Abby was a nurturing

woman. He'd never known one, not since his mother had died. He wasn't sure he liked it. He'd been alone so long that he was used to it. But she was right about tonight. He couldn't bear the thought of sitting in his living room on the sofa that Anyu had shared when he'd just buried her.

"How's the bank robbery investigation going?" she asked when they were almost to the ranch.

"Slowly," he said. "We can't find any local connections at all. But it's early days. We'll solve it."

She laughed. "I know you will. Your cousin says you're the most dogged investigator he's ever known."

"Bart's a good guy."

"Yes, he is." She glanced at him. "So is our Don Blalock. I don't know how I'd manage without him. I don't know the first thing about running a ranch."

"You're very honest, aren't you?" he asked suddenly, his bloodshot dark eyes on her profile.

"Lies are a waste of time and effort," she said simply.

He laughed. "Well, yes, I guess they are."

"I suppose you hear a lot of them, in your profession."

"I do. Nobody's ever guilty of a crime, you see. It was persecution by the police, or they were only looking at something they were accused of stealing." He shook his head. "This one guy was in a car dealership's parking lot trying to hotwire one of those new Broncos to steal it." He sighed. "Now, if that's just looking, I'm a grizzly bear."

She glanced at him amusedly. "You don't look like a grizzly bear. Well, not so much," she conceded.

"Thanks. I think."

She grinned. "You're welcome. And we're home!"

They got out and went in through the kitchen, as Abby usually did. "We're home," she called out, not catching the sudden glimmer in the eyes of the man beside her.

Lucy came running, with the puppy in her arms, cuddled tight. "Hi, Sheriff Banks! You going to spend the night with us?"

He couldn't help but smile at that excited little face. "Yes, I am."

"Hannah made up the bed," she said. "And we're having stroganoff for supper!"

"That sounds good," Cody said. But his eyes were on the puppy. She really didn't look anything like Anyu, who was black-and-white. This little thing was pure white with just a little black on the tips of its ears.

"This is Snow," Lucy told him. "Mr. Blalock found her all alone in the snow and brought her to us. So she's called Snow."

"She's very pretty," Cody said, smiling down at the child.

Lucy moved a little closer, hesitant. "Would you like to hold her?" she asked shyly.

"I'd like that very much, Lucy," he replied quietly.

She handed him the puppy. It looked up at him with bright blue eyes and when he drew it closer, it licked his face. He laughed, some of the anguish gone out of him as he cuddled the tiny thing.

Lucy smiled with relief. She wanted to comfort the sheriff, who still looked sad. But the puppy made him smile, so it was all right.

Abby watched the man with the puppy and thought suddenly what a wonderful father he'd make. He was so tender with the little animal.

He looked up at that moment and saw the odd look on her face. His eyebrows went up.

"What?" she asked.

"That expression," he said, smoothing his big hand over the soft fur of the puppy. "What were you thinking?"

She grimaced. Well, he'd asked. "What a wonderful father you'd make," she confessed and flushed a little, because it sounded very personal.

He just looked at her, his eyes dark and soft, his expression puzzling. "I love kids," he said after a minute. He shrugged. "Debby was determined to be the best in her field, so kids were sort of out of the question."

"I see." She saw a lot more than she was willing to admit, so she smiled and asked if he'd like to have a cup of coffee.

"I would," he said with a long sigh. "I'm feeling pretty empty. Here's your baby back, Lucy. She's a sweet girl. Like you."

Lucy beamed. "Thanks, Sheriff Banks." She took the puppy back and cuddled it close. "We got cats, too. Lots of cats!"

"I've got cats of my own, out in the barn. We call them the mouser brigade. They keep the mice away, for sure."

"I got a cat of my own. He sleeps with me. He's named Patrick."

He smiled. The child fascinated him. He hadn't had much to do with children, except in tragic circumstances that went with his job. Lucy was far and away the most interesting child he'd come across.

Hannah came into the kitchen to help put cookies on the tray with the coffee and cream and sugar.

"Thanks, Hannah," Abby said, and she started to lift the tray.

"My job," Cody said, taking it from her with a gentle smile.

The smile hit her in the chest, confused and delighted her. She flushed again and cleared her throat. "Thanks."

"No problem." He led the way into the living room and put the tray down on the coffee table.

They drank the coffee and nibbled on the cookies without speaking for a few minutes, while Lucy cuddled her puppy nearby and sipped her hot chocolate.

"Homemade cookies," Cody sighed. "I haven't had a home-made cookie since my mother died."

Abby laughed. "Hannah's a terrific cook."

"So are you, Aunt Abby," Lucy piped in. "She can make French pastries," she told the sheriff. "And homemade bread!"

Cody groaned. "I love homemade bread. We used to have a baker here that made it, but he moved to California three years ago."

"I'll bake you a loaf of your very own," Abby promised.

He smiled at her. "That would be nice of you."

"I'm mostly nice," she said.

His eyebrows arched. "Mostly?"

She glanced at her niece. "Lucy, would you give the puppy a little water? She's panting."

"It's warm in here," Lucy said, nodding. She jumped up. "I'll be right back."

"I had to go see the principal at Lucy's school in Denver," Abby told him, "just after the little girl was assaulted. The boys had made a comment to Lucy that she didn't even un-derstand. She told it to me and I went marching up to the school. The principal got an earful, and I sent a registered let-ter to the president of the school board as well." She pursed her lips. "I added the name and address of my attorney at the bottom. I had all sorts of apologies and promises, but in the meantime our cousin Butler died and we moved here." She shook her head. "It's so different here," she added. "I was too young to appreciate it when we moved away, but since I've been back, I can't imagine living anywhere else. Lucy loves her teacher and her school, and she's made many new friends."

He nodded. "It's unique as a community. More like a fam-ily, really, a big, spread-out family. Debby hated it here. She only visited when she had to." His mouth twisted. "I always thought she fell in love with the uniform instead of me." He looked up to see if she understood the remark.

She smiled. "We all know about the uniform and how it attracts women. It's that you law enforcement types are usually pretty muscular, because you have to be, and the uniform shows it off. But more than one officer has lost his job for giving in to that hero worship."

He smiled back. "It draws women," he agreed. He sighed, sipping coffee. "I've had my own problems with it over the years. While I was married, I just ignored it. Now, it can complicate a simple investigation."

"You can't help it that you're good-looking," she said bluntly.

Both eyebrows arched again. "Me?"

She gave him a glowering look. "Of course, you. You're a dish, and don't tell me nobody's ever mentioned it to you."

His eyes narrowed and his lips pursed.

"Not me," she said in a long-suffering tone. "Other women."

"Oh." He sipped more coffee, not looking at her. "Why not you?"

"I don't want to get mixed up with a man, ever," she said honestly.

"Abby, you're a grown woman now…"

"My father was a vicious drunk. My mother said he seemed like the sweetest man on earth when she married him. But when the door closed out the world, he wasn't the same man." She looked up at him, her eyes troubled. "How do you know? You never really see people the way they actually are unless you live with them. And by then, it's too late."

He scowled. He hadn't considered how badly her childhood had colored her attitudes about men. And then there had been his rampage, outside the hospital…

"I made it worse," he said bluntly, watching the faint color come into her cheeks. "I'm not like that," he tried to explain. "I was absolutely consumed by grief, torn apart with it. I've never been sorrier about anything than blaming you and Lucy for something that wasn't even your fault. I left you both with scars." He shook his head. "I wish there was some way to make up for it."

"We pick ourselves up and go on," she said simply.

"You haven't," he pointed out. "You're alone."

"By choice." She smiled. "I have a good job, people around me who care about me, a little girl to raise, cats in the barn, a new puppy—what else do I need?" She laughed.

"Children of your own," he said, and he didn't smile. His dark eyes were piercing, and she couldn't manage to look away from them.

She tingled all over. Her pulse raced. This wasn't at all what she'd planned when she'd asked him to come home with her. She was vulnerable! It was unexpected, and a little scary.

"I have Lucy," she repeated.

"Lucy's a little doll," he said, and he smiled. "But it's not quite the same thing."

She searched his strong face. "Did you want children?"

"Oh, yes. I wanted them very badly." His mouth pulled down. "Debby didn't. She was very career-minded." He sighed. "I don't think she meant to get married at all. We met at a festival, when she was visiting a friend, and got married two days later. She always seemed shocked at herself. She'd mentioned once that she had a sort of relationship where she worked, but she never said anything about it again after we married. It was probably a flash in the pan." He smiled sadly. "I loved her obsessively. She only managed to get home a few days a year. There was always a seminar or a workshop or just plain work. I tried to give her the freedom she needed. I never tied her down." He grimaced. "Maybe I should have." He looked up. "It's almost like I got married, but she didn't, you know?" And it was the first time he'd ever said anything negative about his late wife, ever.

"Some women don't settle well," she replied. "We had an attorney in practice at my brother's office in Denver. He got married, but his wife was out with the girls, supposedly, every single weekend while he was working on briefs. One day, she left and never came back. They had two little girls, and she just left them." She shook her head. "I'll never understand that sort of attitude. Parenting is a sacred trust."

"It's largely gone missing in our society. With both parents working, the kids are sort of raised by daycare and teachers and peers and television and video games. A goodly number of them are never taken to church, they aren't taught manners and courtesy, their school curriculum is narrowed down to what the government thinks they need to know. Back in the old days, parents taught their kids morals and manners. Now, it's like juvenile hall on any big city street in America. And these are the kids who'll inherit the world."

"God help the people who have to live in it with them."

"That's why I'm in Catelow," he said. "Times don't change here."

She smiled. "I guess it's why I'm here, too. I don't like change."

He cocked his head and studied her. She wasn't beautiful. Her eyes were. She had a pretty figure, and he loved that long hair. But what he liked most was her big heart. She was unlike any woman he'd ever had in his life.

"Have I got a wart on my nose?" she asked, uneasy at the scrutiny.

He chuckled. "No. I was thinking that you've got a heart as big as your house."

"Oh." She flushed.

"This was nice of you," he said quietly. "I think I'd have gone crazy trying to stay at home tonight." His dark eyes were sad. "I don't know how to manage without her."

Lucy came running back, her puppy in her arms. "Snow

had some milk!" she said. "Now she's all sleepy. Can she stay in my room tonight?"

"Of course she can."

Lucy sat down beside Cody's chair and looked up at him with soft, pretty eyes and a smile. "You can hold Snow anytime you like," she offered.

"That's really sweet of you, Lucy," he replied, smiling back.

"I never got to have pets before," she said. "We lived in an awful place. You couldn't even have a cat. The people weren't like they are here. It's just super that we got to come and live on the ranch!"

Cody laughed in spite of himself. "I'm not much for big cities, either, Lucy."

Hannah came into the room wiping her hands on her apron. "I'm just starting on the stroganoff," she announced with a grin. "Just time enough to go out and see the barn cats, if you've a mind to."

"Yes!" Lucy exclaimed. "They're so cute!"

"I would love to see the barn cats," Cody agreed.

"Super!" Lucy got to her feet and ran to the back door ahead of them.

"I might need a bit of support, if you don't mind," Cody said under his breath. "I'm not used to alcohol. I might have imbibed just a little too much."

"Not to worry, Sheriff," Abby said, getting under one muscular arm to help guide him. "Think of me as a warm crutch."

He looked down at her with twinkling eyes. "Soft, too," he teased, and on an impulse he didn't understand, bent and kissed just the tip of her nose.

"Don't let me trip over anything big, okay?" he asked, going right along as if he hadn't done anything outrageous at all.

Inside, Abby was churning. Such a simple caress to make her go trembly inside. She wasn't used to men. That had to be what it was. And the sheriff was strong and dishy and smelled of leather and a nice aftershave.

"If I see a steer in time, I'll guide you right away from it so you won't trip," she promised.

He laughed. It was a rare sound, one she'd hardly ever heard from him. "I'm not that drunk. I think."

She grinned. The wind was getting up. It whipped through her hair, lifting it away from her face and shoulders. She smiled, and closed her eyes, and lifted her face to it.

"You're an elemental," he murmured, watching her.

Her eyes opened. "What?"

"You like wind and rain and storms."

"Well, yes."

"So do I," he said.

It was hard to breathe normally, especially when his arm contracted just a little.

"Big rock," he said before she could decide what to do next.

She blinked. There was a very big rock, and she'd walked him right into it.

"There goes your guide-walking license," he said.

She laughed. "Rub it in. I wasn't paying attention. And yes, I do love wind and storms and rain." She sighed. "And snow, most of all."

"Good thing. We get more than our share of it every winter," he pointed out.

In fact, snowflakes were coming down again, in little swirls. "More snow incoming, I'll bet," she mused.

"Probably a lot," he replied. "I hope my crew can handle the wrecks without me. I'm not on call tonight, but if they get overwhelmed, they'll be in touch."

"You're in no shape to drive, or work wrecks," she pointed out softly.

He grimaced. "I know."

She stopped walking and looked up at him through the tiny

swirls of snow. "You can have a twenty-four-hour stomach virus. We're nursing you over here because somebody told us you were sick."

"Why, you little liar," he teased. "And that's so creative."

She grinned. "I practice by telling Lucy lies about Santa Claus and the Easter Bunny being real," she whispered.

He hugged her close. "Thanks," he said huskily.

She smiled up at him, her face radiant, her eyes sparkling. "What are friends for?"

He searched her face, fighting a really strong impulse to bend down and kiss the breath out of her. He caught himself just in time, and then Lucy was running toward them.

"Myra's nursing her kittens!" she exclaimed. "And she doesn't mind Snow!"

"Myra's very laid-back," Abby laughed.

He didn't reply. He was deep in thought. So quickly, Abby had made a place for herself in his life, she and Lucy. He didn't understand it, but he accepted it with gratitude. It was nice, not to be totally alone anymore.

They sat and watched Myra with the kittens while Snow ran around on her little fat legs and curled up in Lucy's lap.

"Snow's going to be a big girl," Cody remarked, studying her.

"How can you tell?" Lucy asked.

"She's got big paws and a blocky chest," he said. He smiled. "I'm not sure what she's mixed with, but she's certainly got malamute or husky in her bloodlines somewhere."

"One of our cowboys has a female malamute," Abby remarked. "She had a litter of puppies, and Don told us that one had gone missing. I called him and told him about Snow, he said she was ours with his blessing. He also said that they're not sure what the father is." She pursed her lips. "They think it might be a wolf."

"A wolf?!" Lucy was all eyes. "I love wolves!"

"Yeah, me, too," Cody confessed. "They get a lot of bad press, but we've got at least two packs of them out here in the country. They're tagged and monitored, and none of them have ever been caught bringing down cattle."

"That's nice to know," Abby said. "Not that I'd want one killed even for doing that. We'd just ask to have it relocated."

"You'll need a trainer for Snow, if she's got wolf in her," Cody said. "Wolves are big, too."

"Maisie's brother trains K-9 dogs. Don's going to give me his phone number."

"That's a very good idea," he replied. "Not that I think Snow will be dangerous. But a little training never hurts."

"They had a Russian wolf on YouTube," Lucy said. "He was soooo big! He was white, too."

"Snow may grow very large. The biggest issue you'll have with her is trying to make sure she doesn't escape." He laughed softly. "Huskies are escape artists. It's hard to confine them. Anyu got away from me one time and I found her five miles away, playing with some other dogs." He stopped, because the memory hurt.

Abby slid her hand into his unobtrusively and gave it a squeeze. "It gets easier," she said under her breath.

He looked down at her and drew in a long breath. "So they say."

"Did Debby like dogs?" Abby asked.

He scowled. "Well, no. In fact, she didn't like animals at all. The dog was a huge surprise. Just after she…passed," he almost choked on the word, "I was directed to a nurse who lived nearby. Debby had left a note that said she had a present for the most precious man in her life at that nurse's apartment. I went over to pick it up, and it turned out to be a puppy. The nurse seemed uneasy about giving me the dog, even after I showed her the note," he added on a laugh. "Funny that I only just remembered that."

"She probably thought you'd love a dog, to keep you company," Abby said.

He sighed. "So many things don't make sense six years down the road," he said enigmatically.

"That's life," Abby replied. "How about some hot coffee? And hot chocolate," she added, smiling at Lucy.

"That would be great! Shall I go inside and tell Hannah?"

"You do that, sweetheart," Abby said, smiling at the little girl.

"Okay!" She picked up Snow and made for the house.

"She's a sweet child," Cody said. "All big eyes and heart."

"Yes. She misses her parents, but it gets easier, as time goes by."

"You must miss them, too. They were the last of your family."

She nodded. "Lawrence and I had each other, at least, and we both had Mary." She smiled wistfully. "She was a wonderful person. Lucy's a lot like her."

"So are you. All heart."

She laughed. "It's a drawback, from time to time. They used to say I was too naïve to live, at the office in Denver. People would come in off the street, looking for handouts, and I'd always have a dollar or two to spare."

"If that's being naïve, I love it," he said. "I'd never turn away a person in need."

"I figured that, about you," she replied. "They said your opponent in the last sheriff's race groaned to anybody who'd listen that your reputation would keep him out of office. In fact, he only got one percent of the vote, so I'd have to agree that he was right."

"This is my second term in office, although I was a deputy for some time before I ended up behind a desk." His eyes were thoughtful. "I'm not sure I'd want to run again. It's a rewarding job, but if I can get the ranch going, I might consider alternatives."

"Didn't Debby mind your job?" she asked hesitantly. "I mean, it's dangerous. Really dangerous."

He looked down at her with affection. "She never thought about it."

She started to speak and thought better of it.

He frowned. "You'd think about it," he said.

She grimaced. "Well, yes. I mean if I was married to somebody who wore a badge, I'd think about it a lot. I'd be sitting up at two in the morning with black coffee and bags under my eyes worrying."

That shocked him. He'd never considered how much Debby's lack of concern for him had mattered. She didn't miss him when she went back to work. She didn't worry that he might get shot. She never told him to take care of himself. If he was sick, she told him to pull himself together and get back to work.

"I shouldn't have said anything. Sorry…" she began.

He got up and pulled her up, turning her toward him. His hands on her coat sleeves were warm and strong. "She never worried about me." He drew in a troubled breath, his eyes on Abby's face. "If she'd been here when Anyu…when I lost her, she'd have been irritated that I grieved. She had no sympathy for people who were hurt."

"But she was a doctor…!"

"I know. I never understood it, either. I was madly in love for the first time in my life, blind with need. I never saw her the way she was," he explained. "Six years afterward, I've questioned a lot of things I never noticed before." He cocked his head and his dark eyes softened. "You should have married and had half a dozen kids, Abby," he said gently. "You'd be out in the yard playing baseball with them while dinner burned on the stove," he chuckled.

"I'd love a big family," she replied. "Lawrence was a lot older than me. When he left home, it was like being an only child, like Lucy is now. I think big families must be wonderful, especially at holidays, like Christmas."

"I've always thought that, too. It's lonely, being the only kid in the house."

She studied his face and wondered what his children would look like. She smiled faintly. "They'd have brown eyes," she said, thinking aloud.

He chuckled. "What?"

"Your kids. They'd have brown eyes."

"Not necessarily," he replied. "My maternal grandfather had blue eyes and my maternal grandmother had brown ones, and my mother had green eyes!"

"Wow."

His big hand smoothed against her cheek and rested there. "I've never seen skin like yours," he remarked slowly. "Not a blemish anywhere."

"I get that from my grandmother," she said, smiling sadly. "She had beautiful skin."

His thumb smoothed over her soft mouth, making it tremble. "No lipstick, either, and you don't need it."

She felt trembly inside. It was getting hard to breathe. He was very tall. She looked up at him with conflicting emotions.

His head bent while his thumb made soft patterns on her mouth, kindling hungers she hadn't felt before.

"We should...we should really...go...inside," she faltered.

"We probably should," he replied huskily, as his mouth lowered to hers and slowly, very slowly, teased her lips apart.

She went stiff and one hand on his coat sleeve contracted suddenly. But she didn't move away. It had been years since she'd been kissed, and she hadn't liked it. This was different. Very different...

He smiled. "You taste like coffee and chocolate cookies," he whispered. "Delicious..."

While she was registering the comment, his mouth opened just a little and moved down onto her lips. She could feel the sudden change in his breathing as his mouth grew slowly more insistent.

The hunger he was feeling transferred itself to her. She caught her breath and stood very still, going on tiptoe to keep him from lifting his face away.

Both big hands went to her waist and he lifted her up just a little. "We're both out of practice," he said huskily.

"Yes..."

"I have a really good solution to that."

"You do?"

"We can practice on each other..."

He kissed her again. She let go of his coat sleeve and wrapped her arms around his neck and held on for dear life.

It was a long, slow, sweet kiss that went on and on until suddenly a small voice called out the back door, "Where are you guys? Hannah's got coffee!"

They jerked apart, both a little uneasy.

"Just coming, sweetheart!" Abby called, her voice a little too high-pitched.

Cody took her hand in his and drew in a deep breath. "Yup," he remarked as he led her through the barn door. "We're going to need a lot of practice!"

CHAPTER SEVEN

Abby had bought a Monopoly set some days ago so that she and Lucy would have a way to entertain themselves. Lucy watched cartoons on Saturday morning, but neither of them liked to just sit and watch TV.

So Abby got out the game and set it on the table after Hannah had cleared away the dishes and washed them.

"Come on, Hannah, we can't play with just three people," Abby called.

"I'm not good at board games," the older woman muttered.

"That's wonderful! I have a better chance of winning," Abby said, grinning.

"I love Monopoly. Me and Aunt Abby used to play it at night when we lived in the city!" Lucy trilled.

Cody chuckled. "I used to play it with the police chief when we were kids," he said.

"They said at school that he had a new baby," Lucy replied.

"They have a little boy," Abby said, smiling. "He's friends with Mr. Owens, too."

"They'll have plenty more, if I know his wife," Hannah chuckled. "She loves babies."

"Oh, so do I," Abby mused to herself. "I'll have to find an excuse to go see them so I can hold him."

"You won't get near the front door until he's at least two months old," Hannah said with a grin. "His wife is terrified that the baby will catch a cold or get a stray germ..."

"I'd be the same way, I expect," Abby replied. "Especially with the first one."

Hannah rolled the dice and groaned. "Oh, no!"

She'd landed on Park Place, where Abby had two hotels.

"Oh, isn't that just sad?" Abby mused. She grinned at Hannah. "And that's going to cost you a bundle, I promise!"

"Maybe the bank could give me a loan?" Hannah teased.

Abby moved the bank off the table and made a face. "Just to keep you honest!" she said, tongue-in-cheek.

"Well, I like that! You just wait. I'll cook you liver and onions tomorrow!"

"No!" Abby put the box right back on the table.

Cody, watching the byplay, chuckled.

The theme from a popular action movie blasted into the silence. Cody pulled his phone out of his pocket and looked at the number. "It's Bill Harris," he said, and started to open the phone.

Abby took it from him and put her forefinger to her lips, silencing everybody. "Hi, Bill," she said, answering it. "We've got Cody over here. He's sick with a stomach virus and he didn't have anybody to take care of him. So we are."

There was a reply and a laugh. She listened, nodding. "I'll tell him. I'm sure he'll be back tomorrow. He's feeling better already."

There was another comment and she hung up. "Bill says they've got a suspect in the bank robbery."

Cody scowled. She looked worried. "Who is it?"

"Our friend from Miami," she said sadly.

"Oh, good grief, he's no bank robber!" Cody said.

She sighed. "Bill says there's an eyewitness."

Cody pursed his lips. "We have this really good defense attorney at your office. I'll bet he'd rush right over to represent Mr. Whatley."

She smiled. "Yes, I'll bet he would. There's no way Mr. Whatley would rob a bank, for heaven's sake! He doesn't need money!"

"We'll work it out tomorrow. For now, I'm going to buy another railroad," he said, and they went back to the game with a vengeance.

Later, as everybody got ready to turn in, a much more sober Cody paused in the living room and took Abby's hand in his.

"I just want you to know how grateful I am…"

"There's no need," she said softly and she smiled up at him. "Neighbors help each other. We've enjoyed having you around. You might have noticed a lack of male companionship around here," she added, tongue-in-cheek.

He chuckled softly. "Yes, I have." He cocked his head and looked down at her. "I like it."

Her eyebrows went up. "You like what?"

"Having a lack of other men here." He couldn't believe he'd said that. He cleared his throat. "I mean, you never know what you'd end up with. Some men aren't what they seem. If a man's a gambler or a playboy or a wife-beater, how would you know unless you lived with him?" His face saddened. "I've been to so many wrecked homes," he confided. "Wrecked homes, wrecked lives. It goes with the job, but I never get used to it."

"And you never have anybody to talk to when you get home," she said softly.

He sighed. "I had Anyu." He fought the pincushion in his throat. The grief was very new, and almost unbearable. "She'd sit on the sofa with me and laugh at me while I talked to her."

She put a hand on his arm. "It takes time to get over a loss. It hurts so much, when it's new."

They stared at each other, remembering loved ones they'd lost.

"I'd have liked a dozen kids and a wife who wanted to just stay home and take care of them." One side of his mouth pulled down. "Debby didn't want that. She didn't like kids. She didn't like dogs, either." He frowned and laughed. "Funny, isn't it, that she'd give me a puppy."

"She knew you liked animals, I imagine."

"She didn't know anything about me, really," he said. "We got married in a fever, but it was only a physical thing, at first." He grimaced. "She didn't want to get married, but I did. I'm painfully conventional. I couldn't just live with a woman I wasn't married to. I go to church," he added softly. "She thought that was outdated. She came up here very rarely. I knew her career came first. It was hard to get used to being second place in her life." He sighed. "I guess she was a good doctor. I wasn't allowed to come to her apartment. Well, I went there once and she fidgeted and danced around so that I felt uncomfortable and left."

Abby was frowning. "That sounds odd."

"It does, doesn't it? Like there was something she didn't want me to know about."

Or someone, Abby thought to herself. It sounded very much as if Debby was seeing somebody in Denver. Somebody her husband wasn't allowed to see or know about.

"Or someone," Cody said suddenly. His eyebrows drew together. "There was this doctor she talked about, her mentor in neurology. He came to the funeral. He was crying. He made it known that she wanted to be buried in Denver, not here. Crazy, I never thought about that before."

"I don't think people in love notice things like that." She laughed softly. "I wouldn't know. I've never been in love. Infatuated, yes, a time or two. But never like in books, where the heroine can't bear to be separated from the hero even for a few minutes." She sighed. "Lawrence and Mary had that kind of love for each other, especially after Lucy was born."

"I love kids," Cody said.

"Oh, me, too," Abby said, her voice soft with longing. "Lucy has been the greatest blessing of my life. I love her so much."

"It would be nice if she had kids to play with."

She nodded. She was thinking about children. Her sadness showed in her face.

"What's wrong?" Cody asked tenderly.

She looked up at him. "I would never put Lucy in a foster home," she said. "But no sane man is going to want a ready-made family, if you know what I mean."

He smiled slowly. "Give it time. You've only been here for a few weeks."

She laughed. "That's true. We get some very handsome men at the office on occasion. Mostly they're married, but there's this one guy." She looked thoughtful. "He's private security for someone local, he wouldn't say who. He was a dish. Tall and dark-haired-and-eyed. Every woman in the place, even the married ones, couldn't take their eyes off him. He could play leading roles in movies, that's how good-looking he is."

Cody felt a sudden and devastating pain. Was it jealousy? He couldn't remember ever feeling it before. "I may know the man you mean," he said after a minute. "He's working a case with me. With our department," he corrected. "His name is Lassiter. His father owns a detective agency in Houston."

"Houston? Then why is he here?" she asked.

"No idea. He and I are tracking down the same escaped fugitive. We think he may be hiding in the area." He couldn't say more. It was a case that might have classified significance.

The man was so ordinary-looking that he could conceal himself even in a small town. He'd done murder and worse than murder. He wasn't going to be easy to find.

"You're very thoughtful," she said.

He smiled. "Sorry. I was wrapped up in the case for a minute. You be careful going out alone," he said, and the smile faded. "That goes for all of you. The man has said that he isn't going back to prison, so he'll probably try suicide by cop. He won't care if he has to kill again to get money to stay alive. You understand?"

"I understand." She smiled at him. "Thanks. For caring, I mean," she added, embarrassed. "All Lucy and I have is each other and Hannah."

"You have me," he said surprisingly. He touched her cheek with his big hand. "I'll be around if you need me."

She looked up at him with soft, puzzled eyes. "And we'll be around if you need us. Like today."

He smiled back. He drew in a long breath. "I'm almost sober again."

"And we don't keep liquor here," she said firmly.

He chuckled. "I wasn't asking for any more. I'm kind of tired of rushing to the bathroom to throw up." He grew solemn. "Thank you, for what you did. Some people would laugh about a man who goes nuts when his dog dies."

"Only people with no heart," she said quietly. "She was a beautiful dog and you had her for six long, good years," she added. "If you remember the good times, and you're grateful that you had her for so long, it might make this easier. And you'll see her again," she added with absolute faith. She smiled. "When you pass over, when it's your time, she'll be waiting for you at the gate."

He sighed. "You make it so much easier."

"I'm glad."

He grimaced. "I guess we should go to bed. It's very late. I enjoyed tonight," he added. "It was fun."

She grinned. "You can come over and play Monopoly with us any night you're free. We don't watch TV. Only when there's bad weather."

"I'll remember. Good night."

"Good night, Cody."

"Good night, Abby."

The sound of her name on his lips made her feel special. She smiled. Unexpectedly, he bent and kissed her, very gently. Before she could say a word, he was upstairs and into the guest room with the door closed.

She stayed awake a long time, thinking about that kiss. When she finally slept, her dreams were sweet.

Breakfast was delightful. Hannah made fresh biscuits with sausages and scrambled eggs, and served them up with homemade strawberry and fig preserves.

"This sure beats burned toast and bouncy eggs," Cody remarked as he opened a second biscuit to spread it with butter and strawberry preserves.

"Come on over and I'll teach you how to cook," Hannah teased. "Or," she added with a mischievous glance at Abby, "you could just come for breakfast every day."

"Oh, I'd like that," Abby said before she thought, and then flushed at being so forward.

"I'd like that, too!" Lucy piped in. She reached down and petted the pretty white dog with the laughing eyes. "My puppy would like it, too. See? Snow's laughing!"

All the adults laughed as well. Cody looked down at the little dog with a pained sigh. It brought back memories of Anyu.

Abby slipped a soft hand over his on the table. "Lucy will need help with the puppy. Breakfast is a good time to talk about it." She hesitated. He was hard to read. "If you'd like to, I mean…"

His hand turned and squeezed hers. "I'd like to. If I wouldn't be in the way."

"In the way," Hannah huffed. "If you knew how many things went wrong in the house that only men know how to deal with. She is hopeless with a screwdriver," she indicated Abby, "and dangerous with a wrench."

Cody burst out laughing. "In that case, I'll be very grateful for breakfast and in return, I'll fix anything that needs it."

"That's a very generous offer," Hannah said, and she smiled at him.

"Very generous indeed," Abby seconded. She grinned. "Especially since I think the belt on the dryer is coming loose."

"I'll have a look at it soon."

"And if I don't get my homework finished on time, maybe you could help me with it at breakfast?" Lucy asked with big eyes.

He smiled at the little girl. "I would be glad to do that, Lucy."

She grinned at him and dug into her breakfast.

He was beginning to feel like a member of the family. It was nice, belonging. He'd never felt it with Debby. He could have kicked himself for that thought. She'd loved him, just as he'd loved her. It was unworthy of him to think such a thing.

He finished breakfast, got his overnight bag, and went out the door, followed by most of the household. He paused on the steps because he'd just remembered that he had no way to get home. Abby had driven him over here.

Behind him, car keys rattled. Abby grinned at him. "Ready to go? I don't have to take Lucy to school for almost an hour."

"Okay. And thanks. For everything."

"Neighbors take care of each other," she said, smiling. "Let's go."

★ ★ ★

She let him out at his front porch. He didn't linger. He just smiled, thanked her again, and went into his house.

She drove away with a sense of unfinished business. He was still grieving for Anyu, the loss was so near. He was probably grieving for Debby, too. Losing his dog, and its connection to her, would make the grief worse. She was sorry for him. She wanted to stay and comfort him, but he'd made it clear without a single word being spoken that he was fine and just needed to be left alone.

Well, he'd go to work, that was for sure, and that would keep his mind busy. Besides, he'd said that he'd come to breakfast, so that made her feel lighter and happier. She wondered why? He was a nice man, and she liked him. But she felt empty when he wasn't around. Odd feeling, and she didn't have time to think about it, because she'd be late getting Lucy to school and she'd be late to work, which was unthinkable!

She mentioned possible charges against Mr. Whatley to Mr. Owens, adding the part about the escaped criminal who hadn't been found and who was desperate for money. It could very well be him who'd robbed the bank, but Mr. Whatley was being blamed in local gossip. No arrest so far, which was good, but couldn't Mr. Owens assign a lawyer to defend him?

Yes, he could, he said at once, but he'd need to see Mr. Whatley and make sure it was all right with him. Strange, how relieved he'd looked when she mentioned the criminal who was loose, but she went to work and forgot all about it.

Horace Whatley, meanwhile, was almost in a panic mode. He'd overheard swatches of conversation in town about the bank robber being almost exactly his height. They knew him from his attempt to impersonate a cattle foreman and a detective who swore he'd found a body, which was proof, they said, that he didn't see a problem breaking the law. If he did those things, couldn't he escalate to bank robbing? He seemed to have a cash flow problem lately as well. One of his checks to the local hardware store bounced. He used his credit card at the grocery store and it was refused. A man desperate for money was a viable suspect when the bank was robbed.

Abby heard those snippets of gossip and was appalled by them. Mr. Whatley, while eccentric, was not a mean person. And she did wonder why his money wasn't available. Her cattle foreman, Don, who'd checked him out, said that he was worth a fortune. His older sister lived on the estate in Florida, where she doled out money to her brother in Wyoming. Don had added that she didn't sound like a mean person, either, because he'd called and spoken to her about her brother. She seemed to truly care about Mr. Whatley and only wanted what was best for him. He did have mental health issues, but the drugs he took worked on those, if he'd just take them; he'd had a patient advocate who helped him refuse the treatment, including the drugs.

Abby wondered if his sister knew about the cattle ranch he'd purchased, which was actually making money for him. Someone should call and question him, she decided.

So at breakfast the next morning, she brought the subject up with Cody.

He just grinned. "Sorry, honey, I'm one step ahead of you." He paused and cleared his throat. That endearment had just slipped out. He ignored it and plowed ahead. "His sister has a boyfriend with very expensive tastes. She's indulging him at Mr. Whatley's expense. Her suitor says she has no real need to keep up her little brother and he should be making his own living without touching estate money."

Cody had reminded her that Mr. Whatley, while eccentric, was not dangerous, and that if she kept holding back funds he was entitled to, he was perfectly capable of filing a lawsuit which might deprive her of all the estate money.

It had shocked her to hear that. She'd stammered that she didn't want to stop the checks but that her new boyfriend had advised her to. She promised to start sending them again very soon, probably through her lawyer so her boyfriend wouldn't know.

Cody, who could sense injustice from his experience with the law, asked for her boyfriend's name, almost casually. She gave it to him without thinking, Bobby Grant, and when he asked what sort of work the man did for a living, she stammered and said that he just had some sort of investments he oversaw, and he was urging her to put most of her money into them. Cody said that she should talk that over, in private, with her attorneys before she did any such thing.

She agreed that it sounded like a very good idea and that she would do that. Cody said he'd check back with her if it was all right. He was working a case in town that might involve her brother. She asked what sort, and he told her. There was a very shocked pause.

"He would never rob a bank! Never! He's never done anything to harm a single living soul. He even stops in the middle of the road to move turtles out of it. He's innocent! I've known him all my life, and I know what he will and won't do. He's no thief!"

That was when Cody mentioned that a check her brother had written had bounced and that his credit card didn't work.

There was a sudden deep mumble from behind her. "I'll, uh, I'll see about that at once. I have to go. If you need any more information, you can call me."

"Thanks, I'll do that. If anything…unusual happens, will you call me anyway?"

There was a pause and another, more impatient mumble. "Yes. Goodbye."

She hung up leaving Cody with a worried look and growing suspicion. He put her boyfriend's name and location into the VICAP program and waited for it to sort through multiple suspects.

At last, he found two possible matches, both in Dade County. One was a well-known Grand Prix racer, whose character was apparently beyond question. The other match was for a man who had a record of taking money from lonely single women under a variety of guises. He'd been arrested and charged twice, and convicted just once on a misdemeanor charge that was just shy of theft. In at least five arrests, the victims refused to prosecute. He had charm, it seemed, and knew how to use it. There was one assault with deadly weapon charge, involving one of his victims. Her brother had charged him with theft, and he'd attacked the man. Later, the brother's tires were slashed, his home broken into and damaged, but there had been no proof that could convict him of the damages. It didn't matter, because the assault charge stuck and he served two years in jail. That raised Cody's eyebrows. He phoned the police chief where the assault took place and learned that there was some gossip that the gigolo might have been looking for a way to get rid of the brother. If he could, he could marry the woman and have her fortune to himself. If her brother vanished, and she did as well, the man would have lived on easy street for life.

Cody said that required a jump in logic. The police chief said it didn't. This opportunist was suspected in the death of a sister to a woman he'd previously courted in Denver, and intended to marry. The suspicion surrounding the death caused the woman to withdraw from any contact with the man, saying that she'd come to her senses too late to save her poor sister. If he was willing to kill the other heir to get to the money, he had no problem with it. The police chief was still furious that he hadn't been able to make the murder charge stick. He just didn't have enough evidence to take to a grand jury.

Then he did an odd thing. He warned Cody about little Horace Whatley. He didn't really have serious mental issues, he said, he just had some behavioral problems that went away when he stayed on drugs. He also warned him about the man who was now courting Mr. Whatley's sister, who was in her forties and hugely infatuated by the attentions of the much-younger, charming man she was dating.

"I know about Nita Whatley's new boyfriend. I spoke to her on the phone before I called you. She sounds very nice. Sort of naïve, if you know what I mean."

"She is naïve. Very sweet, too," the chief added quietly. "She lives on my street, here in Miami. Well, she lives on an estate and I live in a small apartment in a complex nearby," he chuckled. "I can't afford a mansion on my salary."

"Join the club," Cody laughed. "But, then, we don't do the job for the money."

"Exactly. How about watching over our Mr. Whatley? I'm fond of him, too."

"I'll keep an eye on him," Cody promised. "He bought a ranch here, and he's become sort of a mascot to the town. It's a very small town, very clannish, but he fits right in. And he's actually doing a good job of ranch management. He had some radical ideas that we all downplayed, but he's put them into effect on his ranch and it's making money for him. Pretty soon, he'll be solvent."

"Nice to know. I always liked him. Nita Whatley had a fiancé who was killed in the Middle East during the invasion of Iraq, one of the men in my unit. She never got over it. She wouldn't even talk to men for all those years. Then she met this high-flying opportunist a few weeks ago and now she's a teenager again, in her mind," he growled. "Pity. She's a sweet, levelheaded woman, usually. She deserves better."

"I hope you're keeping an eye on him," Cody said.

"You'd better believe I am." He paused. "You know, there was a similar case, when I checked him out on VICAP, in Denver, of all places. He was courting a woman there. A death was involved, her sister, but he denied ever having anything to do with it. The police checked him out but couldn't find enough evidence to prosecute and he left the state soon after and I inherited him when he moved to Dade County. If you want to drive over there to Denver and check it out, I'll give you the woman's address."

He thought about his late wife, Debby, living in Denver. He wanted to go to her old apartment and talk to people who knew her. It would comfort him. He still loved her and missed her. He missed Anyu, too.

"I'll do that," Cody said. "Can you text me the information? This is my cell phone number." He gave it to the other man. "And I'll appreciate any other information you get. I'm working a bank robbery, of all things, in Catelow. It's the first one we've had in years."

"Good luck. We had two this week. Crime doesn't take a vacation. I wish it did. We're overworked and underfunded."

"Aren't we all," Cody chuckled. "Thanks for the help."

"Any time."

Cody went out to the Whatley Ranch, which was called "Pride's Run," of all things, to talk to Horace Whatley.

He was met at the door by a smiling woman, Julia Donovan, Whatley's housekeeper. "Sheriff Banks, how nice to see you! Come on in."

She led him into the kitchen, where her boss was drinking coffee and reading a newspaper.

He looked up and smiled. "Sheriff! Nice to see you! Coffee?"

"I'd love a cup," Cody replied, sailing his hat into an empty chair before he sat down. "It's been a long day."

"How do you take it, Sheriff?" Julia asked.

"Black and strong," he replied. He laughed. "It keeps me awake."

"What can I do for you?" Mr. Whatley asked, and he smiled. No indecision, no fidgeting, no signs that the sheriff's visit might be a bad sign.

"I spoke to your sister."

Whatley's smile fell and he sighed. "Yes. So did I. That man! He sold our mother's favorite antique painting and she let him! I'm so mad!"

Cody thanked Julia for the coffee. He took a sip. It was perfect, strong and flavorful. "Your sister's boyfriend has a rap sheet," he said, and Mr. Whatley perked up at once.

"He's been convicted of something?" the other man asked, interested.

Cody nodded. "Assault. He attacked and almost killed his girlfriend's only sibling, her brother. There was gossip that he wanted the estate and the only way he could get it was to get her very suspicious brother out of the way."

"Oh, my gosh!"

"That's not all. We think he killed the sister of another victim, in Denver. He escaped any charges in that one, but it was known that the sister opposed him and was the only other heir to the fortune."

"My poor sister," Whatley said softly. "She's been alone so long. I guess she was vulnerable to sudden attention from a man and he took advantage of it."

"That's what I think. It's what the local police chief thinks as well."

"He's in love with her. Always has been. But he was the commanding officer in the unit her fiancé was in when he died. The association killed any hopes he had. But now she's fancy-free. He might have a chance. Sadly, her fortune is what holds him back. He doesn't want to be accused of courting her for her money."

"Oh, that sounds familiar," Cody said. "That happened to a friend of mine, years ago. But they overcame it."

"That reminds me. Do you know anybody with the wildlife service locally? I need to talk to somebody about a moose that got attracted to our milk cow. I don't want it harmed," he added quickly, "I just want to see if it could be transported to a national forest somewhere and released."

Cody chuckled. "Welcome to the fascinating world of ranching, Mr. Whatley. You have qualities. Indeed, you do."

"Thanks." Whatley sighed. "Now if I could just solve my poor sister's problem before her no-good boyfriend bankrupts us both and sends us living on the streets."

"That won't happen. I spoke to your sister and mentioned there might be serious complications if she continued to stop your checks and refuse payment on your credit card. She's starting them up again, but through her attorney. I think she's afraid of her new boyfriend but too enamored to admit it."

"That's what I think, too. It's a relief, about the money," he added quietly. "I'm in debt up to my ears. I'd even maxed my credit card. Without those checks coming regularly, I guarantee I'd be on the streets already."

"Nope. You'll never end up on the street, not here. One of us would adopt you and take you in."

Whatley flushed. "What?"

"You'd have a place to live, and plenty of choices." Cody smiled. "You have no idea how much you're liked. You fit in."

He looked up, still flushed. "This is the first time, ever, you know, that I lived in a place where I fit in. I'm eccentric. I got joked about and made fun of back home by the friends we had."

"Then they weren't friends, were they?"

"No, I don't think they were," he replied slowly. "My sister has never been a good judge of character. She's flighty. She took in a homeless woman, who proceeded to bring all her friends in, and my sister had to call the police to evict them. They did a lot of damage. She was too afraid of them to ask them to leave. I coaxed her into calling the police, because I knew Dan Brady would go out there himself and take care of the problem. If only Nita would look at him! He's a good man. Just what she needs."

"He's the police chief? I knew the last name but not the first. You like him."

"I do. He's a fine man. Even though he did arrest me once for a robbery, but the owner took my part and said I'd never steal anything. They found the man who did it and he confessed, a few weeks later." He looked up. "If it wasn't for nice people, I guess I'd be serving time in place of the real culprit."

"Not here in Catelow," Cody said. "Not ever. Not on my watch."

"Which brings me to the question, why are you here, Sheriff?"

Cody chuckled. "The bank robbery."

"Oh! Somebody thinks I did it?" he asked and didn't even seem nervous. He smiled.

"Your name was mentioned, along with several others." His eyebrows rose and he smiled, too. "One of them was the Methodist minister. He was, to say it mildly, shocked."

Whatley burst out laughing. "Who accused him?!"

"A member of the congregation who was angry that he wasn't moving forward and doing what all the big-city churches are doing."

"It's a small town and we're still God-fearing people," Whatley said with conviction. "If the minister was ever homeless, he could move right in with me. I hope he sticks to his guns. The government should keep its nose out of medicine and religion. It's not qualified to handle either."

"I couldn't agree more." Cody got up and picked up his hat.

"If you had me down as a suspect, why didn't you interrogate me?" Whatley asked on the way out.

Cody poised on the top step and looked back at him with twinkling eyes. "I just did. A more innocent man I'd have to hunt hard to find. Have a nice day."

"You, too, Sheriff." And Mr. Whatley smiled, too.

CHAPTER EIGHT

Cody had permission from the town fathers to go to Denver, expenses paid, to interrogate the victim of the opportunist's attentions, since it tied in with a bank robbery suspect, Horace Whatley, in Catelow. It was a tenuous connection at best, but a solid one. If this opportunist had an accomplice who was trying to frame Horace Whatley for the theft, he could be put away and the gigolo would have Nita Whatley all alone with no family to get in his way, and he'd have her money.

Cody told his girls, as he thought of Abby and Lucy and Hannah, that he'd be away a few days to investigate a charge against a local man's sister's boyfriend, who'd left a victim in nearby Denver.

"That would be Mr. Whatley's sister, back in Florida," Abby said at once, nodding.

His mouth fell open slightly. "How did you know that?"

"Oh, somebody told somebody, who told somebody else, who heard it from somebody in the local café. That sort of thing. There's a nasty schemer after Miss Whatley. I hope they rope him to a tree and put a sign on his chest telling what he did."

"Medieval," he said, making a face as he ate his way through the delicious omelet Hannah had made.

"We need medieval back again," Hannah huffed. "All the things people get away with these days, not to mention what politicians get away with. And why is our country being run by a bunch of senile old men anyway?"

"Hannah!" Abby exclaimed. "We have a number of really fine older men in politics, and they do a world of good."

"I'm not talking about them. I'm talking about the noisy scalawags who are always in front of a camera, running down people with opposing viewpoints!"

"You should stop watching the news," Abby advised. "Find a nice old movie to watch instead." She sighed. "Living in Catelow is the best we can do, to live like old-fashioned people did, when they were closer to the earth and God."

"Amen," Hannah said.

"Well, we have to live with what we have," Cody said philosophically. "I'll miss breakfast tomorrow. I'll miss all of you as well."

"I hope you find something that will help you with the case," Abby said.

"So do I."

He didn't say, but Abby knew, that he'd spend some of that time reminiscing about Debby, who'd died at the hospital in Denver. It would be familiar to him, because he'd visited her there, though not often. She hoped it might help him heal. He was still living in the past with his beautiful ghost. No living woman could compete with the perfection of a memory. Abby would have liked to, but she was gun-shy, just as he was. He was friendly now, but only friendly. Maybe a visit to Denver would help him to forget, finally. It would certainly get him away from home, where he still grieved for Anyu.

"I hope you have a nice trip, despite the reason for going," Abby said as they all waved him goodbye on the front porch.

"I won't be away long. If you need anything, you call my undersheriff. He knows what to do."

"I will. You be careful," Abby advised.

He smiled. "I'm always careful. See you in a few days."

He was gone, with a wave of his hand. Abby stayed and watched him drive away, until he was out of sight, while the other two people in the house went back to the kitchen for more biscuits.

It was like going back in time for Cody when he drove into Denver. He'd only been here to visit Debby at work a handful of times during their marriage. He remembered the hospital where she'd died most of all. He'd been out of his mind with grief, lashing out at everybody around her as nurses and residents worked to save her life. He'd lashed out at Abby and Lucy, too, and left scars, something that still shamed him.

In the hospital they'd done the best they could, but Debby couldn't be saved. Her last words had been incomprehensible. Odd, that he'd remember them now, as he pulled into the parking lot of a motel near the hospital. She'd said for Honeybear to remember to feed Muttsy. Who the hell was Honeybear? And who, or what, was Muttsy?

He hadn't thought about that in six years. Now, it came back into his mind with a vengeance. She'd been delirious with fever, of course, and that had probably clouded her thoughts. It could have been something from her childhood. He remembered, so vividly, his last sight of her as she lapsed into unconsciousness. At least she'd recognized him. She'd managed a tired smile and said she was sorry. What was that about?

It had been so long that he'd lived with Debby's memory. He'd been buried in his grief for years, without questioning anything in the past. But now that he was here in Denver, he was remembering strange things, strange behaviors, that he'd buried with Debby.

One of the biggest was Anyu. She'd come with a note that only said Debby meant her for the most precious man in her life. Of course that meant Cody. He was sure of it. So he went looking for the nurse who'd been keeping the puppy in her apartment temporarily. Cody had gone to see her to get it. He was overwhelmed with the little dog, absolutely delighted. Debby had left him this beautiful bundle of soft fur and blue eyes, and he fell in love at once.

The nurse had behaved oddly when he went to get the dog. He'd handed her the note and said that an aide at the hospital had told him that a surprise was waiting for him at this nurse's apartment, and that Debby's last wish was that Cody should have it.

The nurse had regained her composure and said of course Debby meant the dog for her husband, although she'd been shocked when Cody spoke of their marriage and her ambition and his grief. The nurse had known Debby well, and she was grieving, too. The puppy made up for a lot for Cody. He took it home with him after Debby's funeral and named it Anyu, and it had been his confidant, his treasure, until her recent death. Losing Anyu was like losing Debby all over again.

He signed in at the motel and thought about why he'd come. He had questions that he wanted answers to about Debby, but he was here to do a job, so he'd better get to it.

His first visit was to a woman named Violet Henry, and it was worrisome to get her to answer even the most basic questions.

"I killed my sister," she said bluntly after she'd refused to answer any of Cody's careful questions. She wasn't a pretty woman. She was slight and thin and had a few gray hairs mixed in with the warm brown of her long hair. She was fidgety and uneasy, even now, talking about what had happened.

"Miss Henry, life happens," Cody said quietly. "We all do things that we wish we could take back, and we can't. You can't rewind life. You just have to put one foot in front of the other and go on. And no, you didn't kill your sister," he added curtly. "You fell in love with a man who turned out to be the worst sort of person. That was beyond your control."

Tears stung her eyes. She lifted her coffee cup to her lips. She'd offered Cody a cup, but he'd refused. He was still full of coffee from breakfast.

"He seemed like the answer to a prayer," she began. "He was so handsome. It shocked me that a man like that could see anything to love in me." She flushed. "I'm not pretty," she said, and smiled. "But he made me feel pretty. He brought me little presents, took me to restaurants and dancing." She laughed sadly. "I never noticed that he was letting me pay for all those things. I even staked him in a high-ticket casino game and he lost thirty thousand dollars on a spin of the roulette wheel." She grimaced. "My sister, Candy, didn't like him and told me so. She said he was after my money. She even hired a private detective. At least she said she did, I never knew about that until after she was…after she died. The police told me there had been an investigation and that he was involved in some criminal behavior. It was too late by then. Poor Candy." She stopped and put a handkerchief to her eyes. "She loved me. She was the only family I had left, and he took her from me." Her brown eyes blazed with revenge. "I'd love to see him in the electric chair, if they still have those things, and I'd pull the handle if they'd let me!"

"It's lethal injection these days," Cody replied. "But just as effective."

"I guess." She drew in a long breath. "I have all Candy's things." She looked at him with dead eyes. "She was right all along. I wish I'd listened to her."

"Could you look through her things and see if there's any

paper trail that might lead me to the detective she hired?" he asked.

"Would it help you catch the man who did it?"

"I think it very well might," he replied with confidence.

She managed a smile. "Then I'll go through them tonight. Do you have a cell phone number?"

"I do." He gave it to her. "I'll be in town for at least two or three days. I'm staying at the Starlight Motel, over on Spruce Lane."

She nodded. "I'll get on it very soon." She studied him. "Is he at it again, with some other poor woman?"

"Yes. A rich heiress in Florida. Her brother is apparently his next target, since he's the only next-of-kin she's got." He shook his head. "I've never been rich, and never will be. I can't imagine doing something so hideous to a nice woman and her family just to get money."

"Neither can I," Miss Henry replied. "The man is a monster, and he'll keep on until he really does kill somebody." Her eyes clouded. "I still think he killed my sister, but I'll never be able to prove it."

"With a little luck, I'll help you prove it," Cody told her. "The man he's after lives in my county." He smiled wistfully. "He's a little off-center mentally, but he's a kind, sweet man. I'd hate to see him framed for a crime he didn't commit just to get him out of the way of a fortune hunter."

"If I can be of any help, I certainly will," Miss Henry told him. "I'll even testify in court if you need me to. A man like that shouldn't be allowed to get away with murder. It's very possible that the detective found proof of at least some crime my former boyfriend committed."

"I don't doubt it." He sighed. "I don't sleep much, so you can text me at two in the morning if you come up with anything."

Her head cocked and she studied him. "Have you just lost someone?"

He nodded. "My husky. Her name was Anyu and she was my only family. She was just six years old."

"You poor man," she said softly. "I lost my Nicky. He was just an alley cat, but I had him for sixteen years. He was so sweet. I grieved for weeks." She glanced at Cody. "I had to leave him with a neighbor when Bobby came over. That was his name, Bobby Grant, my ex-boyfriend. He hated animals and children. I'd forgotten that."

Cody was taking notes again. "This may help us. Do you recall anything else?"

"Well, yes. When he started complaining that my sister was jealous of me and planned to have me committed, I told him she'd never do any such thing. He got, well, sort of violent. He backed me into a wall and got right in my face and said he could prove it. He started to leave then. He said if I wanted to spend the rest of my life in a mental institution, that was my business, not his." She smiled sadly. "Of course I begged him to stay. And it frightened me. I had these little spells where I'd see invisible people, things like that. My sister knew. It wasn't so far-fetched that she might think along those lines. She wouldn't have, but he scared me." She lowered her eyes. "Not long after that, Candy didn't come home from a date one night. They found her in the river a few days later." Her eyes closed and she shivered. "Candy was more afraid of drowning than anything else in the world. We never found out who her date was."

"I can make an educated guess," Cody said.

"Me, too. I'll bet Candy went out with him and confronted him with what she and her detective had found out, and he killed her." She ground her teeth together. "She was always the toughest one of us." She shook her head. "I'll never forgive myself for what happened to her. But if you can find anything to pin on that…that…that heartless cheater, I'll be grateful to you for the rest of my life."

"I promise you that I'll do my best," Cody said, getting to his feet. "Thank you for taking the time to talk to me, Miss Henry."

"It was my pleasure, Sheriff Banks. If I find anything, I promise I'll get it right to you."

"I'll appreciate that. Sorry to bring up so many bad memories."

"It isn't as if I don't think about it every day. But life goes on," she added sadly.

He nodded. "Indeed it does."

He went back to the motel. He had supper in a restaurant next door and thought over what Miss Henry had told him. If the detective had found proof that the scoundrel had taken out Miss Henry's sister, and subsequently killed her, it would help to keep Mr. Whatley out of jail.

Apparently this man had been around the world a couple of times, and he was as slippery as a greased pig. Certainly he'd managed to save himself from a murder charge, although he'd taken off for Florida when Miss Henry mentioned that detective.

He was thinking that the detective, if he could find the person, might be able to tie up a lot of loose ends. He hoped Miss Henry would be able to dig up at least a phone number or a name.

Meanwhile, he was tired and worn out and he went to bed early. The next morning, he had breakfast. There had been no message from Miss Henry, so he decided to see the city detective who'd handled the murder investigation.

The man was out until the next day, but promised to make time to talk to Cody. Since he had a little time free, Cody went to the apartment building where Debby had lived and asked the manager if he might see the apartment, if it was vacant.

By a stroke of luck it was. The older man led the way to it. "Nobody stays in it long," the manager told him, and laughed. "Can't imagine why. We did have one tenant who lived here for the better part of two years. She was married, but her husband only spent the odd night here. Odd people. They seemed committed. Both of them were doctors. They worked at the hospital down the road."

Cody felt his heart stop. "Would one of them have been Deborah Banks?" he asked.

"Deborah, sure, but that's not the last name she gave me. It was Stern. The other doctor was Craig Stern." Beside him, Cody's whole body tensed. That had been the doctor at Debby's funeral. "She wore a wedding band, so I assumed they were married," he continued as they walked, unaware of the shock on the other man's face. "Good tenants, too. Always paid on time, never messed up the apartment. She died of some virus or other. Her husband went stark-staring mad, they had to take him to the hospital and sedate him. He moved out about a week later. Never saw anybody take a death that hard. Poor guy."

Cody was feeling sick to his stomach. His life, his memories, were crashing around his head.

The manager unlocked the door. "It's fully furnished," he said, leading Cody inside. "Just the way it was left when the doctor died. The other doctor didn't want anything here, and left it for the next tenant. Well, he did take his dog when he left, a furry little dog named Muttsy. Cute dog. He loved it. The other doctor just tolerated it." He chuckled. "Isn't that the way of things? I guess maybe she was jealous of the attention the doctor gave the dog."

"I guess so," Cody said in a haunted tone, because he remembered what Debby had said as she was dying, tell Honeybear to take care of Muttsy.

"Well, look around all you like," the manager said. "Come get me when you're done and I'll lock up again." He paused. "You knew the doctors?"

"Not really," Cody said dully, and it was true. "The woman doctor lived in my town in Wyoming briefly. I'm here on an unrelated case."

"Oh. I see. Well, I'll be around."

He went out and closed the door. Cody wandered through the rooms. The furniture was modern and the only picture in the room was a big still life over the mantel place. He walked through the kitchen, which looked as if it had never been used. Then he looked into the bedrooms. One was big, very big, and one was small. They looked like guest rooms in the motel he was staying in. He didn't linger.

He'd grieved for his late wife for years. Now, he was told that she was living with another man and pretending to be married to him. Why not divorce Cody and marry the other doctor for real? He had no answer to that.

Perhaps there was a reason the other doctor couldn't marry Debby. His lips thinned as he considered it. What if the other doctor was married, too, and Debby's long-distance marriage to Cody gave their relationship at work respectability, and freedom from any suspicion that they were running around with each other.

Cody remembered painfully what the manager had just told him, that the couple was apparently married, but only the woman stayed there full-time. The other doctor, apparently her husband, was only around rarely. It made sense. Cody was furious. He hated Craig Stern with a passion. He wanted to hunt the man down and do him an injury. Two years Cody had spent in Carne County, Wyoming, married to a woman who was an absentee wife, who didn't want him to visit her in

Denver, who rarely ever came home. He'd spent those years passionately in love, so infatuated that he'd have done anything to keep her. And for years she'd lived a lie, in the arms of another man, pretending to be his legal wife.

He didn't plan to go to the hospital, but his feet led him there. He went to the information desk and asked for Dr. Craig Stern. The receptionist smiled and asked if he was an acquaintance. Yes, Cody replied, the man was a good friend of his late wife. He was in town and wanted to pay his respects.

The doctor was in his office, just across from the hospital in a smaller building. She gave Cody the room number.

Cody went to the office, spoke to the receptionist. And a minute later, Cody was taken back to see Dr. Stern.

It was a shock. The doctor actually went pale. They recognized each other from Debby's funeral.

Cody was enraged and had to control it. "My wife called you Honeybear, I believe?" Cody asked coldly, taking the fight into the enemy camp at once.

Dr. Stern took a long breath and sat down behind his desk. "Yes," he said heavily. He looked at Cody with sad eyes. "I'm married. She drinks like a fish and hates my work and most of the time, she's off traveling with a few of her friends. I tried to divorce her and she pitched a fit and threatened to accuse me of perversion so that she could make sure I never saw my daughter again." He looked up, his face a study in torment. "I wanted Debby to ask you for a divorce, but she said her marriage made it look as if we were both tied to other people, so we wouldn't be gossiped about. I loved her more than my life. She loved me as well. I'm so sorry," he added finally. "It wasn't the way I wanted things to happen. But we were both tied, in our own ways, and you were collateral damage."

"She never loved me," Cody said, finally realizing the truth.

"She was fond of you, and she hated deceiving you," Stern replied quietly. "I was her mentor in neurology. She was absolutely brilliant. She had a great future ahead of her." He leaned back in his chair. "My life ended when she died. I love my job. It's the only thing that keeps me from jumping off the roof of some tall building."

"I didn't know any of this," Cody said, ice in his tone. "I never dreamed that she was unfaithful, that she was leading a double life. I loved her more than anything in this world. She left me a puppy..."

"Yes, the husky," the doctor said, his eyes dull with memory. "She was meant for me, a last gift, but the nurse got the message wrong and gave her to you instead. She was to be company for Muttsy." He glanced at Cody's taut face. "I love dogs. She didn't like animals, but she tolerated the dog when I went to see her." He grimaced. "My wife hates dogs. She hates me, too."

Cody was too unsettled to feel sorry for the other man. He was still reeling with what he'd learned about his perfect marriage.

The doctor saw that. "Are you staying for a couple of days?"

"Yes," Cody bit off. "I'm investigating a murder that may tie in to a criminal case I'm working in Wyoming."

The doctor nodded. "Go back to your motel room, have a stiff drink, and go to bed for a few hours. You've had a shock. I'm very sorry for my part in it, but I couldn't have helped what happened. I loved Debby, too, you see. I loved her more than my own life." He choked up and looked away.

Cody was fighting through betrayal, shock, anger and half a dozen less traumatic emotions. He remembered the doctor almost collapsing at Debby's funeral. He remembered what he'd been told, that they'd had to sedate the doctor and hospitalize him when Debby died because he was so devastated.

"I guess we were both victims," Cody said aloud after a minute.

The doctor nodded.

Cody took a deep breath, nodded, and left the office. He walked and walked, until he was too tired to do anything else. He went back to the restaurant near his motel, ordered a stiff drink at the bar and drank it. He went back to his motel room and collapsed on the bed.

When he woke up, there were two messages on his cell phone. One was from Miss Henry, asking him to phone her when he had time. The other was a text message from Abby. It simply said, Are you okay? We're all worried about you. Take care of yourself.

The text message, so brief, lifted his heart and made him feel ten feet taller. Abby was worried about him. He smiled to himself. The one woman in the world who had really good reasons to hate him, was concerned for him. And not only Abby, but Lucy and Hannah as well. His girls. He smiled.

But he had to take care of business before he could contemplate anything else. He phoned Miss Henry.

"I found something," she said after he'd identified himself. "It's not much, just a note she was writing to the detective agency, apparently the night she went out on a date with the murderer and never came home," she said, sadness in her tone. "But the detective agency is in Houston, Texas," she began.

"Lassiter," Cody exploded, recalling that a detective by that name had been in Catelow on business.

"Well, yes, how did you know?" Miss Hunter asked.

"The biggest detective agency in Houston is Lassiter's. It was a leap of logic."

"A very nice one, Sheriff. This detective is the son of the founder of the agency, judging from what my sister wrote. Is that some help to you?"

"It is, indeed. Please, keep looking. Did she keep a diary?"

There was a faint gasp. "Yes! I haven't even looked for it. I'm certain that the killer wouldn't have found it. She had a

secret hiding place that only the two of us knew about. I'll
go look there right now. If I find it, I'll call you back."

"Please do! And thank you."

"We're sort of on the same side," she replied, and hung up.

Finally, Cody thought, maybe a break in the case. Now if
they could just put the gigolo on the defensive and save Mr.
Whatley...

He drew in a long breath. No sense in wearing himself out
with things that might not even happen. He knew that the
law had to proceed one step at a time.

Meanwhile, he had to deal with the reopening of Debby's
death and the doctor's presence in her life.

He thought Debby was faithful to him. God knew, he'd
been faithful to her. A lawman certainly had opportunities to
be something less than that. Many a female suspect was willing to do almost anything to get out of a charge that could
lead to a stint in jail. Then, too, there were the obsessed
women who fell for the uniform and the muscles that filled it
out. Cody had never even been tempted. He was crazy about
his wife. He was so happy just to be married to her that he
overlooked all sorts of red flags that might have led him to
the truth years ago.

Now he had to face it and live with it, and he didn't know
how he was going to manage. He'd lived on memories for so
long. He and Anyu, who wasn't even really meant for him
at all. He'd lost Debby and Anyu both. He had nothing left
of the life he thought he was living; a life full of joy and sorrow that was a sham. Debby had been in love with another
man, a man she could never have. The doctor she loved was
in the same position.

Cody had been, how had Dr. Stern put it, collateral damage. He was the one who'd been hurt the most, but he hadn't
known. If he'd stayed in Wyoming, if he'd never come here

on this case, trying to save Horace Whatley's life, he'd never have known about Debby and her lover.

He felt the pain like lightning going through his body. He sat down with his elbows on his knees, his head in his hands. "Why?" he groaned out loud. "For God's sake, Debby, why didn't you just tell me?!"

She couldn't have. He saw that clearly now. She had to keep her marriage in order to protect the man she really loved, a man who was part of a world that Cody didn't live in.

He felt a cold emptiness inside himself that he'd never known. He understood that he'd need time to process the new reality, to get used to it. He had to have time.

But he couldn't let his personal problems stand in the way of a murder investigation. If he could, he had to save Mr. Whatley. Because that gigolo was very possibly going to do his best to get rid of the little man, so that he had full access to Miss Whatley's fortune. If he'd done that, and succeeded, with Miss Henry's sister, he was more than capable of trying again. It would have given him a sense of invulnerability, to escape a murder charge and start a whole new life in Florida, with a new victim.

That might give Cody and Dade County Police Chief Dan Brady an edge, because they now had information that Bobby Grant didn't know about. If only Miss Henry could find that diary, he thought. It might solve a world of problems.

But she phoned him back within half an hour.

"She moved it," Miss Henry said miserably. "I know that was where she kept it. We shared a fondness for hiding places and secrets. She lived with me, of course, so we shared the secrets. I don't think he could have found it," she added. "He was never alone long enough to do any real searching, and he had no idea that Candy even kept a diary. But if I can't find it, there's no way to know what she put in it."

"Did she discuss it with you?" he asked.

"Not really." There was a pause. "I'm afraid I was rather hostile to her. She was vocal about Bobby Grant. She hated him. She wouldn't even stay in the apartment when he came to get me for a date. Certainly she wouldn't have told him that she kept a diary. There would have been no reason."

"Not unless she threatened him with it," Cody said quietly.

There was a long sigh. "I didn't think about that," she replied. "I'm so sorry. I was sure it was in her hiding place. I'll keep looking," she added quickly. "I'm not giving up."

"Did she have a safe-deposit box?" he asked.

"Well, yes, but she only used it for family heirlooms. Diamond jewelry, mostly. I had occasion to go into the box a week ago. The jewels were still there. I had wondered, you see, if he knew about them, if he might have made a copy of the key."

"Would he have known where you kept it?" he asked.

She sighed again. "He didn't know I had the box. I was too busy listening to him brag about himself to mention that Candy and I inherited a fortune in gems from our grandparents."

"Just as well," Cody said.

"Yes. But it's cold comfort. I'd rather have lost the money than my only sister," she said sadly.

"If you have any luck with the diary, please call me. Any time."

"I promise I'll do that," she said.

"And just a thought, you might speak to the bank manager and see if anyone besides you and your sister had a look in that safe-deposit box."

"That would be what you call a long shot," she replied with a faint smile in her voice. "But I suppose it wouldn't hurt to ask. However, I know all the tellers in the bank, and anyone who goes in there has to sign to be permitted access. The signatures are checked as well."

"I didn't know that," Cody said, and was surprised. He didn't have a safe-deposit box. He didn't have anything valuable enough to warrant paying for one.

"We learn something new every day," she replied. "If you put that man behind bars, please tell me. I'll throw a big party. You can come and bring all your friends."

He laughed. It was the first time he'd felt like laughing in the past twenty-four hours. "I'll make a point of it," he promised.

He phoned the Lassiter Detective Agency in Houston, Texas, and spoke to Dane Lassiter, who'd founded it.

The other man recognized the name. "You were involved in a case concerning the Kirk brothers," he said at once. "A murder investigation. One of our operatives, Ty Harding, was there."

"I remember the case," Cody replied. "We don't have that many murders in my part of the world," he added.

"I imagine not. It's a small community."

"Very small. This case," he added, "involves a playboy whom I think is trying to frame a member of our community for a bank robbery. He may also have plans to eliminate him. There's a fortune at stake and he's got the female heir infatuated enough to give him everything she and her brother own."

"Isn't that a coincidence," Lassiter said thoughtfully. "Because my son is investigating a murder in Denver that may tie into your case!"

CHAPTER NINE

"I don't ordinarily share information on an active investigation," Lassiter told Cody, "but this case is one of the more disturbing ones we've been involved with. I think the man in question killed the sister of his victim in an attempt to gain control of her fortune. The sister was the only other heir, and she was suspicious of the perp. It's a tragic thing. We're almost certain he got away with murder, but my son hasn't been able to find enough proof to take to local authorities." He sighed. "Besides that, the perp has left town and vanished."

"No, he hasn't," Cody replied. "He's safe and sound, living in a small Florida town, and he's trying to convince his latest victim to cut her brother out of the family fortune. Since that didn't succeed, I'm fairly certain that he'll have a backup plan involving eliminating our local character."

"There's a missing diary," Lassiter said.

"I know. I just got off the phone with Violet Henry. She gave me the information about your agency's connection to my case."

"Isn't it a small world?" Lassiter mused.

"Very small," Cody replied. "Is your son able to take time

to come up to Wyoming and discuss the case with me? I'm sure that we can afford to pay him." I hope, Cody added silently.

"Since it's already an active case, we won't require additional payment from your department," Dane told him. He laughed. "I started out as a cop in Houston, Texas. I do know about budgets, even in small towns. I had some contact with sheriff's offices in rural areas. In fact, I still have contact with them."

"We're poor, but honest," Cody told him.

"I'll have my son come and see you Friday, will that do? He lives over in Wapiti Ridge, only about an hour's drive from Catelow. That's why he's working on Miss Henry's case. He's closer to her than I am, in Houston, where my agency's headquarters are based."

"Miss Henry is an interesting person," Cody said. "I like her."

"So does my son," came the reply. "Hell of a shame, what happened to her sister. This perp needs to be stopped, before he can cause any more deaths."

"I'll be happy to work with you, any way I can."

"I know that. Thanks. We'll be in touch." He hung up.

Cody felt better about the case, but he was concerned for Horace Whatley. The little man had some mental health challenges, and he needed protection. Cody bristled when he thought about some slick-talking opportunist looking for ways to frame his victim's brother, or outright kill him, to get his hands on the Whatley fortune. Since he'd been thwarted in Denver, it would likely make him far more determined to strike while the iron was hot. He must be aware that Violet Henry wouldn't stop trying to prove he killed her sister. He'd be looking for a grubstake. A big one.

Thank God Cody had the case to occupy his mind, while

he dealt with the new information he'd dug out about his late wife and her lover. He'd refused to think about it at all while he was pursuing the case. He'd also put Anyu's death to the back of his mind, because he didn't have time to indulge the grief he felt. Work was the great panacea, he thought, a way to get through his anguish. If he stayed busy, he had less time to brood.

But he wanted, needed, to talk to somebody about it. He had no family left, really, except for his cousin Bart Riddle. They were good friends, but he hesitated to share such deeply personal information with anyone else. Then he remembered Abby, holding him while he dealt with Anyu's loss, taking him home with her, looking after him. Warmth spread all through his body at the memory. She was unlike any woman he'd known, except his late mother, who had been a little saint. Abby was like that. She cared deeply about the people around her. She would listen, and without being judgmental. He smiled to himself. So, he had someone to talk to after all. Someone who'd listen and care as well.

He packed his bag and left Denver without a backward glance. It would take time to process what he'd learned about Debby and Dr. Stern. He did feel sorry for the man, but he hated what he and Debby had done. Sneaking around in a clandestine relationship wasn't something Cody would ever have considered, not even with Debby, whom he'd loved so much.

It occurred to him that he was one of those people who loved deeply and forever, and only once. He couldn't imagine loving another woman. He was fond of Abby, of course. She was a good person, and she'd turned into a good friend. But he wasn't going to let his attraction to her monopolize his life. There was no future in it. He didn't want to get married again, to risk being torn apart like this again. He'd lived in a paradise in his own mind for so long now. He was happily married to a brilliant doctor who loved him equally and wanted to spend the rest of her life as his wife. And it was a lie. All of it. Even her last thought, the gift of a puppy to the man she loved, hadn't concerned Cody at all. The puppy had been meant for Dr. Stern. He laughed coldly. No wonder the nurse, Debby's friend, had been so unsettled when Cody came to get the puppy. She might not even have known that Cody was Debby's husband. Or, she might have known everything, which was why she was entrusted with the puppy, on orders to give it to the man Debby loved most in the world. And that man wasn't Cody Banks.

All those years of lies. He groaned inwardly as he drove himself back up to Catelow. He must be the world's biggest sucker, he decided. If he was that bad a judge of character, he was hardly qualified for the important job he held. On the other hand, anyone could make a mistake. If so, his was the biggest mistake of his life. He should have realized when Debby stopped coming home on the weekends that she had other connections. He should have asked questions at least. He hadn't, because having her home once in a while was far preferable to never seeing her again. He'd been afraid to push her too far, for fear of losing her altogether. But he had been a little suspicious. His visit to her apartment, where she'd looked around worriedly the whole time he was there. His visit to her hospital, where she'd been uptight and rushed him through the visit.

He'd been so much in love with her. He'd had crushes on girls in high school, and once there had been a receptionist at one of the local agencies with whom he'd been infatuated until she confessed that she'd fallen in love with someone else—one of his deputies, in fact, and she'd been dating Cody so that she could see the other man. They'd married. Cody, with no hard feelings, had even gone to the wedding. His love life hadn't been very successful. And now here he was, with Debby dead and gone, and he was faced with the reality that his wife had never loved or wanted him, and that she'd been living with another man, a married man.

It was late when he got home. He called the office, to be told that there was nothing of significance to be passed on to him. His deputies were handling the few minor disturbances of the day.

He smiled as he went to make coffee. Law enforcement was like that. You'd have days and days of routine things, traffic citations, domestic disturbances, nuisance calls, threats. And then you'd have a few days when it seemed that every criminal act in the book was being committed, and there were never enough deputies to handle the overflow. He'd had to call in mutual aid a few times, especially during a memorable car chase that had made the news as far north as Billings, Montana. He shook his head. It was the variety of the job that kept him interested. He couldn't imagine sitting at a desk for weeks on end, facing the same boring routine each day. It was very satisfying to never know what the day would bring.

However, it was a shock to walk into his office the next morning and discover that Horace Whatley had been arrested and was residing at the county detention center.

Cody gaped at his undersheriff. "What the hell...?!"

"Now, now," Jeb Chandler said soothingly, "it's not as bad as it seems."

"What was he arrested for?" Cody demanded angrily.

"Bank robbery."

"Oh, come on...!" Cody exploded.

"There's an eyewitness who saw him put on a mask and pull out a gun before he walked into the bank," Jeb continued.

Cody was lost for words. He thought up quite a few, but he didn't get them out before Jeb started again.

"It was the private detective's idea to keep him at the detention center as a potential suspect. He'll be safer in lockup than he will at his house, and he's not likely to meet with any fatal accidents," Jeb said.

Cody wasn't sure that he liked the idea of a visiting detective making decisions for his department. On the other hand, it was a good idea. Certainly the perp or one of his friends couldn't very well get to Whatley where he was.

"Do we know who the eyewitness is yet?" Cody pursued.

"Oh, yes," Jeb said, and his eyes twinkled.

"Well?" Cody prompted impatiently.

"The eyewitness is Cappy Blarden," he said with pursed lips.

"Cappy. Cappy." Cody was thunderstruck.

"Cappy couldn't manage a true statement if he was paid even more than he was paid as an eyewitness to our town character's bank robbery. That private detective from that Houston agency is sharp! He's already checked out Cappy's bank account." He smiled pleasantly.

Cody knew that smile. He relaxed. "I gather there was a recent deposit."

"Yes, drawn on a bank account in Florida."

"Finally, a paper trail!"

"It was a cashier's check, but Lassiter had somebody in Dade County check it out, and the teller described the purchaser to him. In fact, she knew him. It seems that he often withdraws money from a Miss Nita Whatley's account in the same bank."

"Glory!" Cody exploded, laughing.

"So the bank robbery charge is a sham."

"Of course. Nita Whatley was belligerent when I told her that her little brother was a suspect in a bank robbery. She knew he wasn't the culprit."

"You know, we still don't have a culprit…a suspect," Jeb corrected with a grin.

"I know. But we'll get there. Rome wasn't built in a day."

Jeb just shrugged. "Oh, Lassiter left a number and asked if you'd phone him when you got in. He said he spoke to his father last night about the case."

"I spoke to his father, as well," Cody said. "Brilliant man. His agency has a sterling reputation."

"Lassiter walked in just as two of the Corrie girls were here asking about that part-time job we have open for a receptionist." He shook his head. "They just stood there with their mouths open. He's a striking man, I have to admit. If I wasn't sweet on the eldest Corrie girl, Michelle, I might even have liked him."

Cody laughed to himself. Jeb didn't like women much, but he was openly charming to Michelle Corrie when he saw her, especially at the café where she worked part-time as a waitress. The family, once wealthy, had fallen on hard times. There were three sisters. The youngest was still in school, but the two older ones worked and took care of the youngest. Their dad had died some years ago. Their mother was a semi-invalid. Jeb liked all of them.

"I am, fortunately, not involved with either Corrie girl, so I can't say that concerns me," he returned with a faintly smug glance.

Jeb pursed his lips. "Miss Brennan was in here at the same time with a note from her boss, Mr. Owens, for you. She left it with Missy." Missy was the current receptionist, working short time because she was heavily pregnant. "Lassiter was very attentive to Abby. In fact," he added, with a sly glance at his boss, who seemed to be simmering, "he had her blushing."

Something exploded inside him. Lassiter, here in Catelow, flirting with Cody's girl? He just stood where he was, like a statue, while jealousy burned like a flame in his belly.

Jeb noticed that expression with satisfaction. "So I guess nobody's girl is safe while he's in town. Oh, and he has a degree from MIT, by the way," Jeb added, and turned to go back into his own office.

Missy came out of her office with an empty cup. "Oh, welcome back, Sheriff Banks," she enthused. "Did you have a nice trip?"

"It wasn't a vacation, Missy," he muttered.

"Oh, I know that, but Denver's big and sprawling and I expect there's a lot to do there," she added.

"I was there on a murder investigation," he added.

"Well, you don't spend the whole day and night investigating one little thing, do you?" She looked at him vacantly, and smiled.

He just sighed and went into his office, shaking his head. Missy was a little vague about what the sheriff and his deputies did on an investigation. She was a little vague about everything except her husband, Mike, whom she adored.

He envied her. She was never upset, never got ruffled, was always smiling and pleasant. She made worried parents of lawbreakers feel better with her attitude when they came to inquire about charges. It was why she was good at her job. Cody thought about the elder Corrie girl working here and expected that Jeb wouldn't get a thing done. He'd spend his days staring at her and sighing.

He sat down at his desk with a cup of hot coffee that he'd picked up in the small detention kitchen on the way there and checked his cell phone.

The message from Abby was still there. He hadn't phoned her since he came home. He hadn't texted her, either. He was uneasy about Lassiter's effect on her. Abby was quiet and old-fashioned and kept to herself. She'd lived and worked in Denver, but he knew that she hadn't been around men much. He grimaced, recalling why. A man like Lassiter, handsome and brilliant, and flattering, might get close to her. He'd move on, but Abby would be left with a broken heart. He could picture Abby in floods of tears as a carefree detective Lassiter drove out of town.

His dark eyes glittered with feeling. He hadn't even met the man and he was certain that he wasn't going to like him.

He went home after a long day, and still hadn't called Lassiter. He'd put it off until he could cool down and stop thinking evil thoughts about him.

While he was looking at the cans of chili and soup in the cabinet as he thought about supper, his cell phone rang.

He answered the call, his mind still on soup or chili. "Banks," he murmured absently.

"I'm here to steal your girl. I'm going to break her heart and leave her mentally distraught. Meanwhile, your under-sheriff is going to lose his hopeful girlfriend to me, and he's thinking about flights to Tahiti…am I somewhere near the mark?" came a deep, dry voice over the phone.

Cody just stood still. "The CIA had a program where their operatives read minds," he said curtly. "I'll bet you know more about that than you're ever going to tell me."

There was a chuckle. "I don't read minds. I listen when people tell me things. Your undersheriff doesn't like me. He even said why. But you're both off the mark. I'm off women. Period."

"You like men?" Cody mused.

"I like pie."

Cody blinked. "Excuse me?"

"Pie."

"Apple or cherry?" Cody replied.

"Pi, as the measure of circumference," came the reply. "I love physics. Hate women."

"In that case," Cody said, "welcome to Catelow. And if you'd like to repeat that phrase to Miss Corrie, Miss Brennan, and any other potential conquest, I know the undersheriff and I would be happy to take you out for a hamburger and fries."

The chuckle was uninhibited. "I'd like to come and see you in the morning. You might caution any women friends to avoid the office until after I leave. I mean, having them hang onto my ankles as I go out through doors is really very embarrassing."

"Interesting how your father is as sober as a judge, from what I've been told," Cody said.

"We're not much alike. Now my sister takes after him, but she works in an office from nine to five. I'd go nuts."

Cody chuckled. "Me, too. It's why I love this job." He sobered. "Not a bad idea, having Mr. Whatley inside for a while."

"It was the best idea I could come up with, after your undersheriff and I put our heads together," the other man replied quietly. "He seems like a sweet man. A little challenged, sort of a living-in-the-clouds mentality, but not dangerous to anyone. I liked his sister, too."

"You've been to Florida?"

"No, I spoke to her on the phone earlier. She's livid about his arrest. And I had to leave her that way. We can't have her spilling the beans to her significant other until we can nail him for murder."

"I like the way you think."

"Tell my dad. Please. He thinks I'm five degrees off-center." He paused. "He's probably right."

Cody thought about that.

"I'd like to come and visit you in the morning," Lassiter continued. "Could you have one of your squad cars pick me up?"

"Where are you?" Cody asked.

"At the Three Rings Motel."

"That's about half a block from here..."

Lassiter agreed. "Yes, it is. And I'd like your deputy to handcuff me. I'll make a fuss. You know, I'm not guilty of anything, I'm just passing through, why are you harassing me? That sort of thing."

"Why would I want to handcuff you?" Cody was all at sea.

"So I'll have a reason to call Nita Whatley back and tell her that her poor brother's locked up and so am I, and I was only trying to help him out."

"Okay, I'm getting a serious headache," Cody began.

"I'm going to have her tell me about her boyfriend and then I'm going to suggest that I might know a way to have her brother give up his claim to the family fortune. Well, for a cut, you know. I can say that Mr. Whatley told me all about his mental challenges and his sister, and how her boyfriend is going to take care of her so her brother won't worry."

"Man, you should write fiction," Cody said when Lassiter finished.

"Never works. I'm left-brained. Too much theory and exposition to make a good writer. I know one. My best friend's mother. She's about twenty degrees west of center, but she has a mind like a steel trap. She plays video games, rides condemned roller coasters, and drives a Jaguar sedan so fast that she's set a new record for speeding tickets in her county."

Cody burst out laughing. "Why couldn't I meet a woman like that?" he asked.

"Well, she's seventy-four..." Lassiter said slowly.

Cody laughed harder.

"I did hear some local gossip about you and one of the paralegals in the Owens law group in town," Lassiter fished. "Abby Brennan. I met her today in your office."

Cody was fighting some odd, new emotions. He wasn't sure what to say. As if he'd looked for divine intervention, the office phone rang and his receptionist called out. "There's a wreck out on the highway. Injuries, they said. Bad ones."

"Okay, thanks," he told her. "I have to go," he told Lassiter.

"No problem. We can talk in the morning. Don't forget.
Resisting arrest. Bad attitude. Bring handcuffs. Right?"

"Right," Cody agreed. He just shook his head. He'd never
met anyone like Lassiter.

Abby Brennan was having similar thoughts. She'd missed
Cody. She knew he was back in town, but he hadn't phoned
her or texted her or anything. She felt empty inside. Was he
having second thoughts about the attraction he felt for her?
It wouldn't be surprising. Abby knew how much he'd loved
Debby. He might feel guilty. Abby had read about men who
lost their wives having a hard time starting a new relationship with a different woman. The problem was that they still
felt married.

Abby sighed. It would be like living with a ghost, she
thought sadly. No woman would ever be able to measure up to
the Debby of Cody's dreams. She lived inside him, lived with
him, and she came between him and any new relationship.

Not that Abby wanted to have a relationship with him.
He did kiss very nicely, she conceded, but a marriage needed
more than just kisses.

She almost gasped out loud at the track of her own thoughts.
Cody certainly wouldn't be thinking about marriage. Everybody knew how he felt about Debby. He absolutely worshiped
her. He'd gone crazy when she died. How could any ordinary woman fight a ghost?

They'd seemed so close before he left for Denver, as if they
were starting something together. Now, it seemed as if he
wanted to put some distance between them. He hadn't even
called to tell her he was home.

Well, let him ignore her, she thought irritably. That detective, Lassiter, had seemed very personable and she'd liked
him on sight. They'd had an instant rapport. He seemed very
interested in her.

She smiled to herself. It had been a long time between compliments of the sort he'd made. Cody had been caring and tender, but it was an absent sort of affection, as if he was far away from her and liked it that way. Lassiter was a new proposition. He was immediately charming and blatantly interested in Abby.

Mr. Lassiter was a stranger, but he obviously wanted to get to know Abby. She liked what she saw of him. She wanted to see more. And if Sheriff Banks wanted to live in the past with his pretty ghost, why should Abby be concerned about it? There were plenty of men in the sea, which had tossed Mr. Lassiter up all dressed and mounted and everything.

There was a prominent cough. Abby looked up. Mr. Owens was standing at her desk.

"Oh, gosh, I'm so sorry," she blurted out, because it was obvious that he'd been standing there more than a minute.

"No problem," he said quietly. His face was drawn. He looked his age. "Abby, I need you to look up a precedent for me in the law library in the courthouse." He named the case and waited for her to write it down. He added the details he needed as well. "And if you could get that back to me today, I'd really appreciate it. I know it's short notice..."

"Doing things on the spur of the moment is what you pay me for, Mr. Owens," she said with a smile. "I don't mind at all. I'll get right on it."

He smiled from a tired face. "Thanks, Abby. Call me when you finish, all right? Better yet, text me. Our nephew is staying with us for a couple of weeks and he has odd sleeping habits."

"I'll be glad to do that for you," she replied.

"And this involves a sensitive case, so don't mention it to anyone," he added. "Especially the sheriff."

Odd request, she thought, but she only smiled. "I'll keep it under my hat," she replied.

He sighed. "Life is so damned complicated sometimes," he began, running a hand through his hair. He paused and glanced at Abby. "What's this I hear about the sheriff sleeping over at your place?" he added with twinkling eyes.

She flushed. "Well, you see, he'd just lost his dog and he was feeling really down. So I took him home with me, and Lucy and Hannah and I cheered him up. It's hard losing a pet," she added.

"I know. I lost my fourteen-year-old golden retriever last month." He shook his head. "I never thought I'd get through the first few days afterward."

"I'm so sorry. Was she sick?"

"My nephew ran over her," he said tautly. He drew in a deep breath. "I promised my brother on his deathbed that I'd take care of him. It's harder than it sounds. Of course, he didn't mean to run over the dog. He loved Goldie, just as we did. He actually cried. He'd been in a hurry to get to some meeting or other, and he didn't look as he backed up. It could have been one of my grandkids. I'm afraid I was rather short with him."

"So would I have been," she replied. "It hurts to give up a fur baby. I had a dog when I was a little girl. I cried for days after I lost him…" She didn't say another word, and the look on her face didn't encourage questions.

Owens knew about her fraught childhood and her brutal father. He knew, as many other longtime citizens of Catelow knew, that Abby's father had killed her dog over an argument. It was a sick thing to do. In fact, the sheriff at that time actually arrested Abby's father for animal cruelty and pressed charges against him. It was the beginning of tragedy after tragedy for Abby.

Abby got up and grabbed her purse and her coat and a notepad and pen. "I'll look up the information, then I'll look for legal opinions online."

"You're a wonder, Abby," he told her. "I'm constantly amazed at how much information you can glean from the most vague subject matter."

She laughed. "It amazes me, too," she confessed. "I'll be in touch as soon as I track this down."

"Thanks again."

"I don't mind," she told him. "I like the challenge."

"You should have gone to law school," he said.

"I did think about it," she said. "But I couldn't bear the thought of getting up in front of so many people in a court-room without stark terror smothering me. I do best in areas where I don't have to give speeches." She sobered. "It's a deadly thing, defending someone for a capital crime. You have to have the guts to argue the case, to present facts in a manner that the jury will understand, you have to be able to speak to witnesses and drag the truth out of them." She shook her head. "I'd be a dead loss."

"Not likely," he said. "You'd be great at it. You have to believe in yourself, Abby."

"There's another problem area." She grinned.

He just laughed.

"I'll text you as soon as I dig out some information. It may be late," she cautioned.

"Won't bother me," he said, and he smiled.

She was curious about the area of law that was involved in the cases Mr. Owens was working on. He was a tax lawyer and he also specialized in estate law. What he wanted was a precedent in a criminal case, a point of law that excluded certain people from legal penalties if convicted.

But that was Mr. Owens's business, she told herself firmly. She knew that he had plenty of friends in legal circles, so per-haps a friend had asked him to check it out and keep the in-formation to himself.

She liked Mr. Owens a lot. He was a good boss. She felt like part of a family in the law practice. It was a good feeling.

Cody dragged home late that night, his head reeling with what he'd learned about Debby's secret life. He'd hoped to phone Abby and talk to her for a few minutes. But after hearing about her and Lassiter, he wasn't confident enough to do it. She might be embarrassed if he brought it up—especially if she really was attracted to the man.

So he sat down on his sofa, looking absently for Anyu and realizing immediately that she would never be there again, looking up at him and laughing with her blue eyes so steady on his face. He ground his teeth together. He had to stop thinking about it or he'd certainly go mad.

He'd finished a dish of scrambled eggs and sausage and was looking forward to early bedtime when he was called out to a desperate hostage situation, involving a young man and a pre-teenage girl whom he'd taken prisoner and was trying to carry away. Her father had come outside with a gun and threatened the young man, and the girl was screaming her head off trying to get away from him. A knife at her throat stopped both the screaming and her father, who was just leveling the gun.

Cody found the address on his computer and signaled dispatch that he was en route. Jeb was on the scene, along with another deputy and about three Catelow police officers who'd been listening to the chat and rushed over to help. Cody was grateful for the backup, but afraid so many law enforcement people might cause the perp to do something desperate.

He motioned them all into a huddle. "Do we have anybody here who's ever done negotiation?"

One of the police officers raised his hand. "I worked in Denver for a while, and I thought I'd like being a negotiator, so I trained for it. Gave it up, though, it was just too much work."

"Can you bargain with the perp?" Cody asked.

The man sighed. "Well, I trained to do it about twenty years ago."

A car pulled up nearby and a tall, dark, incredibly handsome man got out of it. He was wearing a tee shirt that said Shrödinger's Cat is Alive/Dead. A geek shirt, for sure. He joined the group.

"I'm J.R. Lassiter," he introduced himself. "Hostage situation? I'm a trained negotiator. Let me do this."

Cody was seething inside. The man was handsome. He hated him already. "Okay," he said, though, knowing the other man was more qualified.

"What's his name, do you know?" Lassiter asked.

"No idea. Hey," he called to the man holding the girl prisoner. "What's your name?"

"Tony. Why?" came the belligerent reply.

"His name is Tony," Cody told Lassiter. "Go get him."

"My pleasure." He started walking toward the perp as lazily as if he had all day.

"Hey, stop coming closer. Who are you?" the man demanded.

"I'm your new best friend," Lassiter said. "You're holding that knife all wrong, if you want to impress the lawmen over there."

The man blinked at him, so surprised that he didn't notice just how close Lassiter had come to him. "Huh?" he muttered, distracted. "Why would I want to impress them?"

"They're trying to impress you. Look at that!" He turned his head and pointed to the distance.

The man, predictably, turned his head. Lassiter whirled

around, caught his arm in a graceful arc, twisted the knife out, tossed the perp to the ground, and sat on him.

"Okay, guys, he's all yours!" he called to Cody and the other officers. And he was even smiling.

CHAPTER TEN

"Interesting tee shirt," Cody said when the prisoner was in the detention center and they were waiting for the FBI to get there to take the man into federal custody.

Lassiter just grinned. "It gets noticed."

"I did a physics course in college," Cody said. "But I had to drop it. I couldn't pass the tests."

"It's a tricky subject. I love it. It was a toss-up, following my dad into detective work or teaching. I decided that trying to keep order in a classroom without ending up in handcuffs wasn't for me. I'm not politically correct."

"Neither am I," Cody had to agree. "You're not hand-cuffed."

"Of course not," he replied. "Your deputy took me to jail already and I made bail."

"It's good of you to help," Cody said. "I feel sorry for Miss Whatley. Even sorrier for her brother. The whole town has kind of adopted him. He fits in here very well."

"I'll have to be arrested again, of course," Lassiter told him. "I heard one of the deputies talking about the standoff and I phoned Dad to bail me out. I've done hostage negotiation for years."

"You seem to be very good at it," the lawman said, with a definite interest.

"I was CIA," came the surprising reply. "Dad was furious when I left town and pursued a new career. I went overseas and worked for one of the world's deadliest madmen getting the goods on him. I did a stint as an enforcer for another sheriff's father-in-law in Texas." He chuckled. "He's a drug lord. Nice guy. Didn't put a foot wrong on this side of the border. He has a new granddaughter and he's not risking his visiting privileges."

"You get around," Cody mused.

Lassiter chuckled. "Yes, I do. I finally went back with the agency so Dad's hair wouldn't have yet more silver in it. He and my mom worry."

"It must be nice to have parents. Mine are both gone."

"I'm truly sorry," Lassiter told him. "I don't know what I'd do without mine."

"Well, we'd better get you back into a cell with Mr. Whatley," Cody said after a minute. "If anybody asks, you took a swing at me."

Lassiter chuckled. "That's even believable. Thanks. I was looking for a way back in."

Cody's eyes twinkled. "I do like the way you negotiate."

"It works better with a hide gun," he said, grinning. "But in a desperate case, tae kwon do and judo will stand you in good stead. I was a master trainer in the service."

"Which branch?"

"Marine Corps," he replied. "I thought about staying in, but I was in the last Middle East campaign. I saw enough dead bodies to last me a lifetime."

"Join the club. Army," Cody told him. "I was stationed there for just a little while, but it was more than enough."

Mr. Whatley was sitting on the lower bunk in his cell, looking lost. He looked up at Cody hopefully, but when he saw Lassiter, he just sighed and rested his head in his hands, propped on his knees.

"Back again," Lassiter said merrily as Cody locked him in. "How's it going, Horace?"

"I thought you made bail!"

"He did until he threw a punch at me," Cody said curtly.

Mr. Whatley only sighed again. "Is my sister going to bail me out?" he asked Cody hopefully.

"Not just yet," the sheriff told him. "Listen, you're safe in here. Nobody is going to hurt you."

"You bet," Lassiter said, and his face was solemn.

Mr. Whatley was surprised, but he looked from one face to the other and relaxed a bit. He didn't say out loud what he was thinking. This felt a lot like protective custody, and the man across from him didn't look like any criminal he'd ever seen. He was too clean-cut and authoritative. He looked at the two men and smiled.

Cody smiled back. "I'll be around," he promised, and left them to talk.

Abby had her head wrapped in a towel when she came to answer the door.

"Cody!" she exclaimed, and her face lit up like a Christmas tree.

The dark world suddenly lightened for him. He smiled back. "Glad to see me?" he teased.

"So glad! Come on in. Hannah can make coffee while I finish drying my hair…"

"Give me that towel." He took it from her and led her to an easy chair in the living room. He took the towel and started drying her hair with it. She had beautiful hair, long and thick and very soft. He smiled as he dried one strand after another.

Abby was trying to calm down. It was impossible with his body so close, his face so close as he worked on her hair.

"I love your hair," he murmured as he worked.

She smiled. "It's a nuisance to wash. I thought about having it cut, but I'm so used to the length that I'd miss it."

"I'd miss it, too," he said softly. "I love long hair."

"How did it go in Denver?" she asked.

He froze for a few seconds. "Oh, you mean the investigation," he realized finally.

She turned toward him. "Yes. Was there something else?"

He started to speak as Hannah came back from the laundry room. "Oh, hi, Sheriff Banks! We missed you!"

He chuckled. "Thanks. Where's my best girl?" he asked suddenly, looking around. "And the puppy?"

"Puppy's in the guest room sound asleep and Lucy's gone to a birthday party."

"How about some coffee and cake?" Hannah asked. "It's chocolate."

"My very favorite," Cody said, finishing his chore with Abby's long hair.

"Mine, too," Abby replied. She took the towel from him. "Thanks. Now all it needs is a scrunchie."

He frowned. "A what?"

"It holds your hair up," she said, smiling. "Back in a jiffy."

He was sipping coffee and nibbling cake by the time she got back.

Hannah had her coffee and cake all ready for her.

"I'll be working in the back bedroom if you need me," Hannah called as she went.

"This is good cake."

"Thank you," Abby said with a shy smile. "I made it."

His eyebrows arched. "You can do a lot of things."

"I've had to," she pointed out. "Now, how about Denver?"

He finished his cake and sipped coffee. He looked up at

her. He sighed. She was beautiful, in her own special way, and he loved the way she looked at him. "Debby had a lover," he blurted out.

Her lips fell open. "She what?" she exclaimed.

"She had a lover. They pretended to be married." He leaned back, his eyes far away. "He was a doctor, too, working in the same field. He was married and there was no hope of a divorce, so they had an apartment they shared."

"I'm so sorry," she said, hurting for him. He'd loved Debby so much. It was heartless, what she'd done to him.

"She never meant for me to find out," he said. "And Anyu was actually meant for the doctor she lived with." His eyes closed. "It was a very bad day. I learned things I wish I'd never learned."

Abby didn't know what to say. She just looked at him, with her heart in her eyes. "Need a hug?" she asked softly.

He didn't answer her. He just opened his arms.

She went to him and he pulled her down into his arms and hugged her close, rocking her. "I didn't know how much I needed a hug until just now," he murmured into the thick, soft, sweet-smelling hair at her throat. "I lived a lie and never knew it. Debby came up here once in a while so I'd think she still cared. But she never did. She'd leave me when I was sick and never think a thing about it. She chided me when I had to shoot someone I knew."

"Why?" she wondered.

"Because she never loved me," he said, and it tore his heart to admit it. "I was a nice smokescreen for her illicit affair. Since she was married and he was married, they put on a good show for the public. But that was all a sham."

"She should have divorced you, even if she couldn't marry him," Abby said huffily.

"I was a fool."

"No," she said softly, smoothing her hand over his shirt. "You were just a man in love."

He drew in a long breath, held her very close for a minute, and then loosened his arms so she could sit up, but he held her gently on his lap. "Speaking of men, what about Lassiter?"

"Lassiter." She frowned. "Oh, the new guy who was in your office."

"He's in the jail now, actually," he muttered. "He threw a punch at me."

"Funny, he doesn't strike me as a lawbreaker. A geek, yes," she chuckled. "Did you see his shirt?"

He nodded. "He's an odd bird. I put him in with Mr. Whatley."

"Good idea. He'll take care of him. Did you find out anything that would help his sister?"

"Quite a lot," he said. "It got pushed to the back burner while I was finding out unpleasant things about my late wife."

"I'm truly sorry about that," she said, studying his dark eyes. "I know it must hurt like the very devil."

"It did. Now I feel a little better. Thanks," he added softly, and bent to kiss her very gently on her mouth. "You make the worst problems seem small."

She smiled. The kiss had shaken her, but she marshalled her resistance and didn't let it show. "I'm glad. Any time," she added, smiling. "I don't mind listening."

"I noticed." He tapped her on the end of her nose.

She grinned. "What about Mr. Whatley's sister?"

"That's an interesting tale, and I can't share it just yet. I'm working on a plan to help save her."

She pursed her lips. "I won't ask how. Or who." Her eyes sparkled. "I have a good hunch about what's going on. But I won't say a word. I promise."

He bent and kissed her again. "This is becoming habit-forming," he murmured against her soft lips.

Her arms slid around his neck. "Is it?"

He chuckled as his lips opened on hers. "Very…!"

The kiss caught fire. They clung to each other in the quiet room, the kiss growing deeper and harder and more insistent by the minute.

Abby moaned. He pulled her up and stood up with her, putting her back just a little with his hands on her shoulders.

He cleared his throat. "We might ration these things. You know, so they don't get too intense."

"Whatever you want," she said, still reeling from his ardor.

He looked down at her face and smiled slowly. He liked the way she looked, a little dazed and more than a little interested in him. "But we might practice a little every so often, so we don't forget how."

She laughed softly. "I'd like that."

"So would I. I have to get back to work."

"Lucy wants you to come to supper Saturday," she said abruptly. "She made you something at school."

"Did she?" His face brightened. "I'd love to come to supper Saturday, in that case."

"Then we'll expect you. About six?"

He bent and rubbed his nose against hers. "About six. And don't you go kissing other men."

Her eyebrows arched. "Well, I never!"

He grinned and started to speak.

"I never did that yet, either, and you stop right there!" she said firmly. "And don't you go kissing other women," she added huffily.

"What other women?" he asked, and his eyes were soft and probing.

She cleared her throat again. "Saturday."

He nodded. He smiled. "Saturday."

She watched him drive away with her heart in her throat. It was, so far, the best day of her recent life.

★ ★ ★

Horace Whatley wanted to be bailed out of jail. Lassiter calmed him down.

"Listen," he told his cellmate, "you're the only person standing between your sister's new boyfriend and your inheritance. If he can land you in prison or, better yet, find a way to kill you, he can marry her and then she can have an accident."

Horace gasped. "No! Surely he wouldn't hurt her! She's such a gentle person!"

"He assaulted another woman in Denver and almost killed her," Lassiter replied. "She had him prosecuted. He served two years of a six-year sentence. His lawyer got him out on appeal."

He groaned. "Can't we do anything to save her?" he asked miserably.

"We're working on that. Meanwhile, you're in here with me and, believe me, nobody's touching you."

Horace stared at the other man with wide, innocent eyes. "You don't even know me," he began.

"Mr. Whatley, everybody in Catelow knows you," he said. "You're important to the people who live here."

"M-me?" the other man stammered, flushing. "But I lied about my experience with cattle management, and I made up a story about a body..." The flush got worse.

"We don't always like people for their perfections, you know," Lassiter replied. "You've given people jobs who needed them desperately, like your poor housekeeper who was brutalized by her late husband. You've hired on people you really didn't even need because they needed you." He smiled. "You'd be surprised at the people who've protested your arrest. One of them was the police chief himself."

"The police chief?"

Lassiter nodded. "He said he'd be glad to testify as a character witness. His wife said she would, too."

"But I only loaned them a piece of equipment when theirs broke down," he said.

"And sent a mechanic with them to do the job," came the amused reply. "Then, too, there were the orphan boys who had no place to go when their parents died. And you and Julia, your housekeeper, kept them until their out-of-state relatives came to take them to an aunt who wanted them." He shook his head. "You've already got a reputation for good works. So, yes, your arrest is not popular. But the reason for it has to be kept quiet, and you have to stay in custody."

"Why?" the other man asked.

"Because the gigolo couldn't get your sister to stop your checks. We figure that his next move will be either an attempt to plant evidence against you in the form of an eyewitness, and we've got one of those already, or get you out of the way permanently."

"I don't like either one of those options," Horace confessed.

"Neither do the sheriff and I. So, you're here for the duration. I'll either be in here with you or close by, along with one or two of our local operatives. Nobody's touching you on my watch."

Horace let out a long breath and smiled. "Thanks," he said.

"No problem. You're helping us with a related case."

"Somebody like me?"

"Not so much." Lassiter made himself more comfortable on his bunk. "One of his victims had a sister who was suspicious of him. She died under rather mysterious circumstances. The victim almost lost her mind. He left town running because he was afraid she might try to prove he was guilty of murder. He ran right into your sister in Florida and now he thinks he's set for life."

"He won't hurt my sister, will he?" he asked plaintively.

"It's unlikely, because if he did, you'd still inherit. We think he'll come after you."

"Well, if I had a choice, I'd rather it was me than my sister," he replied. "I don't mind staying here if you think it's all right." He ground his teeth together. "But what about Julia?" he added worriedly. "She's at the ranch all alone!"

"Not really. We've got a guy who's just hired on as a ranch hand. He's sleeping in the bunkhouse. Your foreman doesn't know his true background, which is just as well. He'll make sure that nothing happens either to Julia or to your ranch."

"Thanks!"

"All in a day's work," Lassiter replied. He smiled as he noted the other man's relieved expression. He was beginning to see why Horace Whatley had become something of a town mascot in Catelow.

Cody was worried about Horace Whatley's sister. Lassiter had passed along the conversation he'd had with the man in jail.

"Probably he's biding his time to see if Mr. Whatley is arraigned and charged with the bank robbery," Lassiter told him. "I'm certain that Miss Whatley would have informed him that her brother was under suspicion."

"He already knows it," Cody said. "Jeb told me about the cashier's check that was placed in the bank account of the so-called witness who said he saw Mr. Whatley rob the bank."

"So you could get Mr. Whatley out of jail any time you like."

Cody nodded. "Which would place him right back in the hot seat. The boyfriend will be keeping tabs on what's happening here. I'm sure Nita Whatley will tell him everything she knows."

"It must be hell, to love like that," Lassiter said, shaking his head. "I'm glad that I'm immune to it."

Cody didn't reply. He knew a lot about obsessive love. He'd been a victim of it.

"So we just plug along for the time being and do nothing to spring Mr. Whatley?" Lassiter asked.

Cody nodded. "That way we can keep him alive while we try to tie her boyfriend to the murdered woman in Denver."

"I have a friend who's a fed. He has ties with the police chief who's sweet on Nita Whatley."

"She'd smell a rat if an outsider poked his nose in," Cody said.

"Only if he really was an outsider. He and the police chief are first cousins, and he grew up with Nita." His black eyes twinkled. "It seems the police chief is rather desperate to save Nita Whatley from the clutches of the gigolo."

"I hope we can do that," Cody said. "I've taken a liking to Mr. Whatley. I'd hate to see him killed."

"So would I," Lassiter replied. "I'm going to check with my dad and see if he's had any luck running down that diary of Violet Henry's."

"That would be a nice little piece of evidence, if it has anything to say about Bobby Grant and his obsession with Miss Henry's fortune."

"Her sister was only trying to protect her," Lassiter said. "What a hell of a thing to have happen. I'd love to see the man pay for it."

"So would I," Cody said. "It's not really my case, I'm just investigating Mr. Whatley's charges, but if the Denver authorities could find a way to send Mr. Grant up for life, I'd be happy to help put him there."

"Join the club!"

Abby wasn't told why Mr. Whatley was still in jail, but she was an intelligent woman and she had an idea about it that she wasn't sharing in public.

She and Lucy went ice-skating in the local rink later in the week. There was a teacher workday on Friday, so Abby took a couple of hours off and went skating with her niece.

As luck would have it, Mrs. Micah Torrence was out on the ice doing lazy loops and spins and laybacks while her stepdaughter watched with rapt fascination.

"One day, I'm going to be as good as you are!" Janey Torrence told her and hugged her warmly.

Karina Torrence laughed. "Yes, you are, my darling," she agreed. "As long as you keep practicing!"

"Oh, there's Lucy!" Janey exclaimed. "She's new at our school. She's got a new puppy and kittens!"

They skated over to be introduced.

"We've certainly heard of you," Abby chuckled. "Our very own Wyoming legend. You're the only Olympic gold medalist I've ever met in my life! I'm stagestruck!"

Karina laughed. "I'm just an ordinary woman these days," she protested. "Our son is two years old. Janey and I fight over who gets to feed him," she teased, drawing her stepdaughter close.

"But mostly we share him," Janey said, all smiles.

"How do you like life in Catelow?" Karina asked.

"After living in Denver? It's just great!" Abby replied. "We had a miserable little apartment and no social life at all." She shook her head. "The schools here are great. Lucy loves her teacher."

"All the teachers are nice," Janey said with a big smile.

"Yes, and we get to live on a ranch!" Lucy exclaimed. "I have a kitty and a puppy...and Aunt Abby is going to teach me how to ride a horse!"

They all smiled at the child's enthusiasm.

"It really is like home," Abby said, without going into any detail about her past and the fact that she'd been brought up in Catelow, under tragic circumstances. That was in the past.

"I love to watch you skate. Both of you," Lucy told them. She shook her head. "I'd never have enough nerve to try and do jumps. I just like sliding along," she added with twinkling eyes.

"Different strokes," Abby teased, and hugged her.

"It was nice to meet you," Lucy said, a little shyly.

"Very nice," Abby seconded.

"Nice to meet you, too. Oops, looks like somebody wants us to come home now," Karina teased, indicating a big, husky man in a shepherd's coat, jeans and boots who was standing in the doorway with his hands on his hips looking toward them.

"He's just lonely," Karina said. "But we'd better go. If he's here, Burt's babysitting our son, and Burt will have him spoiled rotten before we can get halfway home!"

Burt, the housekeeper, was something of a local legend himself. Karina and Micah bragged on him constantly. Not only a good babysitter, they enthused, he was a terrific cook.

The big man at the door broke into a huge smile as Karina put the sliders on her skates and ran to him. He scooped her up and kissed her enthusiastically, regardless of his audience. The three of them left very soon, Karina and Janey turning to wave goodbye to their new acquaintances.

"They're terrific people," Lucy said.

"Yes, they are," Abby sighed. "I'll never be able to skate like that. But I like gliding around, too, just like you!"

Lucy grinned at her.

Abby skated around the rink slowly, her mind on her work. Mr. Owens had been unusually nervous all day. Concerned, Abby had asked if she could help.

He'd flushed and said that no, he was fine. He'd thanked her for her concern. But he didn't say what was upsetting him. Abby wondered if it had anything to do with his nephew. The boy had been picked up on suspicion of theft several

days earlier. Mr. Owens had bailed him out, all the time as-
serting his innocence. Abby wasn't so certain that the boy
was innocent. He had a shifty look about him, and he didn't
seem quite sober, although she never smelled alcohol on him.
Poor Mr. Owens. He had such a nice family, except for this
rude, belligerent nephew. But it was nothing to do with her.
Somehow, Mr. Owens would work it out. She'd given him
the piece of information he wanted, that she'd found a precedent for. It didn't seem to relieve his nervousness. If anything, it added to it. She wondered how such a law-abiding,
upstanding man could have such a scruffy, morose man for a
nephew. The boy apparently didn't work and was always in
the office asking for a loan, which Mr. Owens always gave.
But there again, it wasn't her business.

Snow was great fun. Lucy loved the pup, spending every
free minute she had with her. Snow responded to all the love
and petting by turning into a well-mannered, affectionate
little animal.

Saturday evening, just before Cody Banks was due to eat
dinner with them, Abby put on a clean pair of blue jeans and
a loose blue patterned cotton shirt and combed her hair so
that it fell long and soft around her shoulders. She put on just
a little bit of lipstick and not much more.

"You look pretty," Lucy said with a sigh.

"Thanks, sweetheart."

"I think the sheriff likes you," she said solemnly.

Abby smiled at her. "I like him, too."

"So do I. He's a nice man. I'll bet he still misses his dog,"
she added suddenly.

Abby nodded. "It's hard to lose a pet that you've had for a
long time," she agreed, and her eyes were sad.

"We won't lose Snow, will we?" the child asked worriedly.

Abby pulled her close and hugged her. "Not a chance. She'll

live inside with us, and whenever she has to go out, one of us will be with her, or one of the cowboys will. She won't get the chance to run away. I promise."

Lucy relaxed. "Okay. Thanks."

Cody had looked forward to having dinner with his girls. He didn't dress up, but he did make sure he wore nice slacks and a trendy shirt when he slid on his coat and hat and started for the front door.

Sadly, he never made it that far. The phone rang and he answered it quickly.

"Sheriff?" It was Bill Harris, the assistant police chief.

"Yes. What is it, Bill?"

"We've got a wreck, a really bad one," came the quiet reply. "Can you come and help out?"

He thought about the girls and dinner, but surely this wouldn't take a long time. Besides, it was his job. "Sure thing. Where is it?"

The deputy gave directions and hung up.

It should have been simple, but it wasn't. Several people were hurt, two critically, which meant Cody had to track down relatives and explain what had happened. There were other questions which had to be answered as well, and he had to call in investigators to do a re-creation of the accident, because one driver was definitely at fault and the insurance companies, and lawyers, would certainly be involved.

By the time he was through, it was dark. And just as he started for Abby's ranch, there was yet another call with yet another wreck. Life, Cody thought as he drove to the scene of the second accident, was getting harder by the day.

CHAPTER ELEVEN

Abby had Hannah wait to put dinner on the table until Cody arrived. But one hour passed, and then another, and still he didn't come.

"Are you sure you told him this Saturday night?" Hannah asked.

"I thought I said tonight," Abby replied. She bit her lower lip. She was feeling let down. Cody had no obligation to them, of course, and he could do what he pleased. But usually when he gave his word, he kept it.

"Maybe something came up," Abby said.

"Wouldn't he have called us?" Lucy asked sadly. "Could you call him instead?"

Abby flushed a little. "Well, I might interrupt him if he's working," she said. "He probably is, and he's forgotten everything else. Something bad might have happened," she added, and now she was really concerned. Had he been in a wreck? Had he been hurt?

She bit her lower lip, wondering what to do.

Cody, just leaving the hospital, suddenly remembered that he'd promised to have supper with the girls. He looked at his watch and groaned. It was eight o'clock. They'd probably long since had supper and gotten ready for bed. He didn't feel comfortable going over there this late.

He thought about it, though, and just as he'd decided to swing by and apologize, he spotted flashing lights on the highway. He pulled in behind a state police car and noted a struggle going on.

He jumped out of his SUV and rushed to render aid. The perp had his hand on the trooper's gun and was trying with all his strength to gain control of it. Cody caught his arm, twisted it around, came under him and threw him up against the patrol car, his hand going quickly to his handcuffs. The trooper, a very small blonde woman, thanked him profusely.

"Your first cuff, huh?" he teased her gently, and he smiled. She was very pretty.

She laughed. "I'm afraid so. It was so much easier when my training officer was riding with me," she confessed. "Thanks for the assist."

"No problem." He eased the suspect into the back seat, careful not to let him bump his head on the way in. The man was obviously inebriated and unruly, despite the handcuffs.

"Don't lose those cuffs," he told her. "It's the first pair I ever owned. Call it sentiment."

"I'll do better than that, Sheriff," she said, her eyes flirting with his. "I'll drop them by your office in a few minutes, as soon as I get this guy to lockup."

"Thanks," he said, smiling.

"No sweat. Thanks again." She got in under the steering wheel, ignoring the furious obscene language coming from the back seat. She waved and drove off.

And she had returned them, pausing to talk to Cody. She had to wait for a few minutes, but apparently she didn't keep her eye on the clock, or worry about not getting right back to work. It had been an interesting visit. She was very pretty. Not that Cody noticed other women, but it was kind of nice to know that a woman that pretty found him attractive.

Cody checked his watch. Definitely too late for supper now, but he had to explain why he was so late. So he swung by the ranch despite the lateness of the hour.

Snow was drifting down now, in big, soft flakes. The ranch road ran like a ribbon toward the ranch house. All around were lodgepole pines covered in snow. It was like a winter wonderland to Abby, who was sitting on the back stoop, looking out over the garden spot, wrapped cozily in a down coat with a hood. She sighed. She wondered why Cody hadn't come to supper. Maybe he'd just lost interest in her, she decided. Or maybe he felt that he shouldn't get too close to the family. She was full of questions that had no obvious answers.

"You'll freeze out here," Cody said gently.

She jumped. She hadn't heard the SUV drive up. Her face was radiant before she worked belatedly to look less excited. She smiled. "We thought you weren't coming," she said.

"I almost didn't," he agreed, dropping down beside her on the step. "I had to help work two wrecks, and afterward there was a state trooper being overpowered by a prisoner, so I stopped to help. It's been a long night," he concluded with a sigh.

"Have you eaten anything?" she asked.

"Well, there really wasn't time…"

She stood up and caught his big, lean hand in hers. "We had plenty of leftovers," she said. "Come in and have something to eat."

"If it's no trouble," he began.

She just smiled. She led him into the kitchen and indicated the small table there. She took things out of the fridge, filled a plate, and stuck it in the microwave while she put the rest of the food up. "I hope you like beef stew and biscuits," she murmured absently.

"I love stew and biscuits," he said with a sigh. He took off his shepherd's coat and hung it on the back of his chair. He put his hat, with its plastic cover, on a nearby chair. "This is kind of you, especially after I showed up almost at bedtime."

"You look tired to death," she remarked as she put utensils and a cup of hot black coffee at his elbow.

"I am," he confessed. He smiled sheepishly. "I guess I'd have gone to bed hungry if I'd gone home. I'm too tired to do anything."

"I know that feeling very well," she said with a gentle smile.

"How are you liking your job?" he asked after she'd put the heated plate in front of him, along with a paper towel.

"I love it," she confessed. "I feel that I'm doing useful work here. In Denver, I was more or less an errand girl. I mostly delivered papers and dug out precedents for the other attorneys." She grimaced. "It was my brother's law firm. I got the idea that after he died, they were keeping me on for sentiment more than any real need. I was very uncomfortable there. Poor Lucy hated her school. And then we got left a ranch," she said with a faint chuckle. "I've never been so happy in my whole life," she added. "That goes double for Lucy."

"I'm glad," he told her. He closed his eyes, savoring the stew. "This is out of this world," he murmured. "What in the world did you put in it?"

She laughed. "It's a French stew. I make it with blackberry wine and spices like cinnamon and nutmeg."

He gaped at her.

She just smiled. "It's the way it's made," she continued. "I thought it sounded terrible the first time I read the ingredients, but it's a beautiful dish. Lucy and I love it."

"I love it, too," he told her. "Best stew I ever ate."

"You're just hungry," she teased.

"It's still the best stew I ever ate."

"Got room for dessert?" she asked. "I made an apple pie to go with it."

"I'll manage room for it. Apple pie's my favorite."

She got the pie out of the fridge, unwrapped it, cut him a slice and put it back in its carrier. She put it in front of him, along with a dessert fork.

"That looks good," he murmured as he cut into it. He took a bite and moaned. "Now that's apple pie!" he exclaimed.

She laughed softly. It made her feel good that he enjoyed her cooking. "I've always loved to cook," she confessed. "It was a good thing, too, because when I inherited Lucy, it meant paying a lot more attention to making healthy dishes. She's a growing child."

"You're doing a wonderful job of mothering her," he replied, searching her eyes.

She flushed. "I do the best I can. I know she misses her parents."

"Just like you miss your brother and your sister-in-law," he added.

"Yes."

He reached out a big hand and curled it into hers on the tablecloth. "Thank you for my supper," he said. "And thank you more for just being here, and listening to me when I feel like I'm carrying the weight of the world. I don't know what I would have done when I lost Anyu if you hadn't come looking for me."

Her own fingers curled into his, feeling their warm strength. "Neighbors look out for each other," she said gently.

He hesitated. "Yes," he said. "They do." He got up from his chair. "I have to get up early tomorrow. We're expecting a new patrol officer to start in the morning. I hope he drives better than the last one."

"What did the last one do?" she asked, fascinated.

"Rolled the squad car on his first day," he replied. He shook his head. "Maybe this one can drive."

She laughed. "I'll cross all my fingers for you," she promised. She studied his hard face. "You be careful out there," she said finally.

"You keep your doors locked in here," he replied with twinkling eyes.

There was a scratching sound, followed by a squeaky door opening, and little Snow exploded into the room. She ignored Abby and made a beeline for Cody, rearing up on her hind legs to be petted.

"You little doll," Cody cooed. He picked her up and cuddled her. She was so much like Anyu. "Sweet girl."

"No need to ask who her favorite human is," Abby chuckled.

He glanced at her over the little dog's head. He grinned at her.

"Just you remember who feeds you, young lady," Abby told the dog with mock anger.

Snow wriggled until Cody put her down, and then she wobbled over to Abby and licked her hand.

"Such a tiny girl to be so diplomatic!" Abby said, picking the puppy up to cuddle her. She sniffed and frowned. "Since when do you wear Nina Ricci cologne?" she asked after a minute.

"The trooper," he replied. "She was wearing it."

"What trooper?" Abby asked, trying not to sound jealous.

Cody felt his heart swell. He could see exactly what she was thinking, and it made him warm all over. "I told you about the perp I assisted with. She was almost overpowered by a perp she was trying to get into the back seat of her squad car. I stopped and assisted."

"I see."

He pursed his lips. "She had my handcuffs from an arrest

I helped her with," he added, watching Abby carefully. "She dropped them by the office."

"How nice of her," Abby replied. She forced herself to smile and act nonchalant.

"That was what I thought." He studied Abby. "It was the first set of cuffs I ever owned. They're still the best ones I have."

"I can see that you might get sentimental about a tool of your trade," she replied, seething under her calm expression.

He pursed his lips. "You want to know about the trooper, don't you?" he teased. "She was about five foot five, blond hair, blue eyes and a big, warm smile. Very pretty."

Abby just glared at him. She couldn't even come up with words.

He moved closer, step by step, and caught her by the waist to bring her gently to him. "It wouldn't matter if she was a swimsuit model with a see-through negligee on," he told her, and he wasn't smiling. "I don't look at other women lately, Abby. Just at you."

Her heart took a great leap and landed inside one of her shoes. "Really?" she asked breathlessly.

"Really." He bent his head and kissed her, very tenderly, coaxing her arms up and around his neck before he lifted her off the floor by her waist and kissed her with slow, barely contained hunger.

He drew back almost at once. "Work," he bit off. "Sorry. I have to get back. It's one of those nights when I wish I had ten extra deputies, just to work traffic. One of my deputies is out sick, so I'm on call, even though I can grab a little sleep in between catastrophes," he chuckled.

She leaned forward and kissed him, shyly. "Stay warm," she said. "And watch all around you." Her worried eyes met his. "You must be very careful."

He smiled slowly. "I have a good reason to be careful now,"

he whispered. He kissed her again, one last time, and put her down. "And so do you," he pointed out.

She smiled. "That sounds nice."

He chuckled. "What are you doing tomorrow afternoon?"

"Cooking, mostly."

"Cooking what?"

She sighed. "Whatever you like," she teased.

"Chicken and dumplings."

Her eyebrows arched. "Lucy's favorite Sunday meal," she assured him.

"Mine, too." He studied her. "I wish I could cook it."

"I can," she returned. "You can come help us eat it, if you like."

He grinned. "Okay. What time?"

She told him. "And if you have a wreck to work or something, just text me and we'll wait until you're free to serve it."

He bent and kissed her warmly. "That I'll do. Thanks for the meal. And the company."

He put on his hat.

"No pretty little blonde troopers," she muttered softly.

His eyebrows arched. He grinned. He chuckled. He caught her around the waist, riveted her body to his, and kissed her so hungrily that she moaned.

"I'll see you tomorrow," he said on his way out the door. He paused and his eyes twinkled at her. "And no troopers. I promise."

She watched him leave with her heart in her eyes. She didn't even care if it showed.

Cody had been in the detention center when he went to check on Mr. Whatley, finding him unwell. He was soon hospitalized with a seizure, which was interesting, because he'd never had one before and he certainly didn't have epilepsy—

the doctors' tests were ongoing, but the attending physician was certain that he wasn't epileptic.

"You don't think it was a health problem that caused it?" Cody asked.

"No. We're doing bloodwork, but the first panel indicates that he ingested a poisonous substance."

Bobby Grant, Cody thought immediately. The man had found a way to get to Whatley even in a highly guarded prison cell. It was unnerving.

"Do you know what it was?"

"Not yet. I can tell you that it's not something I'm familiar with. We're sending a sample off to the state crime lab and putting a rush on it. That might tell us more than we know at the moment." He cocked his head. "Nice guy. He apologized to us all for the trouble."

Cody smiled. "He's like that. The whole town has sort of adopted him."

"Does he have enemies?" the doctor asked curiously.

"My mind was running in that same direction. And yes, he does have one, the new boyfriend of his only sister. They're worth millions."

The doctor was quick. "And if he marries her, it would be better if there was only one heir, and it was her?"

"Bingo. So I'll need every piece of evidence you can get me that this was a deliberate poisoning and not something he just happened to eat. We're careful about what we feed our prisoners," he added.

"I don't doubt that," the doctor said and smiled.

Cody gave the doctor his cell phone with pleas for the results as soon as they were obtained.

After he left the hospital, there was a commotion in the local grocery store, where the nephew of Abby's boss, Mr. Owens, was having a meltdown when he was two dollars short of the amount he owed for the groceries he was getting.

He stopped immediately when he saw the sheriff, glared at the checkout girl, and started out the door.

"I'll just go hungry," the boy yelled back at the checkout girl, as if it was her fault. "I never have any money. Well, that's going to change, very soon!"

He stomped out, leaving behind several stunned faces.

"I just told him he was two dollars short," the checkout girl defended herself and burst into tears.

One of the checkout boys gave her a shoulder to cry on.

"It's okay," Cody told her. "Life's little problems intrude every so often, but there are usually compensations," he added. He smiled. "You'll get tougher as you get older, and you won't take things so much to heart."

She smiled. "Thanks, Sheriff Banks," she said.

"It goes with the job." He left the store and climbed into his squad car. It was getting late and he hoped he'd finally be able to go home. Just as he was thinking that, the radio blared with a new wreck, another with injuries.

"Oh, well," he said on a sigh, and cranked the car.

Two mornings later, Cody went by the detention center to see Mr. Whatley, who'd been released from the hospital, but was still being held on a charge of attempted bank robbery. The doctor was having an expert go over the drug panel, but he had found a substance that could induce a seizure. He was being cautious about naming it, but he'd promised to get back to Cody today with the information.

Whatley looked up when the deputy let Cody into his cell. "My sister called," he said miserably. "The deputy took a message but he wouldn't let me talk to her."

That was irritating. He was going to have something to say to the jailer when he left. "What was the message?" Cody asked gently.

He sighed. It was a plaintive, defeated sound. "She says she's marrying the Grant man next week," he replied. He was staring down at his feet, his shoulders hunched.

"Like fun she is," Cody said quietly.

Whatley's head came up and his eyes caught Cody's. His eyebrows arched.

"We'll have something to say about that, or I miss my guess. The detective on your case has been very busy, and no, I can't tell you all of it right now. I have to make a few phone calls." He smiled. "I'll talk to you later."

"Okay. Thanks, Sheriff!" he said, brightening.

"A more important question is how do you feel?" Cody added in a softer tone. "A lot of people heard what happened. They're concerned about you."

Whatley flushed. "Gosh. That's...so nice," he stammered.

"You're part of the family in Catelow, you know," Cody added. "We look out for each other."

"We never were a family, my sister and I," Whatley replied. "Our parents were ice cold with us, when we saw them. We didn't see them much at all. They were jet-setters. They went where the stimulation was better than diapers and bottles. We were raised by the housekeeper." He sighed. "If I ever had kids," he added, "I'd never leave them alone."

"Neither would I," Cody agreed quietly. "Are you feeling all right now?" he added.

"Pretty good. I just don't understand why I had a seizure. I've never had one in..." He stopped dead and looked at Cody. "He got to me, didn't he?"

"I'm afraid so. I don't know how. We keep up with what you have for meals, with anything that might come in from outside the jail. There wasn't anything suspicious."

"It was just my usual meal. I did have a Diet Coke," he added, "a couple days ago. The jailer was kind enough to bring it to me."

"Unopened?" Cody asked narrowly.

"Well, I asked him to open it for me," Whatley confessed. "My hands aren't even strong enough for that. I have arthritis in them."

Bells were ringing in Cody's head, but all he did was nod and wish Whatley a good morning.

Cody had a word with the jailer, but it wasn't the one he'd planned to have. "If his sister calls with any more messages, you call me. Don't tell him anything, not even that she's called. Got that?"

The jailer was all eyes. "Something big going down?" he asked.

"Something like that." Cody cocked his head. "He said you brought him a soda the other night."

"Yeah, even had to open it for the poor guy," he added with a sigh. "He's pretty much a weakling."

"We all noticed that. The soda, that was kind of you," Cody added in a placid tone.

"You know me, Sheriff, always trying to help." He smiled.

Cody smiled back. He didn't know the deputy. But he was willing to bet that Lassiter could compile a dossier on him in about five minutes.

When he got to his office, Lassiter was sitting in front of his desk with a cup of black coffee.

"Good news, I hope," Cody remarked as he paused to pour himself a cup of the deep, rich blend.

"Very good news," he replied, chuckling. "We found the missing diary. What's in it is almost enough to hang Mr. Grant, too. We have names, dates, accusations…everything that can be verified and put him at the bottom of some very nasty threats that resulted in the victim's death." He shook his head. "Her poor sister. Violet was smiling when I left her, however." He reached into the pocket of his jacket and pulled out a small book in a freezer bag. He handed it to Cody. "Have a look."

He sat and sipped coffee while Cody went through the book from one end to the other. He shook his head. "What an investigator she'd have made. And what a pity there was nobody to avenge her."

"Until now," Lassiter replied with a cold smile. "A few days is all I need to wrap this up and have him arrested."

"He's marrying Whatley's sister next week," Cody said through his teeth.

Lassiter finished his coffee and got to his feet. "Okay," he said. "I can do it in two days if I call my dad and ask for help."

"Your dad is an amazing human being," Cody mentioned.

Lassiter smiled. "Yes, he is, and so is my mother. And my baby sister," he added, sighing. "She's a skip tracer."

"That's a job I could never do," Cody confessed.

Lassiter chuckled. "Me, neither," he agreed. "I prefer something a little more up close and personal."

"I'd like a little up close and personal with Mr. Grant," Cody muttered.

"So would the authorities in Denver. Don't sweat it. We can deliver the goods on him, and we will. The boom is about to fall." He cocked his head. "Make sure you don't mention anything about it just yet. We don't want him to run."

Cody remembered the jailer and what he'd told him. "I'll make sure all the bases are covered," he promised, "which reminds me, about my jailer." He proceeded to ask for some information about the man whom he'd hired recently, but about whom he knew nothing. And he added some information about the unexpected seizure and the drug panel that he was supposed to have information on later that day.

"I'll take care of it," Lassiter assured him. And Cody knew that he would. Now that Abby had made her feelings clear, he no longer had any worries about Lassiter stealing his girl. Jeb, now, he thought with a tinge of humor, might not be so lucky.

The minute Lassiter left, Cody was on his way back to the detention center. He found the jailer and pulled him to one side. "Don't forget what I told you. If Miss Whatley calls her brother, tell her he can't come to the phone, take the message, and call me. And don't repeat this to anybody. Not until I tell you, face to face, that it's okay."

The jailer nodded. "And then?" he asked hopefully.

"And then you're going to have some really juicy gossip to pass along," he promised with a grin. "And maybe a patrol job with it."

The jailer's face brightened. "Really?"

"Really. I know watching the jail is boring work. But we've got a patrol deputy nearing retirement, and he's already asked for the job."

"It isn't even Christmas," the jailer said with a long sigh. He grinned from ear to ear. "I didn't hear a word you said, Sheriff," he promised. "And I have never seen you before in my life," he added solemnly, with his hand over his heart.

Cody burst out laughing as he went out the door. But he sobered as he climbed into the patrol car. It was important to act natural, to treat the jailer as if nothing was going on. Lassiter was digging around. Pretty soon, they might know more than they anticipated on the friendly jailer. A lot more.

It was the following Sunday and Hannah and Abby were making chicken and dumplings. Cody gave himself the afternoon off and lay on the rug in the living room with Lucy and Snow, watching the puppy's antics with pure joy in his face.

"Isn't she just the most beautiful puppy on earth?" Lucy sighed. "We could never have a pet where we lived before," she said sadly. "Mama wanted a cat, but it was against the rules for us to have one in the apartment." Her face was sad. "Sheriff Banks, do you think my mommy and daddy went to heaven?" she worried.

"Of course they did," he said gently, and he smiled. "Your aunt says they were wonderful people."

She smiled. "I remember them, but it was a long time ago."

"I'm sure your aunt has photographs of them," he pointed out.

"They make her sad," she confessed, "so I haven't asked her if I could see them."

"We'll work on that," he said. "Don't worry about it, okay?"

"Okay." She went to him and hugged him. "I'm glad you come to see us."

He hugged her back. "I'm glad, too," he said. "I don't have any family left, except for cousins."

"We don't have anybody at all," Lucy said. "Just each other. And you," she added shyly and with a smile.

His heart jumped when she said that. It lightened his mood. He chuckled. "Thanks."

Her eyes asked a question.

"It's nice to have family," he explained.

"Oh." She grinned.

"What's this, about family?" Abby teased as she came to the doorway with a towel in her hands.

"I said that Sheriff Banks is family," Lucy explained. "He is, isn't he, Aunt Abby?"

Abby looked at him and flushed, but she smiled, too. "Yes, he is," she said, her voice very soft.

Cody's chest expanded. He felt like a million dollars. "All this, and chicken and dumplings, too," he murmured. "How much joy can a man stand before he explodes?"

"Let's find out," Abby teased, and she went to him and hugged him, too.

He hugged her back with a sigh. "Be careful. I'll blow up. It will seriously damage the paint on the walls."

She just laughed.

Dinner was an uproarious affair. Abby was telling them about a case she'd been part of back in Denver, some years ago when she was just training as a paralegal. A man had cheated on his wife, and she'd backed the car over him, accidentally she said, three times.

Cody's eyes opened wide. "Accidentally? Three times?"

"That's what she swore," Abby agreed, her eyes dancing with glee. "We were representing her poor husband."

"Who won?" he asked, while Hannah and Lucy sat, eyes wide.

"Well, of course he did," she said. "But that wasn't the end of the case." She laughed. "His mistress thought he'd been sleeping with his wife, so she ran her car over him, but just once, and nobody could prove it wasn't an accident—there was thick fog at the time, there were lots of accidents. She bawled at his funeral, but we always thought that was because his wife got everything in his will. Millions of dollars, several houses, a Rolls-Royce, two Jaguars, and a very large Saint Bernard dog."

"Oh, the irony," Cody laughed.

"What happened to the mistress?" Hannah wanted to know.

"Another irony," Abby commented between bites of chicken and dumpling. "She got into a relationship with another married man, but this time the wife didn't go after her husband, she went after the mistress. She had her arrested for car theft."

They all stopped eating and looked at her.

"See, the husband gave her a Mercedes, but when his wife accused him of it, he denied that he'd given it to her. His name was still on the title, so his wife called the police. The mistress had a good attorney, paid for by the husband, so she got off. But his wife sued for divorce. She had a really good lawyer—my brother—and she got everything, and I mean everything, in the divorce. The mistress deserted him immediately, because the real money in the family was his wife's, an enormous inheritance including land, stocks, bonds, you name it. So the cheating husband was left with absolutely nothing. Which was what he deserved."

Cody smiled at her indignation. His expression was hard to read. He was thinking about Debby and her affair with a married man. Her lover had lost everything, too.

Hannah cleared away the dishes and Lucy took the puppy outside for his walk, leaving Cody and Abby alone at the table.

"I'm sorry," Abby said softly, laying a hand over his big one. "Bad memories?"

He nodded, turning his hand so that he caught her fingers in it. "I was thinking about Debby's married lover," he confessed. He drew in a long breath and looked straight into Abby's eyes. "I felt sorry for him. Can you imagine that? He helped my wife cheat on me, carried on a deception for years, and I felt sorry for him. He really loved her. I think she loved him, too, as much as she was capable of loving anybody." He studied Abby's face. "She wasn't like you. She was all business, about everything. The only thing that mattered to her was prestige and wealth. She didn't really care what she had to sacrifice to get them. She told me one time that if I hadn't come up on her blind side, she'd never have married me. It was an impulse. Now I know why, years too late. She was making sure that she and the doctor wouldn't be suspected of ongoing infidelity." He smoothed his fingers in between Abby's and looked down at her hand. It was small, and the nails were done with clear polish. It was a good hand. "I never cheated on her," he added bitterly, "and there were a few temptations."

"Never?" she asked softly.

He cocked his head and his dark eyes twinkled. "Never. Which means that I went without sex for two years." He pursed his lips at her scarlet blush. "And in fact, Abby, I'm still going without it, six years later."

Her breath was caught somewhere deep in her throat. "Still?"

He nodded. His fingers moved against hers, very sensuously. "I have no plans to change that, either."

"Oh." She looked suddenly crestfallen.

He looked down at her hand. "I could be persuaded, of course," he mentioned without lifting his eyes. "Men are so easy when a determined woman puts on the heat. Like those two pretty women who came in the office recently," he added with a mischievous look in his eyes as he lifted them to Abby's. "And that little blonde trooper…"

"Oh, you…!" She hit him with her free hand.

"Assault on a peace officer," he began.

"I'd love to assault you," she started, the memory of those women making her livid with feelings of possession and jealousy.

"Would you, really?" he asked. He stood up, drawing her close. Then he spread his arms and closed his eyes. "Go ahead," he invited. "I would love for you to assault me!"

She stood there with her mouth open as Hannah and Lucy stopped in the doorway, spellbound.

The silence was broken suddenly with the theme from a new action movie. Cody opened his eyes, put down his arms, his high cheekbones just faintly flushed as he glanced at his audience, and dug into his belt holder for the phone.

"Banks," he said at once.

"Lassiter," came the reply. "And have I got news for you!"

"Where are you?"

"Sitting in your office drinking some of the worst damned coffee I ever tasted in my life!"

"Deputy Jones," he sighed. "I'll take care of that when I get there. Ten minutes." He hung up.

"I have to meet a man," he told the women and the child.

Abby threw up her hands. "And here I thought you were getting attached to me!"

"I am getting attached to you," he said, bending to kiss her in front of them all before he grabbed his jacket and his coat. "Stay out of the car until the snow stops. Don't let Lucy go beyond the yard. And don't take candy from strangers or go around kissing strange men," he added gleefully.

Abby made a face at him and smiled with absolute delight. "Okay. And the same goes for you!" she said, adding, "and that goes especially in reference to strange men! No kissing!"

He grinned at her. "It's Lassiter."

"Oh, my." She sighed loudly. "He really is handsome, isn't he?"

Cody glared at her. "He's off limits."

"Not to you, apparently," she said accusingly.

He made a face at her, grinned, and walked out the door.

Hannah and Lucy were gaping at her. She flushed. "Well, Lassiter is very attractive," she repeated.

"So is a certain sheriff who seems very attached to you," Hannah said with a wry smile.

"I like Sheriff Banks," Lucy said, going to hug her aunt. "I wish he was my uncle." She looked up at Abby. "Hint, hint?"

"You could propose to him when he comes back over," Hannah interjected. "There must be an old ring off a Coke can that you could use for an engagement ring." She frowned. "Your cousin Butler used to smoke cigars, in fact, I'll bet there's a band from a cigar around here somewhere, too!"

"I am not getting engaged," Abby said firmly.

"Not unless you ask him, certainly," Hannah said. She grinned. "I'll just bet he'd say yes."

"I'll bet he would, too," Lucy piped in. "You could make him some more chicken and dumplings and that apple pie he liked, and propose over the pie!"

Abby threw up her hands again and went into the kitchen to help with the dishes.

Lassiter was sitting in the visitor chair in front of Cody's desk when he walked in, with his booted feet propped just on the edge of the desk.

"I made fresh coffee," Lassiter said, indicating the pot. "And I told your deputy what I'd do if he ever touched that coffeepot again."

Cody burst out laughing. "I hope you make good coffee."

"I do." He grinned. "I have some absolutely great news."

"Well, tell me!" Cody invited as he poured himself a cup of coffee, divested himself of hat and jacket, and sat down behind his desk.

"The police chief in Nita Whatley's little town is on his way over to see Mr. Grant, with an arrest warrant."

"If he sees anybody coming…" he interrupted, concerned.

"Miss Whatley had a call from the chief early this morning, while Mr. Grant was sleeping peacefully. He told her exactly what the man had done, calmed her down, and instructed her in what to do next. So Mr. Grant is sound asleep, thanks to a couple of pills that Miss Whatley ground up and doctored his coffee with. And the chief took two newspaper reporters with him."

"Oh, joyful day," Cody said. He sighed. "If this were a musical comedy, I'd get up and burst into song."

Lassiter glared at him. "I've heard you humming. Please don't."

Cody glared back. "I know people say I'm tone deaf. All lies. I even have perfect pitch."

"So do I, and if you burst into song, I'll demonstrate just how well I can pitch."

"Don't you dare, or I'll phone Abby and have her come over to protect me," he replied, with a smug smile.

"It's like that, is it?" Lassiter chuckled. "Story of my life. Too late on the scene. Ah, well, I love my job. I suppose any woman who wanted to marry me would draw the line at the work I usually do."

"Which is?" Cody asked, because he was curious.

"I help my dad go after bail jumpers. The kind that usually have guns, and shoot back," he added, black eyes twinkling. "Dad used to be a Texas Ranger, before a perp shot him to pieces and almost cost him the ability to work. My mom was almost his stepsister, but their parents both died before they could get married. Dad took care of Mom for a long time, until he finally gave in to what he felt for her." He shook his head. "You'd think they were newlyweds," he sighed. "They go out driving and when they get back, the windows are all fogged up."

"You don't hear so much about good marriages these days," Cody said quietly. "I come from a badly broken home. So does Abby."

"Not me," Lassiter said with a smile. "My sister and I had the best childhoods imaginable. Great parents. Dad and I argue once in a while, but only because he worries about me."

"It must be nice to have a son," Cody remarked, and the thought caught fire in his mind. He and Abby could have a child...

The phone rang just as he was thinking about names.

CHAPTER TWELVE

Cody picked up the phone. "Banks," he said.

There was a long sigh. "Sheriff, this is Nita Whatley," she said. "I thought you'd like to know that our Lake Luna police chief, Dan Brady, just picked up Bobby Grant personally and carried him off to jail." Her soft voice was hard with anger. "I have Miss Violet Henry's phone number and I'm going to call and talk to her. I'm so sorry about her sister, Candy. She was taken in, just as I was, by a money-hungry killer. I guess we're both lucky to still be alive." She paused. "Sheriff, what about Horace?" she added quickly. "Bobby said something to me that didn't really make sense. He said that Horace wasn't going to interfere with my life any longer, that he was going to take care of things. I really hope that he was only making a vague threat."

"We can't take that chance, Miss Whatley," Cody said. "Don't you worry. Your brother is in very good hands. We'll keep him safe."

"But you still have him in jail," she said heavily. "I know because I tried to call him and your deputy said I couldn't talk to him."

"On my instructions," Cody said. "We had plans for Mr. Grant and we didn't want to risk having the jailer say anything to you that he shouldn't."

"Oh. So that Bobby wouldn't overhear it. I see."

He hesitated, but he didn't really have a good reason for keeping the information from her. She was his sister, after all.

"There's something else, Miss Whatley. A few nights ago, your brother was taken to the hospital with a seizure," he said gently.

"A seizure!" she exclaimed. "But he's not epileptic. There's nobody in our whole family who ever had epilepsy!"

"We know. They ran a drug panel. There was an exotic substance introduced into a soft drink he was given at bedtime."

"Well, is he all right? Will he recover?!"

"Yes, to both. We got to him in plenty of time. We have an investigator working the case."

"Why wasn't I called at once?" she asked.

"Because I was up to my neck in wrecks, mainly. But I also wanted to be certain of the cause. There was no sense upsetting you at the time. He was perfectly all right, in no danger. But I'm sorry, just the same," he added, wincing. "It was a real oversight on my part."

"It's all right," she replied. "I guess I'm getting used to shocks, they don't affect me as much. But he's fine, you're sure?"

"I'm absolutely sure." He sighed. "I thought my detention center was the safest place for him. I can't tell you how disturbed I am, and how sorry, that such a thing could happen on my watch."

"Who found him?"

"I did once I got the call, and just in time, the doctor said." He hesitated. "Miss Whatley, do you know if your boyfriend had any contacts with access to exotic poisons or substances?"

She hesitated. "Well, there was this blonde woman who came to the house a time or two. He said she lived in South America with her uncle," she related. "I didn't really see her much, he met her at the door and talked to her outside."

"Did he see her recently, do you know?"

"Well, yes, a few days ago. They were talking about a trip she was going to take. I didn't really eavesdrop." She hesitated. "That's a lie. Yes, I did. She was very pretty. But Bobby said she was just a cousin or something and he didn't think of her as a woman."

"That's all you know about her?" he probed.

"Yes. I'm sorry I didn't pay more attention. To a lot of things," she added on a sigh. "Honestly, I feel like I've been in an isolation chamber or something. Infatuation is a very bad thing."

"Very bad indeed. But your brother is doing fine and I've doubled the watch. Believe me, nobody is going to get to him again!"

She laughed softly. "I believe you. Please tell him that I love him and that I'm sorry I've been so horrible to him."

"I will, but it's not necessary. He doesn't hold grudges."

"No. He's the sweetest man I know. Bobby had me do some terrible things, including holding back Horace's checks from the estate. But those are going out regularly now, so he won't have a cash flow problem ever again."

"He'll be happy to hear that."

"I'd love to see Bobby go to prison for what he did to that woman's sister in Colorado," she added shortly. "And I'd really like to speak to her. We share something truly horrible."

"I realize that, but it would be a good idea if you hold off on talking to Violet until we have Mr. Grant booked and locked up."

"He won't make bond?" she asked, horrified.

"Your police chief will make sure that bond is set high

enough that Mr. Grant will have a hell of a time trying to scrape it up."

She groaned. "I gave him a diamond ring," she muttered, "before I found him out. He can hock it for thousands of dollars."

"Won't be enough," Cody assured her. "We're talking at least a million, on suspicion of murder, which is what he's being charged with."

"My goodness! They'll have to take him to Colorado to stand trial, won't they? What if he escapes?"

"I'll be driving him myself," Cody assured her. He glanced at Lassiter, who was shaking his head. "Actually, we'll have federal marshals doing that," he added, after Lassiter had whispered it to him.

"Then he shouldn't be able to get away," she replied, obviously relieved. "I can't tell you how stupid I feel," she added. "I must have been out of my mind."

"Just a thought, but I believe most people in love think they're crazy."

Nita laughed softly. "Perhaps so."

"I'm not sure you know it, but your police chief has a case on you," Cody said, his voice deep and soft.

"Dan does?" She caught her breath. "Really? But he can't stand the sight of me! He won't even come to parties here if I invite him!"

"Have you invited him at a time when Mr. Grant wasn't there?" he asked, amused.

There was a long pause. "Well, actually, I haven't."

"You could invite him over for coffee," Cody remarked. "Just to discuss the case, you understand."

"Yes. Of course, I could. Just to discuss the case." She coughed. "Do you think he'd really come?"

"Indeed, I do," he assured her. "Call him. You'll see."

She laughed softly. "I was just remembering this song

my mother used to love. Looking for love in all the wrong places…"

"Your only wrong place is headed back to Denver to stand trial. You'll very likely be called to testify."

"No problem there," she replied. "I'll enjoy it. I can't believe I was that foolish!"

"People get lonely. Sometimes other people take advantage of it. I'm sorry things happened that way for you," he said. "Miss Henry is very much like you. She's a sweet woman."

"Why, thank you," she stammered.

"You're most welcome. I can assure you that your brother is in excellent health, and the minute we've made certain he's out of danger, I'm letting him go home. You should see his ranch, by the way," he added. "He has some revolutionary ideas about cattle raising. They're turning out better than any of us expected. You should come and see it."

She laughed softly. "I'll do that. I'll look forward to meeting you, and that super detective who was working on the case. Mr. Lassiter, wasn't it? His photo is on his dad's website. What a very dishy man. Pity he isn't older," she sighed.

Cody laughed. "That's life. I'll be in touch. I'm certain that Dan Brady will be in touch, also, and don't forget about the coffee."

"I won't. Thanks, Sheriff Banks."

"All in a day's work. Stay safe. And I'm truly sorry for not calling you about your brother."

"He's all right, so it's not a problem. You take care, too. Goodbye."

He hung up and glanced at Lassiter with a big grin. "Miss Whatley thinks you're dishy," he said.

"Ooops," Lassiter said, grimacing.

"No worries. It's not like that. She said it's a pity you weren't older."

He chuckled. "I'm old enough. And she's a nice woman, but I'm off women for the immediate future."

Cody didn't ask. He changed the subject to Bobby Grant's arrest and what they both expected to happen next.

The little blonde trooper stopped by just as he was going out the door.

"Hi," she said. "Got time for a cup of coffee?"

He grimaced, checking his watch. "Sorry, I've got a commitment tonight."

"No problem," she replied. "I'm by this way a lot now," she added with a grin. "So I'll try again another time."

He smiled back. She was cheerful for a woman in law enforcement, he thought. He waved her goodbye and went to his truck.

He drove out to the ranch to see Abby, his mind on Whatley's near miss. Cody ground his teeth together as he realized that Bobby Grant himself couldn't have made the attempt on Horace Whatley's life, because he'd been in Florida with Whatley's sister the whole time. Which meant he had somebody in Catelow who was willing to commit murder for him. He wondered who, and how Grant intended to pay the person when he was now in jail himself and charged with attempted murder and, if the charges in Colorado were added, and could be proven by evidence, first-degree murder.

He remembered his jailer's kind offer to get Mr. Whatley a soft drink the night he was rushed to the hospital. That was, again, his first choice of suspects. He knew next to nothing about the man except for what a light background check had told him when he was hired. He'd never been in trouble with the law, the check revealed, and he was considered trustworthy by his former employer, a police chief in a neighboring state.

That didn't help a lot. When the doctor had finally touched

base with Cody, late last night, he was only able to tell him that the substance used was a rare and exotic powder which contained a neurotoxin. And, yes, it could cause seizures. Sometimes fatal ones, depending on how much was given to the victim.

Cody felt vaguely guilty, because the cute little blonde trooper had come by to return Cody's handcuffs and he'd been talking to her while his jailer, presumably, had been poisoning Mr. Whatley. Well, honestly, he hadn't been talking to her all that time. She'd waited in the office while he went out on a quick call to break up a fight in a nearby diner.

She'd been a little flushed when he returned, and he wondered absently if Lassiter had come by, because that was how women usually appeared when he'd been around. But when he asked, she said, no, nobody had come in and none of the prisoners had been unruly. She'd been thumbing through a pamphlet on drugs that she found on the sheriff's desk. Nobody else had come in, although she could hear the jailer moving around in his area, away from the sheriff's office.

Cody had enjoyed talking to her. She was very attractive and a little nervous. He felt guilty, because he was getting more attached to Abby by the day, and he shouldn't be paying attention to other women.

Not that the trooper overly flirted. She was matter-of-fact about her job, although she seemed not to know the name of the trooper who was assigned to this area. But she was new, he considered, so that wasn't really surprising.

She'd only stayed for a few minutes, and then she was off, smiling and shaking hands before she walked out to her car. She wasn't driving a prowler, but then, she wouldn't be, when she was off duty, and there was a shadowy figure in the passenger seat.

Tonight, she'd been alone, but she was driving what looked like a sports car. Must be nice, he thought, and wished he'd taken time to ask her about that soft drink the jailer had given Whatley. On the other hand, might be a better idea not to spread information around, even to another law enforcement officer.

He thought back to the sports car she'd been driving. But it didn't mean much. He'd noticed that some other law enforcement departments didn't approve of lawmen taking their squad cars home with them. Cody thought it a good idea for his deputies, especially in bad weather, when they might be called out at any hour. Police cars, and sheriff's cars, were built to different specifications than regular ones. They had wider wheel bases and several other minor adjustments that allowed them to outrun anything less than a Jaguar or a Lamborghini.

He'd finished his reports after the pretty blonde trooper left, just after the jailer had given Whatley the soft drink. He'd gone to check on Mr. Whatley one last time before he went by Abby's to explain about missing supper. It was a lucky thing that he had. The little man, in the middle of a sentence, went into a seizure. Lassiter had been on his phone taking care of business until then Cody had called for an ambulance and rushed Mr. Whatley to the hospital. They'd saved his life, but the doctor remarked that Cody's quick action had done that. A few minutes more for the poison to work, and no power on earth would have saved him.

Cody stopped by Abby's house, just to see how they all were.

Abby knew that there was something on his mind. Cody was preoccupied, and it showed.

"Is there something I can help with?" she asked gently.

He just smiled. "Afraid not." He grimaced as he drank the sugared and creamed coffee she'd placed before him. "It's our Mr. Whatley. They took him to the hospital a few nights ago with a seizure of some sort."

"Is he epileptic?" she asked, surprised.

"No. And that's the problem."

She was watching him closely. She pursed her lips. "I see. Something bad and top secret that you can't talk about."

"Exactly," he said, and bent to kiss the tip of her nose. "I'm glad you know me so well already!"

She laughed softly. "Not that well."

"Better than most," he corrected. "I'm not an easy man to know," he confessed. "I'm a loner. I like my own company. I'm not used to having anyone around to talk to except..."

His dog. She pushed back a strand of hair that had fallen over his forehead. "You can talk to me," she told him. "I'm a clam. I'm not allowed to talk about anything I do at work. You might say that I've had advanced training in secret-keeping."

He chuckled. "That almost qualifies you for police work," he teased.

Her eyes went to his belt. "You have your handcuffs back," she noticed. They were different from the handcuffs most of the deputies carried. She remembered the cute little blonde trooper and her eyes narrowed. "Has your trooper friend been back?" she asked, and her eyes were like chips of ice.

He chuckled. "Yes, two nights ago," he said, failing to add that the blonde trooper had been by the office today to see him. No use messing things up worse than they were.

"You're laughing," she pointed out. "Why are you laughing?"

"You're jealous," he mused, watching the color come into her cheeks.

"Of course I'm not jealous," she muttered. "I mean, I'm so gorgeous that men stand in line to get dates with me...!"

She stopped midsentence because he had her close and he was kissing her hungrily. "You will never—" he kissed her again "—have any reason to be jealous of—" he kissed her yet again "—any other woman. I swear."

It took her a minute to catch her breath. She was very flushed. "Well..."

"Sheriff Banks!"

Lucy came running and threw herself into his waiting arms. He swung her around, laughing.

"What a welcome!" he exclaimed. "Your aunt just gave me a very nice one, also," he added with a wicked look in Abby's direction, which caused her to blush.

Snow was pawing at his boots.

He put Lucy down and picked up the little dog, laughing as she licked his cheek.

"Snow loves you," Lucy said.

"I noticed." He cuddled the little dog close for a minute. It brought back hard memories of Anyu. Work had kept them at bay for a while, but now they were back. So were memories of Debby, even harder ones.

He was distracted. Abby noticed, but she assumed it was about work. He went home earlier than he had on past visits, promising to come back soon. He was just tired, he told them.

Well, it was partly true. He was tired. But more than that, he was heartsick. He'd pushed Debby's infidelity and Anyu's loss to the back of his mind for too long already. He'd never dealt with either of those problems.

When he got home that night, it all hit him at once. He stared at the sofa where he'd spent so many nights with Anyu curled up beside him, watching movies or DVDs or the occasional science or History Channel episode. He could never forget those gorgeous blue eyes laughing up at him. Anyu was his comfort after Debby was gone; the puppy she'd left to, according to the message, the most important man in her life. But Debby didn't seem to think of him as that important.

She rarely came home because of "obligations" at the Denver hospital where she worked; those obligations being her mentor, the doctor who'd almost killed himself after her death.

He wondered now if her feelings for her colleague were really love or just making sure that she continued to be his protégée, so that she could learn all the revolutionary methods he was teaching her. That education would have put her on a fast track to a much higher position in the medical hierarchy.

Until he'd gone to Denver and accidentally found out about his late wife's social activities, he'd never given that much thought to her advancement in her career. But she was really focused on making a lot of money, and working her way up the medical specialist ladder was the way to do it. She'd shared her dreams with him, going over and over about how important it was to be the best, and for that, she'd added, you needed to be trained by the best. So nice, she'd added, that she had such a good mentor or that he made sure she was up on all the newest techniques in neurosurgery.

That poor doctor was like Cody, a stepping-stone to Debby's success. He'd been so besotted that he hadn't realized how ambitious she was. Apparently, so had her mentor in Denver. She'd used both men for reasons of her own, neither of which had anything to do with love eternal.

Cody could have kicked himself for not realizing it sooner, for not wondering why she never came home, why she was so uncaring about him, why she was so wrapped up in getting to the top of her particular niche in medicine.

He'd had a small beagle dog when he and Debby had started dating. She'd never liked Barney. Now that he looked back, he realized that she didn't like animals at all. She tolerated the dog, but Barney was banished to the kitchen or back porch when Debby came to visit—which wasn't often. Debby had asked him once why he didn't give the dog away. He'd ignored the question, something he'd learned to do a lot while

Debby was in residence. Barney had died not long after he and Debby married.

In bed, she was ice-cold after they'd been married, nothing like the hot-blooded woman who'd gone home with him the night they met. After the wedding, on her rare visits, she only wanted it over. He'd wondered at the time if it was some trauma in her past, but when he'd asked her, point-blank, she'd said that she just couldn't get into something so carnal. She liked discussing history with him, something he was very good at. He had a good brain, even if Debby thought he wasn't living up to his full potential in law enforcement work. She'd never understood why he did the job. He tried to explain his own childhood, in which she was supremely disinterested, and why it predisposed him to a job that involved helping other people out of life-threatening situations. She said that death was a part of life and it just happened. She had no compassion for other people, not even for Cody.

He permitted himself to wonder how such a cold person could be a doctor. Most of them were ultrasensitive to other people, going out of their way to help anyone with physical trauma. Not Debby. She was interested in how much she could earn when she got to the top of the tree.

She talked about it, about the huge fees she could command, about the places she wanted to go, the things she wanted to see. He told her once that he wouldn't be able to take long vacations due to the obligations of his job. She'd given him a blank look and asked why he'd want to go in the first place.

So many red flags, and he'd never seen them. Correction, he'd never wanted to see them. He'd been so much in love, living in his fairy-tale life, with his perfect wife who came sometimes to visit. There were a hundred questions he'd never asked. It was a little late in the day to be asking them now.

He remembered how devastated he'd been when Debby died, raging at Abby and Lucy in the parking lot, yelling at them that they'd killed her. He cringed at the memory. It had left emotional scars on the woman and the child, and for what? He was grieving for a fictional woman who didn't even exist. The real Debby was cold as ice with a cash register for a heart. If Cody had died, she'd have wanted to know how much what he left her was worth, and she wouldn't have blinked an eye at his passing.

He got himself a cold beer out of the refrigerator and sank down on the sofa. He wasn't on call tonight, thank God, or he wouldn't be drinking. He turned on the History Channel and tried to get interested in a program on Alexander the Great, but he was restless and he couldn't settle.

He looked again at the sofa where Anyu had been beside him for that long six years. He'd been mourning old Barney at the time, so Anyu was a delightful surprise. He recalled now that he wasn't even supposed to have Anyu. Debby had meant him for the other doctor, her mentor, and wires had gotten crossed so that Cody ended up with her.

Well, it had been a sweet accident, he told himself wistfully. Anyu had been part of him for all those wonderful years until her death. He'd never had a pet as a child. His alcoholic father would have been deadly to any pet Cody kept in the house, a perfect tool for revenge when Cody called the law on his brutal parent.

Anyu had been a breath of spring. He missed her so much. She was getting some age on her. She hadn't moved as fast as she once did, and it was a chore for her to jump onto the sofa. Cody had finally gotten her a pair of wooden steps. She had arthritis and medicine for it. She must have been in pain a lot, but she always looked up at Cody with those laughing blue eyes. Nothing ever got Anyu down. He missed her terribly, regardless of the act of fate that had put her in his house.

He ran a hand through his thick hair and thought about Abby. Things were getting serious there, but he wasn't certain that he was ready for thoughts of marriage. It was a commitment he wasn't sure he could make. He liked living by himself. He enjoyed just sitting and watching what he pleased on TV. That wouldn't be possible with Abby and Lucy and Hannah around. The cooking would improve, certainly, but his house only had two bedrooms, not nearly enough for four people. Of course, he could move in with Abby. Plenty of room at the ranch...

He had another sip of beer. Plenty of time to think about that later on. He pulled the History Channel back up and finished watching Alexander the Great.

Two days later, he hadn't called Abby or gone to see her. The little blonde trooper had come by, again, just to say hello. She really was lovely, Cody thought, trying not to feel guilty for giving her coffee in his office.

"This is really good coffee," she sighed. "I like Colombian best. Is that what this is?" she added, wide-eyed.

"I don't really know," he began.

"Definitely Colombian," Lassiter said from behind him.

"You're in lockup," Cody said curtly.

"My dad bailed me out again," he replied, his dark eyes going to the pretty blonde trooper, who was looking at him with the same expression most women had when they met him. Cody was quietly irritated.

"J.R. Lassiter, Miss..." He hesitated. "I don't know your name."

She laughed. Even the laughter was pretty. "Bella," she said. "Bella Cain."

"Nice to meet you," Lassiter said, and shook hands, holding hers just a little too long.

"Oh, the pleasure is mine," she replied.

He pulled up a chair and sat down, ignoring Cody's guilty

look. Lassiter knew he was courting Abby, and here he sat
flirting with another woman. It was embarrassing.

"You work around here? Sorry," he added on a laugh, "I'm
not up on small area protocols. I live in Houston."

"Oh, in Texas," she purred. "I have a cousin there."

"What part?"

"Near Dallas," she said, and stopped abruptly. "But I grew
up in Douglas, Arizona," she replied. She leaned forward,
grinning. "Rumor has it that my family dates to the time
Pancho Villa was fighting near there, and that one of my an-
cestors was with Pancho at the time."

"Wow," Lassiter said. "Interesting ancestry there. Do you
speak Spanish?"

She laughed. "Oh, yes." She stared at him. "Do you?"

"Of a certainty. I live in Houston, but I do a good bit of
work in South Texas, ranching country. It comes in handy."

"Yes, it does." She looked at her watch and gasped. "I have
to get back to work!" she exclaimed. "I was on my lunch
hour. I don't like to cost my employer time," she added with
a sly grin.

"Two birds of a feather," Lassiter said, and he and Cody
got to their feet when she got up.

"How gentlemanly," she said with a warm smile. "I enjoyed talking to you."

"Same here."

"That man the jailer spoke of, who was here for bank robbery, did you get him convicted?" she asked innocently.

"Still awaiting trial," Cody said lazily, and didn't give away
the sudden red flag that went up at the question. He knew
that she'd had contact with the jailer the night Whatley had
been taken to the hospital, but he wasn't letting on.

"Ah, the time-consuming legal process in this country,"
she added, shaking her head. "In other parts of the world,
such criminals are dealt with in a more timely fashion. Such

is life. Nice to see you again, Sheriff. And nice to have met you, Mr. . . . Lassiter, was it?"

He nodded and smiled. "Nice to have met you as well."

"I will be seeing you," she told Cody, going close and smiling up at him. "You don't mind if I drop in from time to time?"

He cleared his throat. She smelled delicious. "Not at all."

She smiled at him again, waved as she went out the door.

"Now, that was interesting," Lassiter said when she'd gone.

"What part?"

"Do you know anything about perfumes or colognes for women?"

Cody thought about that for a minute. "Abby said something about the cologne that was on my shirt. She said I smelled of Nina Ricci, whoever that is."

Lassiter chuckled. "It's not a person, it's a fragrance. Co-incidentally, my sister's favorite. Expensive as hell, too. She orders her soaps from Paris and they're about forty bucks a pop," he added, making Cody's eyebrows lift. "Interesting, isn't it, that your trooper friend can afford a fragrance like that on a trooper's pay?"

"Even more interesting," Cody replied, "that she had contact with the jailer the night Whatley went to the hospital. The jailer brought him an opened soft drink."

"Nita Whatley said that a pretty blonde woman from South America used to come to see Bobby Grant at her house."

The sheriff nodded. "Interesting connections."

"I'm beginning to see a few of my own."

"So am I. I think I'd better add on a couple of men to hang around the office when I'm not in it."

"That's not a bad idea. This Grant man is more slippery than an eel. He managed to wriggle his way out of a murder accusation in Denver. I'd imagine he's been in scrapes even before that. He does have that prior for assault that he spent two years in stir with," Lassiter added thoughtfully. "I have some friends who owe me a favor," he added. "Let me contact them and get a man up here to keep the office going when you aren't here."

"I'm not sure our budget will run to..." Cody began.

Lassiter held up a hand. "It won't cost you a penny," he said, grinning. "They owe me a favor and this is where I need it."

Cody chuckled. "You do get around."

"Believe me," Lassiter replied, "when I say you have no idea."

"Oh, I believe it," Cody mused.

He was on his way home from work, still concerned about his feelings for Abby and where he was going to go next in their relationship, when a movement on the side of the road caught his eye.

He stopped, backed up, and pulled onto the shoulder. He got out, curious, because what he saw looked like an animal of some sort, making furtive movements.

As he went closer, he could tell what it was: a malamute, mangy, covered in mats, half-dead of starvation, and it had been hit by a vehicle.

"Poor old man," he said soothingly, because the dog was very obviously a male. "It's okay, old fellow. I'll get you to the vet." He opened the back door of the squad car, took out the blanket he kept in the trunk to protect his back seat from sick drunks, and then went to pick up the dog.

It whimpered, but made no move to bite him. "It's okay," he said. "I won't hurt you. Neither will anybody else. You've had it rough, haven't you?"

He eased the animal onto the back seat. It lay there, looking at him with misery tinged with hope.

"I'll get you to a vet," Cody said. "You'll be fine. I promise."

CHAPTER THIRTEEN

When she saw the dog, the vet, Dr. Clay, was shocked. "I never can understand why animals are allowed to get into this condition. Did you arrest the owner?"

"Don't know who put him out. Found him on the side of the road," Cody corrected. "And I don't think he's had an owner. Not for a long while."

"Well, you could be right."

"He looks like a malamute," he pointed out.

"Yes. Far too big to be a husky," she agreed, going over the dog. "But he's got blue eyes and malamutes are almost always brown. Could be a mixture of both breeds, though..." She winced as the dog yelped. "I think his leg's broken. I'll get X-rays...or do you want me to put him down?" she asked suddenly.

He looked into the old dog's tired eyes and saw hopelessness there. He knew how that felt. He ground his teeth together. Well, his truck could do without those flashy hubcaps he'd been pricing. He wouldn't miss them. "Get X-rays and do whatever else you need to."

She looked at him curiously.

"I'll be responsible for the bill."

"Name," she said.

He started to give his, laughed a little self-consciously, and then looked at the dog with his head cocked. He recalled the History Channel special he'd been watching on television and he pursed his lips. "Alexander," he told the vet, turning to her with a smile. "His name's Alexander. And can you get a groomer to do something about the way he looks? Poor old guy."

"You bet I can," she said. "Our regular groomer's booked for three months, but she's got a trainee, lucky for you. I'll have her do him in a couple of days. He's going to need to be checked for parasites and diseases."

"Do whatever you need to do," Cody said.

The vet smiled. "Going to keep him, huh?"

He nodded.

"She isn't Anyu, I know," she said gently, "but maybe it's a good thing that you don't have a dog who's a carbon copy of her. This will be a new start." She glanced at Alexander, who was trying to wag his tail, as if he understood what was being said. "For both of you."

So Alexander was wormed and groomed and fed and put on a veterinarian diet and taken out to Cody's ranch with his leg in a cast. Now that he was rid of the mats and the infestations, he looked quite handsome. When he was completely healed and his fur grew back, Cody considered, he was going to be a fine-looking dog.

"You don't look so bad right now, old man," Cody told the dog, smiling as he made himself at home on the big rug in front of the television. "We can watch TV together and when you're better, we can go walking."

Alexander looked up at him with pale blue eyes and actually seemed to laugh, just as Anyu had. His eyes misted, but he leaned over and petted the big dog. "You'll fill a hole in my heart," he said quietly. "A very big one. Welcome home, Alex."

The dog wagged his tail.

Of course, it got around Catelow that Cody had a new dog. Abby heard it secondhand, because Cody hadn't come to the ranch in several days.

"Is he mad at us or something?" Lucy asked Abby with real concern.

"I think maybe he's just very busy," Abby said cheerfully, even though she didn't quite feel it.

"He's got a new doggie, too," Lucy said sadly. She petted Snow, her constant companion. "I thought maybe he'd like to show it to us."

"Dog's in a cast," Hannah interrupted. "He found it on the side of the road. It had been hit by a car and was in a miserable condition." She glanced at them. "One of my cousins is the groomer trainee at the vet's." She shrugged. "She said the dog was in the biggest mess she'd ever seen, but when they cleaned him up, he was surprisingly handsome."

"A boy dog?" Lucy asked.

"A boy dog," Hannah replied. "And he's named Alexander."

"What an odd name," Abby said, trying not to show how much it hurt her that Cody had apparently had second thoughts where she was concerned. She'd heard about the latest visit he had from the blonde state trooper, too, and it had hurt. Until then, she hadn't realized how much emotional capital she had invested in the sheriff.

"I'd love to see his dog," Lucy sighed. "Hannah, did your cousin say what sort of dog it was?"

"A malamute," Hannah replied. "They're like huskies but much bigger," she added. "But probably mixed with husky because he's got blue eyes." She smiled.

"I'll bet he's a nice dog," Lucy said.

★ ★ ★

And he was nice. Cody found him to be a charming companion for his lonely evenings. The dog followed him everywhere he went in the house, cast and all, and sat looking at him lovingly the rest of the time.

"You're the best accidental find I've ever had, Alex," he told the old dog and reached down to pet him.

Alex looked up with worshipful eyes, as if to say, that makes two of us.

"When you're healed, we'll go walking."

The big dog howled.

He chuckled. Huskies and malamutes never barked. They howled.

"I'm glad you agree," he told the animal.

He turned on the television, hoping he wouldn't be called out. It was Friday night and he had no place to go. He ground his teeth together. Of course he had a place to go, but he'd been away long enough to be uncomfortable about calling Abby and inviting himself over. She might slam the door in his face, especially if she'd heard about the blonde trooper's latest visit. It was all over town.

He was puzzled by his own behavior. He'd enjoyed being with Abby and Hannah and Lucy, but as time passed and he and Abby grew closer, he grew more wary. You never knew people until you lived with them, he considered. Abby seemed to be an honest, kind, sweet woman. But Debby had seemed like that at first, too. Then she'd turned his life upside down. His pride was still smarting from her affair with her mentor in Denver.

"Maybe Abby's not like that," Cody told Alexander while they watched TV. "But how do you know?"

Alexander looked up at him with laughing pale blue eyes and wagged his tail weakly.

Cody reached down to pet the dog. "You've been through

the wars, haven't you, old man?" he said affectionately. "Don't worry. You'll be safe here."

Alexander sighed and laid his chin down on his extended front paws.

"Safe," Cody murmured to himself. He glanced around at the living room and the dining room, and wondered if he'd ever feel safe. He seriously doubted it.

Horace Whatley's housekeeper, Julia Donovan, came by the jail frequently to bring slices of homemade pies and cakes to her employer. She was very shy and she hadn't much to do with Cody or the jailer.

"I heard what happened to Mr. Whatley," she told Cody on one visit. "You know, about the seizure." She bit her lower lip. "It's okay if you want to have somebody look at the stuff I cook for him," she said in her soft voice. "I mean, I wouldn't mind. I don't want anything to happen to him, but you don't know me from a bug, Sheriff Banks," she added with a faint smile. "So you can check the food anytime. It's okay."

He chuckled. "Miss Donovan, you're the last person I'd ever suspect of trying to off her employer. Really."

She forced a smile. "Thanks. That's nice." She sighed. "I can't believe anybody would accuse Mr. Whatley of trying to rob anybody. I mean he has money of his own and he's just the nicest person you'd ever want to meet." She looked up and caught the sheriff staring at her. She flushed. "He's really good to all of us who work for him. Paid vacations, sick leave, insurance." She laughed unsteadily. "My late husband was brutal to me. Mr. Whatley isn't like that. He's a gentle man."

"Yes, he is, and I don't believe he robbed anybody, either, Miss Donovan, but that's off the record," he added. "I have to deal in facts. He was accused by a supposed eyewitness."

She grimaced. "Yes, and the man's a known liar who'll do anything for money, like that sneaky nephew of Mr. Owens's," she added. "He tried to borrow money from Mr. Whatley. Mr. Whatley was nice and even offered him a job. I've never heard language like that in my life, not even from my husband! I guess working for what he got never appealed to the young man!"

"I guess not," he agreed.

"And Mr. Owens is so nice," she emphasized. "It seems that the sweetest people end up with relatives who only live to try to take away everything they've got."

He stared at her. "Relatives?" His mind had wandered.

"That boy. Mr. Owens's nephew, Jack," she said. "He's a constant embarrassment to his family. Always in trouble of some sort. You'd know about that," she added, "because you have to lock him up from time to time."

He nodded. "I feel sorry for Mr. Owens. He's never put a foot wrong, that I can see."

She agreed. "That new paralegal who works for him, Abby, she's nice," she said, not noticing that Cody had colored just on his cheekbones when she said Abby's name. "Never meets a stranger."

"She's an asset to him, I'm sure," Cody said stiffly.

"Yes. And she and her little niece went out with that nice Mr. Lassiter yesterday, just driving," she added, wondering why the sheriff was suddenly so still. "I'm glad you let him out on bail. I don't understand why a man like that would have problems with the law. He's also gorgeous," she laughed.

Abby was going out with Lassiter? He was overcome with fury. Abby, his Abby, with that philanderer!

Just as he was thinking about putting Lassiter back into a cell and throwing away the key, the office door opened.

And there she was, the pretty little blonde trooper, in uniform. She hesitated. "Did I come at a bad time?" she asked hesitantly.

"Oh, no, I was just leaving. I meant what I said about the food, Sheriff," Julia said with a sweet smile.

"It won't be necessary to check anything you bring. I promise," he assured her.

"Thanks. Well, I'll go home and take care of my chores." She frowned. "You're sure that Horace—Mr. Whatley, I mean—is going to be safe?"

"I'm sure," he lied, because he couldn't promise that.

She smiled. "Okay. Thanks." She gave him a shy smile, tossed one toward the blonde, who ignored her, and went out the door.

"What a plain little woman," the blonde said, laughing.

Cody glared at her. "Beauty is more than surface looks," he said flatly.

"I'm sorry," she backtracked quickly. "I've had a hard morning. Got in a fight with a man I arrested for transporting drugs." She showed him a bruise on her forearm. She winced as she flexed it. "Is law enforcement always so violent?" she asked, looking at him as if he were old and wise and had all the answers. He wondered how old she was. She seemed older than Abby, but she was still very pretty.

"Yes, it can be violent," he said. "But you can always get backup from the local law if you need it."

She gave him a flirty glance. "I thought you might say that. I'm having a hard time getting used to the job. I was hoping you might be free to give me a few pointers over a cup of coffee. That new place on the corner has cappuccino. It's my very favorite."

He felt his heart lift. If Abby could go around with Lassiter, there was no way he was going to feel guilty about buying this pretty little blonde a cup of coffee.

He got up from his desk and picked up his hat. "I'm free enough," he assured her with a smile. "Let's go." He stopped to tell his deputy where he'd be, but he had to take a phone call when they were out on the sidewalk.

"Oops, left my clipboard in the office, be right back!" the blonde whispered while he was explaining a point of law to a man who was complaining about a traffic stop. Cody just nodded, lost in his conversation. It only took him a minute or two, and by the time he hung up, his blonde companion in her neat uniform, was back beside him with the clipboard. He waited while she walked off to stick it in her car and then rejoined him.

Abby, who was on her way to the courthouse, saw them together going into the local coffeehouse. She felt a wounding in her heart that almost provoked tears. She and Cody had gotten along so well. He'd loved being with her and Lucy and Hannah, or so she'd thought, he'd been part of their family. But now here he was with that little blonde trooper and she felt her heart drop into her loafers.

She had no claim on Cody, after all. They were friends. But she'd built a future on a few kisses and some affection, and she'd obviously been wrong. In a fit of temper, angry over Cody's disappearance from her life and gossip that he was still seeing the blonde trooper, she'd accepted an invitation to go riding around the county with Lassiter. She'd hoped news of it would get back to Cody, if for no other reason, to show him that she wasn't sitting home alone hoping he'd come or call. It had backfired. He and the little blonde trooper went into the coffeehouse, both laughing, the sheriff's big hand on her arm.

Well, at least she knew now where she stood, Abby told herself. She'd never really been involved with a man, and she'd hoped there might be a future with Cody. It was a silly dream. Perhaps she'd been too forward with him or taken his presence in her life too much for granted. Or it might be that he got cold feet at the thought of involving himself with a woman who already had a family. He'd seemed to love Lucy, but he could do that without wanting to be responsible for her, if he and Abby married. Married, she thought whimsically. Now there was a pipe dream if there ever was one. Cody had loved his late wife. She might have had a lover, she might have been a totally unpleasant person. But if you loved someone, you loved them regardless of what they did.

She knew he missed Debby, despite what he'd learned about her. She was sorry for him. It must be terrible to love a woman who treated him like dirt, had a lover, ignored him for weeks at a time. Married, and yet not married. And what he'd found out about her had certainly shattered his pride. Perhaps he was just afraid to risk his heart again.

As Abby pondered it, that last issue was the one she settled on for his absence. He must think she was angling for marriage, she, with her ready-made dependent, her niece Lucy. She flushed. She would never have chased after him, but he didn't know her well and he might have thought about it like that.

She could never give up Lucy, not for any man. Maybe it was better that Cody had transferred his affections to another single woman who was alone, like he was. Well, she assumed that the pretty little blonde was single. She gave the departing couple one last wistful look and drove on to the courthouse.

"Why doesn't Sheriff Banks come to see me and Snow anymore?" Lucy asked Abby one Saturday night when she and Hannah were sitting down to dinner with the little girl.

"I expect he's very busy," Abby began.

"Busy taking that little blonde trooper around town," Hannah muttered as she worked her way through perfectly cooked mashed potatoes.

"Little pitchers," Abby cautioned her.

Hannah glanced from her to Lucy and grimaced. "Sorry."

"What's a little pitcher?" Lucy asked curiously.

"A figure of speech," Abby said, and forced a laugh. "After supper, suppose we watch that silly Halloween movie we both like so much?"

"Oh, that would be fun!" the child exclaimed.

"I'd enjoy it myself," Hannah seconded with a smile. "Imagine Martians hearing that old Orson Welles broadcast of War of the Worlds and rushing to invade earth!"

Abby burst out laughing. "I know. It's hilarious."

"I love the little boy in the duck costume," Lucy said. "He's so cute!"

"So sweet, too," Abby commented. "Just like you, Lucy." She reached out and touched the child's soft cheek. "You're such a joy to have around."

"I love you, too, Aunt Abby," Lucy replied with a big smile. "I'm so happy we came to live here on the ranch."

"So am I," Abby said, but with less enthusiasm.

Hannah watched the younger woman pick at her food and felt sorry for her. Cody Banks had obviously had a change of heart, if he was seeing another woman, a prettier woman. It must sting Abby's pride, especially since she had feelings for him. Cody was just scared, she reasoned, of ending up with another Debby, another woman who pretended love and walked away.

Abby wasn't like that. She'd stay until the bitter end, through famine, fire, flood. If Cody had lost everything, Abby would have dug in and helped him regain what he'd lost. But that wasn't going to happen, it seemed. Cody had made essentially a public statement, by taking the blonde trooper out for coffee. In a small town like Catelow, everybody gossiped. It was going to hurt Abby. A lot.

"Suppose I make us some popcorn," Hannah offered. "Nice to eat while watching TV," she added.

Lucy hugged her. "You just think of everything, Hannah!"

"Well, not quite everything," Hannah sighed, glancing at Abby's sad face, which she was trying so valiantly to hide. "Not quite everything."

The little blonde trooper was full of stories about places she'd been, people she'd seen. To a small-town lawman like Cody, it was fascinating. He'd never met anyone like her. She was fancy-free and she didn't want roots, she'd made that very clear.

His dark eyes fell to the chain she was wearing around her neck. It had to be real gold. And there was a charm on the end of it that looked like a hand with the thumb sticking out between the clenched fingers. He knew he'd seen something like it before, but he couldn't remember where or when. She started on another subject and he forgot about it.

This little blonde was fun to be with. She was older than Abby and had obviously been on her own for a long time. But it was Abby his mind kept going back to, even as he smiled at his companion.

They'd feel that he'd deserted them, Abby and Hannah and Lucy. He felt bad about not even going near the ranch. But he thought of Abby with Lucy as a dependent, and his thoughts confused him. He didn't want the responsibility for a family. Not now, probably not ever. He liked having his own space, doing what he pleased. A man got into habits and routine when he lived alone. Abby and Hannah would interfere with that, and Lucy would be an ongoing interruption. The child was...

He grimaced. She was a joy. A sweet, gentle little girl who loved animals and loved Cody. He felt guilty that he hadn't been back to see her. He just wasn't ready. What he'd learned about his late wife hadn't seemed to affect him, but now that the shock had worn off, the pain began. He felt like the world's biggest fool. Debby had played him for a sucker, and he'd let her. He was a small-town sheriff. She'd been a big-city specialist, looking forward to a lucrative practice and high-ticket patients. How would that have played out when she got through with her training? It didn't bear thinking about. He was smart. He'd had some college while he was in the military. But he was a far cry from a neurosurgeon, even a neurologist. Looking back, he realized that it had been the uniform that had caught Debby's eye. She'd been attracted to it, not so much to Cody. She'd even mentioned once, just once, that he was very conventional in bed. He hadn't thought much about the comment at the time, too besotted to think she was complaining. But his experience hadn't been that great, and Debby seemed to know a lot more than he did.

Abby, on the other hand, was naïve. He ground his teeth together, picturing her with Lassiter. She wasn't a pretty woman, in the accepted sense, but she was sweet and kind and compassionate. Obviously, Lassiter saw those qualities in her and found them appealing.

"I said, I have to get back to work," the blonde said, laughing as she waved a hand in front of his face to divert him.

"Oh." He laughed self-consciously. "Sorry. I've had a case on my mind," he said. He got up and paid for the cappuccinos. He noticed that his companion didn't offer to pay her share. Most women these days would have protested. Especially Abby.

He left her at her car. It was a new sports model of a brand he didn't recognize. "Where's your prowler?" he asked.

She blinked. "Oh, it's at my cousin's," she said. "I borrowed his little car to come to town." She grinned. "See you soon."

He watched her drive away and thought of Debby. She'd been like that. Outgoing and smart and fascinating to talk to. He felt like a victim all over again. Not that he planned to get involved with the trooper. He didn't plan to get involved with anyone.

He went back to work, preoccupied, and got on with the day's work. He got up from his desk and went to look at the pictures on the wall, just for something to do. He was worried and bored out of his mind. "I must be going nuts," he told himself.

"Bad habit, talking to yourself," Lassiter mused as he came in the door.

Cody turned and glared at him.

Lassiter didn't need to be told why. It was a small community and gossip must be overwhelming about his ride in the country with Abby and Lucy.

"Don't blame me," Lassiter said, dropping into the chair beside Cody's desk. "You've been going around with a pretty little blonde. A woman like Abby isn't going to sit on the shelf for long." He pursed his lips at the sheriff's black glare, growing worse by the second. "I understand that your cousin, Bart Riddle, even asked her to a community dance."

He hadn't known that. He was even more livid. "I helped the trooper subdue a perp who was giving her a hard time out on the highway," he said shortly.

"Well, there aren't many perps in the local coffee shop, I imagine," Lassiter drawled.

Cody looked away. He was a public official. It would look bad if he threw the other man out onto the sidewalk. Really bad.

"Did you know that Bobby Grant made bail in Florida?" Lassiter asked suddenly, and he was serious.

Cody scowled. "How?" he exclaimed. "The police chief said he was going to make sure that the bail was set so high, Grant couldn't raise it!"

"There was a new judge sitting who felt so sorry for the poor man, jilted and arrested, and charged with crimes that just couldn't be true," Lassiter explained.

"Don't tell me. The judge was a young woman and Grant charmed her."

"Exactly," Lassiter replied. "Remember the diamond ring that Miss Whatley gave him? He sold it. He had more than enough for his reduced bail and to apparently pay somebody to go after Mr. Whatley again. And this time, the perp he sends might be more successful."

Cody's jaw tautened. "I'll double the jailers."

"Won't help," Lassiter returned. "He's got more than one person on his payroll. That's all my operative has been able to find out so far, but he's working on it."

"That's just great," Cody muttered. He glanced at Lassiter. "I don't guess Julia, Whatley's housekeeper, would be one of the people? She's been bringing him food."

"Have it checked," came the cool advice. "Nobody is above suspicion right now."

"Good idea." He sat down behind his desk. "Well, starting tomorrow. He's already had a slice of that pie she sent today. The jailer said he took it in. Even asked if it was okay." He rolled his eyes. "Now, how about Nita Whatley? I hope the police chief is keeping an eye on her."

"He is. Mr. Grant has made threats."

"I'd like to lock him up," Cody said irritably.

"You've got company. The police chief, I'm told, was all but jumping up and down in a rage when Grant was released on bond. But we're still working on enough evidence to get him to trial in Denver. There's an exhumation coming up, Miss Henry's sister, Candy. Violet had to be talked into that. She's deeply religious and she loved her sister. But in the end, she didn't want Grant to get away with murder. We're also checking dates and interviewing people about Candy's last night before she was killed. We think she was having dinner with Bobby Grant just before she died. Remember what I told you, about Grant's blonde visitor when he was living at Nita Whatley's home, the one who had a way with exotic poisons? Some can't be detected."

"I hope that's not the case, if she was poisoned," came the quiet reply.

"So do I. I hate to see a man get away with murder, especially a smug so-and-so like Bobby Grant. He seems to think he's beaten the law, even more so now that he got out on bond. All they could hold him for was assault, and it wasn't a violent one. Even Miss Whatley had to confess that he only tapped her on the cheek." He glanced at Cody. "There was a bruise, of course, but he told the judge that it was pre-existing, that the police chief was enamored of Miss Whatley so naturally he was prejudiced."

"Give me a break!" Cody exploded.

"I think she was afraid to admit how hard he'd hit her," he continued irritably. "He made a lot of threats and, police chief notwithstanding, she's on her own at her home." He leaned back. "I was young and impressionable once," Lassiter sighed. "Seems like a million years ago, now, but I vaguely remember how easily I was led." He chuckled. "That was my excuse for why I had two marijuana cigarettes in my pocket in my junior year of high school. My dad didn't buy it. He grounded me for two weeks. I missed the junior prom, and I had a hot date, too. I raged and cussed and slammed things around. It did no good at all. My father," he added, "is formidable in a temper."

"So was mine," Cody recalled. His face tautened. "He'd pick up anything he could find and use it on me or my mother when he was drinking."

"Not my dad," Lassiter replied, smiling. "He loves all of us, but especially my mom. She was in tears over the illegal cigarettes, which was why Dad came down so hard on me. He reminded me that it was a gateway drug." He rolled his eyes. "Now it's legal in several states. But ten years ago, it wasn't. Mom was heartbroken. She was afraid I'd be arrested and sent to jail."

Cody found that idea unusually appealing, when he recalled Abby riding around with the man. He pulled himself up. This was no time for personal vendettas. "Can't they find some charge to hold Grant on?"

"Believe me, the police chief is working on it. So is an assistant district attorney, who also knows the Whatley family and was outraged on Miss Whatley's behalf." He crossed his long legs. "There's a possibility that a local attorney's nephew is tied to this case."

"Owens's nephew?" he exclaimed. "How?"

"He's been trying to get money out of local people for months, even hounded his uncle for it. Now, all of a sudden, he's wearing new clothes and driving a new car and he just moved into a rental unit. Odd, wouldn't you say?"

"How interesting," Cody mused.

"I've got people working on that, too. My sister, for one. She can get blood out of a turnip. The date Owens's nephew deposited money in his checking account is also interesting. It was the same day Grant was released from jail. And it was a wire transfer."

"This case gets more confusing by the day."

"And more interesting," Lassiter agreed. He sighed. "Well, things being the way they are, you'd better arrest me for loitering or something and get me back in jail next to Horace Whatley. He's not safe on his own, especially now."

"I have to agree. If you're sure you want to be locked up?"

"Don't see that I have much choice," Lassiter replied. "If we want to keep Horace alive, that is."

Cody got up. "Come on back. I'll find you a nice, cozy cell next to Horace."

"How about breakfast in bed, some sports magazines, and a box of gourmet brownies? Oh, and a nice cappuccino? You could take that pretty little blonde with you to buy it," he added with pure malice.

Cody unlocked the cell with a burning glare. "Be careful. You could be confined with all sorts of roommates if you get me really hot."

Lassiter stepped into the cell and watched it close. "You could ask Abby to come visit me," he said innocently. "She's the sort of woman who would wait for years while a man served his time. And she's a terrific cook."

Cody barely kept his temper. He wanted so badly to drag Lassiter out of that cell and throw a punch at him. Unthinkable.

"Hi, Sheriff," Horace Whatley called to him. Cody stopped at his cell, which was next to Lassiter's. "You've arrested Mr. Lassiter again? That makes, let me see, three times, doesn't it?" he asked worriedly. "Have you heard from my sister?"

Cody hesitated, but there was really no reason not to tell him. "Bobby Grant's out of jail on bond. Now, don't worry," he added when the little man's face contorted. "She's got watchers she doesn't even know about, and the police chief will be keeping a very close eye on her."

He nodded. "Dan was always sweet on her. She didn't like guns, you know, so she wouldn't go out with him." He smiled. "I guess times change."

"So do people," he replied.

"You be careful, Sheriff," Whatley said gently. "I mean, if Nita and I are in danger, you could be, too. So could this nice Mr. Lassiter—anybody close to you. Mr. Grant will be furious that he lost my sister's fortune. He may have a hit list."

Cody chuckled. "You watch too many mobster movies, Mr. Whatley," he said. "It's highly unlikely that he'd target a sheriff, even if he had a way to get at me. I'm here in Wyoming and he's in Florida."

"My uncle was CIA during the Cuban Missile Crisis,"

Whatley replied soberly. "There was some talk of mob involvement, you know, about getting rid of Castro. My uncle said there were all sorts of people who were eaten up with revenge and you'd never know it until somebody died mysteriously. I guess he knew what he was talking about, because he died after lunch one day of a heart attack when he'd never even had heart trouble. He talked about a certain mission. Nita and I heard, from a friend in government, that he talked too much. He lived in a small town up in Montana," he added deliberately. "They can get you anywhere."

"I'm sorry," Cody said and meant it. "But this isn't Cuba, and we don't have mobsters around here."

"But you do," Whatley returned, surprised. "That nephew of Mr. Owens was dating a girl who was thick with the Chicago mob until just recently. Didn't you know?"

Cody had a headache. It was new and sudden and he was certain that it was going to fry his brain. The mob. Here? In Catelow?

"I'll check that out," he told the smaller man with a smile. "Don't you worry. We'll keep you safe."

Mr. Whatley hesitated, as if he wanted to say something else. But in the end, he just smiled.

Three days later, Cody went to the dry cleaners to drop off his spare uniform and almost collided with Abby in the doorway.

"Oh, excuse me," she said, and smiled politely, as if he were a stranger.

He hesitated. His heart went wild at just the nearness of her. "Abby," he began, searching for words he was having a hard time finding.

"I'm sorry, I'm on my lunch hour. Good to see you, Sheriff," she added, and walked away.

Cody stared after her with his heart sinking in his chest. He felt a door close. It was like ice down his spine.

That was what his cold feet had gained him. Abby walked by him as if he was a distant stranger. Obviously she knew about the little blonde trooper. But instead of being belligerent, or snooty, or even sarcastic, she'd done something far worse. She'd reduced him to the status of an acquaintance.

And how could he blame her? He'd brought it on himself. She wouldn't know that he'd only taken the trooper for coffee after he heard that she'd been riding around his county with Lassiter. He left his uniform with the dry cleaner and walked out into the cold air, where snowflakes were swirling around. He remembered Abby coming after him when she'd heard Anyu had been put down. She'd taken care of him. He'd mentioned his new dog to the blonde trooper, who'd laughed at him for caring about an old, used-up dog. She didn't even like animals, she'd said, and who would be crazy enough to keep one inside the house?

Cody hadn't said anything, but the comment had gone through him like hot steel. A woman who was that unconcerned for a wounded animal wouldn't have much more compassion for a wounded human. He knew the commanding officer in this area's division, they were in combat together. It might be a good idea to just give him a call. He'd noticed the little trooper's gun was a .32 Smith and Wesson and he knew from experience that the new designated sidearm for troopers in 2021 was a SIG Sauer 9 mm. It was just a little thing, but it stuck in the back of his mind and refused to budge. After all, it never hurt to check out people. He was probably just being paranoid.

And actually, he wasn't. The commanding officer of the area units was absolutely shocked when Cody asked about his newest patrol officer, a cute little blonde. He went on to describe how they'd met.

There was a tense pause in the conversation. "My newest patrol officer isn't a blonde, she's a brunette, mostly Crow with a little Lakota blood, and she's about as cute as a cobra if you're a lawbreaker. Like hell she'd need help with a cuff!"

CHAPTER FOURTEEN

Cody kicked off his boots and padded into the kitchen to make coffee. His unexpected meeting with Abby had knocked the stuffing out of him. She obviously thought he was backing away from her, and she was acting accordingly. She hadn't even met his eyes when they spoke.

She wasn't a pretty woman, despite her nice figure and pretty eyes. She'd probably seen him with the little blonde trooper and realized that the competition was lovely to look at. He could have told her that it was just a casual friendship, but Abby took things to heart. He felt guilty for the way he'd treated her. He could have been honest and told her he was finding it hard to deal with Debby's unfaithfulness, with the danger to Mr. Whatley and his sister, with the murder investigation. But he'd just absented himself from her life without a word. It must have hurt, if she couldn't bear even to look at him now. And if Abby felt that he'd deserted them, how must Lucy feel?

He stopped in the middle of perking coffee to think about that. It made him feel guilty. Lucy was a sweet child, and she'd grown close to him. But he'd put her aside as if she had no value to him at all, just as he'd jettisoned Abby.

He just wasn't ready to deal with all his issues. Not now, at least, when he had so much on his plate at the office. Besides, he reminded himself coldly, she'd been riding around with Lassiter!

He hated the thought of the man. Lassiter was formidable competition. What if the other man was thinking about the future, about the sort of wife Abby would make? Cody had to admit that she'd be an ideal one. She was loving and kind and supportive.

At least, she seemed to be. But he didn't really know her. Not that well. What if she turned out to be like Debby? What if she two-timed him, the way she had with Lassiter?

Alexander hobbled in on his cast and looked up hopefully at the pastrami Cody was loading onto wheat bread with Swiss cheese. He didn't like anything on the sandwiches so there was no mayonnaise or mustard. His new companion seemed to appreciate that.

"Hungry, old man?" he asked gently, and smiled as he paused to reach down and pat the dog's broad head. "You can share the sandwiches with me."

Alexander wagged his tail and laughed up at him.

Cody sighed. "It's nice, having somebody to talk to," he told the dog.

Alexander made a soft howl, as if he understood. Well, why not? Anyu had always seemed to understand what he told her. Huskies and malamutes were intelligent dogs.

He finished the sandwiches and went back into the living room, to sprawl on the couch with sandwiches and milk, while Alexander took up a position at his feet and worked on his starving expression. It probably wasn't even just an expression, Cody thought guiltily. The poor dog had been in such bad shape that most people, seeing him in that condition, would have opted to put him down.

"I like hard luck cases, I guess," Cody said, and smiled.

Alexander howled softly.

"I'll drop by the store tomorrow and get us some more," he said, when he and the dog had finished off all the pastrami and most of the Swiss cheese.

Alexander panted hopefully.

Cody went back to work with a leaden heart. He wanted to phone Abby and explain, or try to explain, why he was standoffish.

About the time he started to lift the receiver of the base phone on the table beside the sofa, there was a call on his radio. Reluctantly, he answered it. Another wreck, this time catastrophic with multiple injuries. The roads were slick and getting slicker with sleet. No wonder there were wrecks, usually when people from low-lying areas tried to drive up here.

"On my way," Cody said, and was glad that he'd had milk instead of the beer he usually liked on his day off.

Cody shared his intel about the imposter blonde trooper with Lassiter after he worked the wreck, speaking in whispers so the jailer, always lingering nearby, couldn't hear.

"Blonde," Lassiter mused.

"Yes. Wasn't Bobby Grant's visitor in Florida a blonde, well-traveled and pretty?"

"She was indeed."

Cody scowled. "I was going to look something up, too, but I forgot. She was wearing a charm that looked like a closed fist with a thumb sticking through it..."

"A Figa," Lassiter said coldly.

"A what?"

"It started out as a vulgar expression in Italy, but it migrated to South America, where it's worn as a protection against evil."

"That's where I saw it," Cody recalled suddenly. "I was watching a special on the Amazon, and one of the visitors was wearing one. The interviewer asked him what it was, and he explained it. No wonder it looked familiar!"

"So now we know who the third member of the Grant party is," Lassiter replied. "Where do we go from here?"

"First things first. There's Owens's nephew, and the blonde, and the so-called witness to the robbery who purportedly saw Mr. Whatley commit a crime. I can't pull somebody in on suspicion without evidence. All I have is suspicion."

"As soon as we get the autopsy report back on Violet Henry's sister, Candy, we may have something to go on. If the blonde's from South America and has a way with poison, there will be a way to connect her to the murder. Depending on whether or not the poison is still in the body, and whether it can be traced to a particular place or person. We'll have to find the paper trail of the blonde's movements. If she's been to Denver in recent times, that's a start."

"Look up airplane tickets," Lassiter said. "What did she say her name was?"

"The name she gave was Bella Cain."

"It's a start," Lassiter said with a smile. "Nice start."

Cody got up. "Yes."

Lassiter eyed him quietly. "You might give that coroner in Denver a call and make sure he keeps enough evidence to share with the FBI crime lab. Those guys can trace a single hair all the way to hell."

Cody chuckled. "So they can. I'll make a point of it." He glanced at Horace, who was dozing. "Don't let your guard down," he advised softly.

"I never do that."

Cody nodded and left him there, his mind on how easily

he'd been taken in by the so-called trooper. He was amazed at his own naivete. She was just like Debby. But this time, he wasn't falling into the trap. He knew better. And always, at the back of his mind, was Abby. He grimaced. Abby, who'd written him off because she thought he'd exchanged her for the little blonde. He was regretting his actions more than ever now.

Abby had been shaken at the sight of Cody, although she'd recovered quickly. She was proud of her indifferent act. It had been a very innocent outing with Lassiter, which Lucy had enjoyed, too. They'd gone to a movie while they were out—a nice cartoon one which Lucy had loved. Lassiter liked kids. That was surprising in such a loner. He was a complex person, and Abby genuinely liked him. But she was in love with Cody Banks, who was now apparently romancing a blonde state trooper.

She sat at her desk working and brooding. Mr. Owens's nephew, Jack, had been in the office begging for money several days ago. But he'd walked in yesterday in a pair of designer jeans and designer shirt, and announced to his uncle that he had a great job now and he could fend for himself. He was obviously high on something, because he made his announcement loudly in front of the entire office staff, with appropriate bad words which made Abby blush even in memory.

Mr. Owens had been oddly preoccupied since then, and she'd seen him in the local café having coffee with one of the assistant district attorneys. She couldn't hear what was said, but afterward, Mr. Owens looked as if he had the weight of the world on his shoulders.

Marie sat down beside Abby when the commotion was over. The nephew had gone slamming out of the building and a worried Mr. Owens had gone back into his office.

"There's some gossip," Marie whispered, "that Mr. Owens's nephew is in league with someone local who's planning to get Mr. Whatley out of the way."

Abby's jaw dropped. "Marie, how in the world do you know...?"

"My husband has some rather shady contacts, not that he's ever been shady, but he is a practicing attorney, you know. Anyway," she continued, "the rumor is that some man in Florida is paying the nephew and two other people, including a woman, to do away with Mr. Whatley so that his sister will be the only person left to inherit that estate."

"You should tell somebody!" she exclaimed.

"Who? If I tell the sheriff, he'll want to know where I got the information," Marie said miserably. "And my husband has already said that he'll deny hearing any of it if he's questioned. He likes his job," she added with a long sigh.

Abby pursed her lips and narrowed her eyes. "I think I know somebody who might be able to help," she said.

"Listen, I know you're friends with Cody Banks...!" Marie began.

"No. It's somebody else, somebody who can keep his mouth shut. He has connections, too. I won't involve you or your husband. I promise," she added.

Marie relaxed a little. "Thanks," she said softly. "All marriages go through stages," she added curiously. "I don't want Matthew to grow up without a father. And I love my idiot husband, warts and all."

Abby just smiled. "You're very lucky," she said wistfully. A marriage with children had been her dream once. Now she had to learn to be content with a young girl who was her niece, not her daughter, and a life that didn't contain a man. Just as well, she thought. Cody obviously didn't give her a thought anymore.

She waited until she knew Cody was due in court to go to the detention center. She had to see Lassiter.

The jailer, a strangely sneaky sort of person, let her into Lassiter's cell, but he stood within earshot, which Abby found strange. Lassiter didn't.

She pretended that she'd just come to see how he was, and if he needed anything. Unexpectedly, the little blonde trooper who'd been pursuing Cody came into the office. Abby saw her, although it would have been difficult for the girl to see her, in Lassiter's cell. She motioned to the jailer, who left the room.

"I'll be quick," Abby said, leaning close to him. "Mr. Owens's nephew is wearing designer clothes. He came into the office and made a terrible scene. Then an acquaintance," she added, protecting Marie, "told me that a man in Florida who was being held in jail got out and paid money to three local people, including James Owens's nephew, Jack Owens, and some woman as well, to take out Mr. Whatley!"

Lassiter didn't even look surprised. He kept it to himself that he knew who the woman was. It was interesting that the little blonde who wasn't a real trooper was speaking earnestly to the jailer even now, so engrossed that she hadn't even looked toward the cell Lassiter and Abby were in.

"Thank you," Lassiter told her. "I'll check that out."

The trooper turned and left abruptly and the jailer, who looked disoriented, turned toward the cells.

"Sorry about this, but it will keep him off the track," Lassiter said, and abruptly pulled Abby to him by the nape of her neck and kissed her with sudden passion.

The jailer, returning and fearing he might have missed overhearing something he needed to know, just stared. He relaxed, laughed under his breath, and coughed. Loudly.

Lassiter lifted his head and looked in his direction.

"She should go now," he said, and indicated Abby.

"Yes, I should," Abby agreed. She grinned at Lassiter. She liked him, but the kiss had been nothing more than vaguely pleasurable. No toots. No whistles. No sudden acceleration of the senses.

Lassiter noted the same reaction on his part. Shame, he thought. She was the kind of woman he'd have adored. But, then, she'd never fit in his violent world.

"Come back and see me," Lassiter said softly.

"I'll certainly do that. I'll bake a nail file into a cake!" she whispered, loud enough for the jailer to hear.

"No nail files," he said curtly. "We have a metal detector." He pointed to it. The door was just outside the cell area.

"Ah, well, I'll think up something more innovative," she said aloud, and gave the jailer a simpering look. He glared at her.

"See you," she told Lassiter.

"Oh, yes, you will," he assured her.

The jailer reported to Cody when he came back that Lassiter had a visitor. "A blonde woman," he began.

"The state trooper?" Cody interrupted, worried that she knew they were suspicious of her.

"No. She came by to see if you wanted to go get something to eat but you weren't here and she had to go back to work, she said. This was another blonde lady. Slender, long hair. She went to see Lassiter. I guess they've got something going, because she was really kissing him in his cell."

Cody felt his insides explode. Riding around with Lassiter was one thing. But Abby's kissing him indicated deeper feelings. He felt as if he'd dropped from a great height. It wasn't a pleasant feeling. He'd lost Abby. And the little blonde trooper who'd seemed to be actively pursuing him was only trying to kill his prisoner and keep him under surveillance. He felt absolutely depressed.

"How about Mr. Whatley?" Cody asked absently.

"Him? Oh, he's been sleeping. A lot."

Cody's heart jumped. He dismissed the jailer and went past Whatley's cell to Lassiter's. "Has anyone been in his cell?" he asked curtly, keeping his voice down.

Lassiter looked up, grimaced and indicated his cell phone. "Sorry. I've been busy. And your jailer moved Horace to a cell farther along while they cleaned the one he was in…"

Cody went back to Horace Whatley's cell with a black scowl and opened the door. Horace was lying on his bunk with his eyes closed.

"Mr. Whatley?" Cody asked curtly.

Horace opened his eyes and blinked. "Oh. Hi, Sheriff," he said. He sat up and yawned. "I haven't been sleeping well at night, so I thought I'd have a nap. I feel much better now."

"Glad to hear it," Cody replied.

"Sheriff, have you got a minute?" Lassiter called as he turned to leave.

He wanted to throw the man out the back door by the seat of his pants. He had to remember that he was a public servant. He moved to the cell.

"Can you come in?" Lassiter added, when Cody seemed glued to the floor.

"You can say what you want through the bars, can't you?" Cody growled.

Lassiter was amused. "Not really."

Cody was weighing the options of going into that cell with a man he wanted badly to lacerate.

"It's not what you think," Lassiter began, noting the other man's bridled fury and guessing at the cause. He lowered his voice. "And if you kill me, somebody will notice you digging a hole behind the detention center."

He had such an angelic look on his face that Cody burst out laughing against his will. He closed the cell door and moved closer.

"Nice assessment," Cody remarked.

"Oh, I'm no stranger to homicidal rage," he said, tongue-in-cheek. He looked past Cody to the jailer.

Cody followed his gaze. "Jones, go get something to eat."

"But, Sheriff, I don't go to lunch for another...!"

"And I said, go now," Cody said, lowering his voice.

The jailer swallowed, hard. The look in those dark eyes was like a loaded gun pointed at him. "I'll go right now."

Cody and Lassiter watched him go hesitantly out the door.

"What?" Cody asked Lassiter.

"He'll be back as quickly as he can wolf down something. He and your trooper friend had a brief conversation, after which he was watching Abby and me like a hawk. And yes, I kissed her, but it was to distract the jailer, nothing more," he added abruptly. "He was listening to every word we said. I don't know what he and the blonde talked about. Plus that, Abby had news."

"What sort?"

"Apparently Mr. Grant has paid two local citizens and a woman—and we both know who the woman is—to take out Mr. Whatley," he said, lowering his voice so that Whatley, in the nearby cell, couldn't overhear.

"What?" Cody exclaimed. "How does she know this?"

"She wouldn't tell me. But she said it's legitimate. She got it from someone whose significant other has mob ties. That means that at least one of Grant's operatives has them as well."

"Damn," Cody said under his breath. "Well, at least we know who they are—Jack Owens and the so-called witness who saw Horace rob the store. The third is now painfully obvious." He shook his head. "I should have checked her out. That was stupid on my part."

"We all make mistakes," Lassiter said. "She even looked legit to me."

"She did to me, too, at first."

"One of my calls was positive. They're doing the autopsy

on Miss Henry's sister this morning. We should have results on that soon. And one of our operatives based in Denver has been questioning people who work in the restaurant where Candy, Miss Henry's sister, had a date the night she disappeared."

"He'd better work fast," Cody said. "Or more people might conveniently disappear…although I can't see the logic in it. Bobby Grant doesn't have Mr. Whatley's sister in his pocket anymore."

"Obviously he thinks he will have," Lassiter replied grimly. "Either by coaxing or force. Nita's afraid of him, remember. They couldn't hold him in Florida for assault because she was too afraid to press charges. After which the bleeding heart judge set him free."

"What a mess," Cody said on a long sigh.

A door slammed and the jailer was back. "I'll be checking the other prisoners, Sheriff," he said helpfully.

"Never saw a man eat that fast who wasn't starving to death," Lassiter remarked dryly, but so that the jailer couldn't hear.

Cody made a face, his back to the jailer. "Well, I'll get back to work, and I'll check with your father about that contact in Florida," he added, his face expressing the fact that he was making up things as he went.

Lassiter quickly caught on. "You do that. He has something on one of Bobby Grant's contacts," he added, just loudly enough that the jailer could overhear.

"I'll check into it. Things are coming to a head very quickly," he added with a chuckle. "Heads will roll, I promise you."

"You keep an eye on yours," Lassiter replied.

"And you quit kissing my girl," Cody said unexpectedly, and then his cheekbones flushed, because that had just slipped out.

Lassiter chuckled. "I'll consider it," he mused. "But you'd

better watch out for your cousin. I'm not into marriage at the moment, but Bart Riddle is. If you get my meaning."

Cody's eyes burned in his tanned face. "And we'll see about that," he muttered as he left the cell. He paused at Horace Whatley's but the little man was sound asleep. He left the two men behind and went into his office.

Minutes later, the jailer stuck his head around the door. "Sheriff, I think there's something wrong with Mr. Whatley," he said.

Cody was out of his chair and down the hall in a flash. He glanced at Lassiter, who was standing at the bars with a solemn expression. He gave Cody a speaking glance.

Cody opened the cell and went in. Horace Whatley was almost comatose. "Get an ambulance," he shot at the jailer. "Tell them to hurry."

"Yes, sir!"

Cody was starting artificial respiration with a tube he carried in his duty belt for emergencies, alternating with chest compression. "Did you see anything?" he asked Lassiter.

"No. And the jailer didn't come near him," Lassiter said worriedly.

Cody kept on with artificial respiration until the ambulance came, and he rode in it to the hospital.

The attending physician was thorough. He called for lab work, X-rays and even an MRI to make sure there were no hidden head injuries.

"Check for poison," Cody told him.

The physician who was mostly on duty in the emergency room had been a combat medic. He was loved in the community.

"Just like last time," the doctor murmured as he worked with his team to get Horace breathing normally.

"Yes, and nobody saw a thing," Cody said furiously.

"You know what comes next."

"I do. A thorough vetting of everyone who brought food and on your part, a precise examination of his stomach contents."

"You got it," the doctor said.

"Will he live?"

"He'll live."

"Just make sure you save enough samples for the FBI lab," Cody told the doctor. "This case is going to involve a lot of people before we're through, and not just here in town."

"I'll do that. You be careful out there," the doctor added.

Cody gave the doctor a thumbs-up sign and went out the door. He was furious. This had happened right under his nose. Twice! But if the jailer wasn't involved, then who was?

He did question his jailer first, however. "The blonde trooper spoke to you this morning," Cody said without preamble. "Lassiter told me she was here."

"Oh, uh, yes, sir, she sure was," he blurted out.

"Why?"

"She was looking for you, sir," he said. "She asked if you were going to be in today because she had something serious to speak to you about. I told her that you'd be here all day," he added.

"What did Mr. Whatley eat today?"

The jailer shrugged. "He didn't have much appetite. He had a piece of fried chicken and some pie that Julia brought him," he said. "But we know she wouldn't poison the boss. I think she's sweet on him," he added.

Cody grimaced. "I need what's left of the pie. I suppose you threw out the piece of chicken?"

"No need to keep it. All that was left was the bone."

"How about the pie?" Cody persisted, and he stared at the other man with eyes that demanded an answer.

"It's, uh, I was about to throw it out. I put it in a bag in the kitchen…"

This was getting worse and worse. Cody barreled past him and found the pie in a gallon baggie sitting just over the trash can. He thanked God that the man hadn't had time to hide what he was almost certain was the evidence.

He grabbed it up. "I'll take care of this," he said shortly.

The jailer flushed. "It's mostly eaten," he persisted.

"I'm not going to eat it," Cody replied curtly. He went out of the room, nodded toward Lassiter, and made a beeline to the hospital.

He had the pie tested and asked the techs not to throw out the remainder, because if it was poisoned, he'd need to send a sample to the FBI crime lab.

That got everyone's attention. That lab was famous.

He waited for the doctor to come out. It didn't take long.

"How's Mr. Whatley?" Cody asked.

"Cussing," the doctor chuckled. "Well, I'd cuss, too, you know. He's had his stomach pumped. I saved samples of it for our lab and the FBI lab. I should have results on the panel we did, any minute…" He was looking at his cell phone while he spoke and there was a ding. He nodded. "A very special poison, from a plant only found in South America," the doctor said smugly.

Cody patted him on the shoulder. "I'll remember you in my will."

"Okay," came the reply. "I'll remember that you said that," he added with a chuckle, "just about time you go hunting and cook another pot of venison stew. I hear it's famous hereabouts."

"That it is." Cody grinned. "Thanks for such quick work. Will Horace be okay?"

He nodded. "We got to it in time. Nasty stuff," he added,

"and not as familiar as, say, curare, which comes from the poison arrow frog." He shook his head. "Damn, Cody, you'd have to be a botanist to even know about the plant this poison comes from."

"You know, I have a feeling I'm about to find that out," Cody told him with a smile. "I'll be in touch."

"We're here if you need us. I don't mind testifying, just FYI."

"Thanks. I'll make the assistant DA on this case aware of that."

It was later that same day that the report came in about Violet Henry's sister. There was poison still detectable in the remains, and it was derived from a rare South American plant.

Cody thanked the doctor who'd phoned him at Violet's request. "We're sending a sample of our poison up to the FBI crime lab. It would be most welcome if you could do the same with the poison you found in Candy Henry."

"I'll be happy to do that."

"I'll phone the Denver authorities for you and have them collect it. And thanks again!"

He hung up and started making more phone calls.

After he finished, he went to Lassiter's cell and unlocked it. "Horace's going to be in the hospital for a couple of days, under guard, so there's no need for you to stay in here," he told the other man.

"Thanks. I was getting a touch of claustrophobia," Lassiter chuckled. "Thank God they were able to find something when they examined Miss Henry's sister. There will be a paper trail. You get anything on the name the blonde gave you?"

"It was a dead end," Cody had to admit. He frowned thoughtfully. "She said she left her prowler at a cousin's house and drove his sports car here to have coffee with me the other day." He glanced at the other man. "I wonder if she does have a relation here?"

He went to his office and looked up a local number. He phoned it. One of his deputies lived near the small rental house occupied by Jack Owens, attorney James Owens's nephew. "Hey, Bob," he said when his officer answered, "I've got a quest for you."

"Hot dog," the officer replied. "What do I get for this quest? Better armor? A bigger sword? Or gold…?"

"You get substandard pay and a pat on the back. If you find out anything, I'll make it two pats on the back," Cody said. "So you're still knee-deep in that fantasy computer game, I see."

"It's great. I'm so glad I discovered it," the man raved. "Of course, I don't eat or sleep, but who cares? I went up ten levels in one day!"

Cody laughed in spite of himself. "Good for you."

"What do you want me to do? Need me to come in?"

"No need. I want you to drive by Jack Owens's rental house and see if there's a green convertible sports car parked in the driveway."

"I wish it was parked in my driveway," Bob sighed. "I'd go racing."

"Not in my county, you wouldn't," Cody retorted. "Get going."

"I'll rush right past it. I need gas in my civilian car anyway."

"Good man. Call me if you see anything."

"Will do."

Cody and Lassiter had a long discussion about computers and how they worked while they waited for the phone to ring. Which it finally did.

"Boss?" Bob said when Cody answered.

"Well?" Cody prompted. "Was it there? A little green sports car?"

"Yes, sir," Bob replied. "And guess what else was there?"

"Tell me!"

"That so-called witness who put Mr. Whatley in jail, apparently living there," Bob said, a grin in his voice. "Two of them were outside shoveling snow so they could get the car out of the driveway. That's going to take a while, too, with it coming down in buckets now. So how's that for catching some fish?" he asked on a quick laugh.

"I'll promote you when we both join the French Foreign Legion and I'm an officer," Cody promised. "Meanwhile, I owe you two pats on the back. Feel free to collect them any time," he added, and hung up.

CHAPTER FIFTEEN

Cody felt that, finally, all the pieces of the puzzle were coming together. He called Dan Brady, the police chief in Lake Luna, Florida, who was deeply involved in the Bobby Grant case.

"Do you know where Bobby Grant is?" Cody asked at once.

"Oh, I hope you have a really good reason for asking," the chief replied. "Do you?"

"Poison," he said. "Candy Henry was poisoned. So was Horace Whatley, again, but this time we know what poison was used." He described it.

"A rare plant in South America. Why does that sound familiar…oh, yes, that blonde I told you about, who was thick with Bobby Grant, her dad's a botanist. He's from Manaus, I think, deep in the Amazon."

"A botanist." Cody smiled.

"I know exactly where Bobby Grant is, and we've got him under constant surveillance."

"You must have a really nice city manager, with all that overtime," Cody remarked.

"Not at all," Dan chuckled. "I have a few friends that most

people wouldn't want to meet. They're helping out while they're between missions."

"Nice to have friends like that!"

"What about Horace?" the chief asked. "Is he all right?"

"Yes. He's under surveillance, too, and we've got your blonde right here in town," he added grimly. "She's part of a triumvirate hired, apparently, by Bobby Grant, to get Horace Whatley out of the way. He has plans, or so I'm told, to get Nita back with flattery or force, whichever works."

"Over my dead body," Dan Brady said furiously.

"All I need is enough evidence to get an arrest warrant," Cody told him. "And I've got help from a former MIT professor," he added with a grin at Lassiter.

"A who?"

"His dad's got a detective agency in Houston, Texas."

"Ah. That young man. Yes, I've met him. He discussed the case with me over the phone when Nita was still involved with Bobby Grant. Brilliant fellow. And he's catching crooks?"

"Our differences are what make the world go round," Cody chuckled.

"So they say. Keep me in the loop."

"No problem. Watch your back."

"You watch yours," Brady said suddenly. "If money changed hands, or was promised and that blonde's involved, anybody around you is going to be in danger when you make the arrest. There might be an accomplice you don't know about. And the blonde has a reputation for vengeance. Nasty vengeance. She'll look for your weakest link."

His mind went immediately to his three girls, Abby and Hannah and little Lucy. He felt a surge of possession as strong as death almost burst inside him. His girls, and his old dog. Those were his weakest links. He'd have to make sure they were safe once he started making arrests.

★ ★ ★

It took a few days while Cody and Lassiter formed a plan of action. Lassiter had a friend who was between jobs, so he made a phone call to ask for help. Cody's deputy was assigned to keep an eye on the triumvirate camping out at Jack Owens's home. And Cody himself went to the Owens law office to pay a call on James Owens, uncle of one of the prime suspects.

Abby was working at her desk when he came in. He paused, but she pretended not to see him. With a sad sigh, he went on to the receptionist and asked to see James Owens.

He was ushered right back into Owens's office without having to wait.

"Have a seat, Cody," Owens said quietly. "I've been expecting you."

"Do you know what your nephew's up to?" Cody asked, when he was seated.

Owens shook his head. "I know that he's involved in something illegal, but not what," he replied. "My brother would roll over in his grave if he could see what his only child had turned out to be. This is what comes of overindulgence and never trying to be a parent. Tom wanted to be his son's best friend. He didn't need a best friend, he needed a father!"

Cody drew in a long breath. "I'm sure he did his best," he replied.

"Jack's mother tried to discipline him, but she died when he was only seven. Then it was just Jack and Tom, and Tom spoiled him rotten. He bailed him out of jail at least five times before he was out of high school, and it was always somebody else's fault. Usually it was the police persecuting the boy," Owens said, rolling his eyes.

"I've had him in a time or two myself," Cody said. "Mostly for petty things. But, Jim, this isn't a petty thing," he added quietly. "It adds up to a conspiracy to commit murder. I don't have to tell you how much time in prison he could be facing on just that charge alone."

Owens nodded his head. "I've already talked to Mark Sessions, our assistant district attorney, about the charges. The DA's investigator is already on the case. You might get in touch with him." He smiled sadly. "He's incorruptible. Just like you."

"I'll do that. I have to go talk to Julia Donovan. Mr. Whatley's most recent close call with poisoning was through one of her pies," Cody told the other man.

"But Julia's crazy about Horace Whatley!" James exclaimed. He laughed at Cody's expression. "My housekeeper knows her," he added. "They share secrets. She said that Horace was noticing Julia more and more, also. A sort of romance in progress. Two lonely people, in the process of finding each other."

"It would be nice if they did," Cody said. "But I have to go through the motions, as distasteful as it is. I hate going out there alone. It will look like I'm trying to intimidate her."

Owens pursed his lips and managed to look innocent. "You might take Abby with you," he said. "She could take down notes, if you need them."

Cody's heart jumped at the thought. It might be his only way back to Abby, to undo some of the damage his avoidance of her had done. He was feeling more guilty by the day. And now of all times, he needed to be around for all of his girls.

"That's a good idea. If she'll go," Cody added quietly. "I've been dealing with a lot of personal issues lately. I've... avoided people."

Owens touched the intercom button. "Abby, will you come in here, please?" he asked.

She replied, and in a couple of minutes, the door opened with a perfunctory knock, and Abby walked in.

Her heart was beating her up, but she managed a calm expression, noting that both men got to their feet as she entered the room. Old-world courtesy, hardly seen in modern times. It made her feel good and she smiled.

"Yes, Mr. Owens?" she asked.

Beside her, Cody was feeling a rush of emotion. It had been too long since he'd smelled that soft, floral unique scent that clung to her skin, since he'd been near her. The blonde trooper had done nothing for his senses, but Abby made them stand on end.

"Cody needs someone to go to see Julia Donovan with him and take notes."

"Oh?" She struggled for words, suddenly tongue-tied.

"I'm investigating an attempted murder," Cody replied.

"Oh. Poor Mr. Whatley," Abby said, nodding, because everybody in the small town already knew that Horace had been poisoned. "Is he okay?"

"He's fine. But the poison was in a pie that Julia brought him..."

"But she loves him," Abby protested, finally meeting Cody's dark eyes with her light ones, which made her flush. "She'd never do anything to hurt him!"

"We know that," Mr. Owens told her. "But any connection to an attempted murder must be investigated and reported."

"I see," Abby replied.

"So, will you go with Cody?" Mr. Owens asked.

She drew in a breath. "If he needs me to," she agreed, ignoring Cody, right beside her.

"I do need you to go with me," Cody said finally. "It will be easier for Julia if there's another woman there. Are you free now?" he added.

"Yes, she is," Owens replied, smiling at Abby. "It's only a couple of hours to quitting time and I don't need the work you're doing until day after tomorrow. Get your things and go with Cody now, if you don't mind."

"I don't mind," she replied, her heart racing.

"Thanks, Abby," Owens said, dismissing her.

"I'll be in touch," Cody added with a grin at Owens.

Owens sighed. "That's what I'm afraid of," he said, but he managed a smile.

Abby sat like a statue next to Cody in the sheriff's car. She couldn't find the right words to express what she felt, and apparently he was struggling with them as well, because he was silent until they reached the crossroads that led toward Horace Whatley's ranch.

"Do you know who actually poisoned Mr. Whatley?" Abby asked at last.

"Yes," he said. "And it isn't Julia."

"Thank goodness," she said.

He watched her hands moving restlessly over the nice slacks she was wearing with black boots and a silky blue blouse and a thick charcoal wool coat. She was obviously nervous with him.

"It's Debby," he said abruptly, and there was a flush high on his cheekbones as he tried to express why he'd absented himself from Abby for so long.

"Debby?" she faltered, turning in the seat to look at him.

He drew in a rough breath. "This is hard. I don't talk about…personal things. Not much. Debby sold me out. I put her on a pedestal all those years. I never knew what she really felt about me, what she was doing in Denver when I wasn't there. I felt like a fool. It took a while for me to deal with it." He hesitated. "That's not true. I'm still dealing with it."

"And you don't trust women anymore."

He grimaced. "That's a little more bluntly than I'd have put it."

"But it's the truth, all the same." She glanced out the window. It was snowing again. "And here I am with a ready-made family."

His heart jumped and fell. "Abby…"

"I dated a very nice man in Denver, not too many months after my brother and his wife were killed," she went on without looking at him. "He said that I was a lovely woman, and he'd love to get involved with me. But that there would be no future in it because of Lucy. He didn't want to raise another man's child. He didn't want the responsibility."

He felt sick to his stomach when she said that. He winced.

"So it's not a surprise," she continued, and even managed to smile. "I'm not giving up Lucy for anyone. She and Hannah and I have a good life, a good income, a place to live and a community of friends," she added. "I'm content. I'm sure that you are, too. You like your own space and a routine that's familiar. So…well, I mean, I wasn't planning to stalk you or anything," she blurted out.

"Abby." It was almost a groan of guilt.

"Look, there's Julia, sweeping off the porch," she said quickly, indicating Horace Whatley's front porch.

He forced himself to look calm. He felt anything but. "Yes. That's her," he said, parking in front of the steps on the newly paved drive.

The house was an old ranch house. It had been in really bad shape when Whatley had purchased it, but now it had a paint job, obvious repairs, and it looked both welcoming and sprawling. The long porch had a swing and several chairs, including a rocking chair. Julia was busy sweeping the last of the autumn leaves, and some stray snowflakes, off the porch.

"Hi, Sheriff," Julia called as he and Abby got out of the patrol car. "Isn't that Abby?" she added. The smile widened. "It's so good to see you! How is Horace, Sheriff?"

"He's doing fine," he was quick to assure her as he and Abby went up onto the porch. He drew in a long breath. "Julia, I have to ask you some questions and they won't be nice ones."

She grimaced. "I already know that it was my pie that put him in the hospital," she said in a sad tone. "If you want to arrest me…"

"Good Lord, no," he said at once.

She caught her breath. "But it was my pie, and you're here…"

He smiled reassuringly. "I just want to know about how the pie traveled, if anyone had access to it, stuff like that," he said. "Julia, you're the last person on earth I'd suspect of trying to poison anyone."

She let out a held breath. "Oh, thank God. I've just been so worried about him," she added self-consciously. She pushed back a strand of dark hair that had escaped the tight bun she kept it in. "He's the kindest human being I've ever known."

"Yes, he is."

"But he's done some crazy things," Julia added, frowning. "He's not deliberately mean, and he only told fibs because he wanted to fit in here so badly," she persisted. "He's never had a real home until now or any place where he really belonged. He's done such a good job with the house and the cattle."

"You're preaching to the choir," he said gently. "I know Horace's good points. Nobody holds his actions against him. He's greatly treasured. I can't tell you how many local citizens have volunteered to act as character witnesses if he needs them."

"There will have to be a trial, I guess," Julia said sadly. "Come in and have coffee, and I'll tell you all I know about my pie," she added. "It's cold out here."

"It will get colder, the weatherman says," Abby added, smiling. "And more snow is in the forecast."

"Well, it's Wyoming," Cody replied on a chuckle. "Snow and cold sort of winter here."

"True," Julia had to agree.

Over coffee at the kitchen table, Julia went over the trans-
port of her pie to the sheriff's office.

"Nobody touched it except me," she said, sipping black
coffee. "I gave it to the jailer and had him cut a slice of it
while I watched."

Cody's mind alerted. "Were you there the whole time he
was cutting it?"

She frowned. "Well, actually, no. There was this small
blonde woman in a uniform," she added. "She said she needed
to tell the jailer something for you, so I went and talked to
Horace until they got done."

Abby's heart jumped when Julia said that. She was jealous of
the little blonde. Ridiculous, because Cody had already made
it clear that he wasn't interested in getting involved with Abby.

Cody saw a path where the jailer and the blonde met; not
a nice one. "I'm going to take that testimony down. I'll have
it typed and you'll need to come in and sign it," he told her.

"Or I could bring it out here for you and let her sign it with
witnesses. I'm a notary public," Abby added, because she'd
never shared that with him.

His eyebrows went up.

She felt silly so she averted her eyes. It was like bragging.
"It's handy to have a notary in our office," she added quickly.

"I wasn't criticizing," Cody said, and the softness of his
deep voice made her pulse race.

"There was one other thing," Julia told him. "Horace said
that blonde woman had been in the office a couple of times
when you weren't there." She bit her lower lip and looked at
Cody imploringly. "Sheriff, there's a lot of gossip about you
and her, but she looks pretty shady to me. She was talking to
that jailer like he was a dog."

"Could you hear what she was saying?" Cody asked.

She shook her head. "But she was mad. You could tell."

"Thanks, Julia, for the coffee and the information. If you'll jot all that down, I'll take it back to the office with me."

"I'll be very happy to," Julia replied.

"No need, I can take dictation, and I'm quick," Abby said. She pulled out her cell phone. "I have a recording app. If you'll just repeat what you told me, I can type it up at the office. I know it will be all right with Mr. Owens, if the sheriff doesn't mind?"

"I don't mind, Abby," he said softly, and he smiled. "Thanks."

"Sure." She cleared her throat, hating the soft blush that turned her delicate features red, and pulled up her recording app.

They were on their way back to town fifteen minutes later.

"That was good coffee," Abby said after a minute.

"Very good." He glanced at her. "How are Lucy and Hannah?"

"Just the same. Lucy misses seeing you," she blurted out.

He drew in a breath as they drove closer to town. "I was trying to tell you, on the way here, that I haven't dealt with Debby's infidelity yet. I was in shock when I came home from Denver with the truth of the matter. It's taken a while for it to hit me. We were married for two years. I was deeply in love for the only time in my life, and I thought I had the perfect marriage. I never dreamed that she had another life in Denver, that she was really in love with another man."

Abby spoke hesitantly, because she could see the pain in his taut face. "How did you know Anyu was meant for the doctor?"

Cody drew in a breath. "I went to see him and he told me all about it. There was a message that Debby left, just before she died. It was that the most important man in her life was to have the puppy. I noticed that when I went to get Anyu, the nurse who had her—Debby's friend—was surprised and almost didn't let the dog go with me. I didn't think anything of it at the time. But now, it makes sense. See, I didn't know that the most important man in Debby's life was her mentor, the neurologist."

"I'm so sorry, Cody," Abby said, and meant it.

"I felt like an utter fool," he said. "I still feel that way. I was sold out in the worst possible way. I'd have given her a divorce if she'd asked for it. But she needed to be married so nobody would suspect she and the doctor were running around on their respective mates." He hesitated. "The doctor said that his wife had threatened to make up lies about him and his daughter if he cheated on her. So he had to keep it quiet. There was no possibility of divorce on his part." He stopped at a traffic light and glanced at Abby. "I felt sorry for the damned man. He was as miserable as I was. He loved her as much as I did. That was confusing and only made things worse. I wanted to hate him. And I couldn't."

"I've never had anybody sell me out," she confided. "Except maybe my dad, because he drank to excess and he was cruel when he drank. It was hard for me to come back here, with that history in Catelow. Small towns," she added with a smile, "where everybody knows everything about you. But nobody even mentions my past. It makes it easier. Lucy was miserable in Denver. So was I. We're both happy here."

"I'm glad of that. And I'm sorry I've been so distant with all of you." His lips compressed as the light changed and he drove on. "I've had the thing with Debby, and Mr. Whatley, and Lassiter for what seems half a lifetime."

"Lassiter?" she asked abruptly.

"He's after my girl," he said shortly.

She swallowed and looked out the window. "Oh, yes. The little blonde trooper."

"Not the trooper. You!"

She actually gasped as he pulled into a vacant business's parking lot, stopped the car, put it in Park, and reached for her.

"Cody..." was all she managed to get out before he was kissing her. Not the soft, sweet, gentle kisses of before, but passionate and insistent and consuming. She went under without even a protest, so much in love that it never occurred to her to ask him to stop.

He nibbled her upper lip as he fought for control. "Sorry," he whispered. "I had a weak moment."

"Did...you?" she faltered, watching his mouth move against hers.

"Umhmm," he whispered, and brushed his lips with maddening patience over hers.

"Do...do you think you could have another weak moment? If I asked," she whispered back.

She saw the faint smile before he curled her close and kissed her into a breathless, wondrous silence. It was a feast after starvation, a drink after hours in the desert. Abby had never known such utter delight. And if the long, insistent kisses she was getting were any indication, Cody was feeling something similar.

It wasn't until his phone started ringing that he managed to lift his mouth away from hers.

He let her go with obvious reluctance and dug for the phone on his duty belt. "Sheriff Banks," he said curtly.

"And where are you, Sheriff?" a sensuous voice drawled. "Your jailer gave me your number. I came over for coffee and advice. Are you available?"

"I'll be there in about ten minutes," he said and hung up.

Abby was still gaping at him. The unexpected interlude had knocked all casual conversation right out of her.

"I have to get back to the office," he said. He sounded as breathless as Abby felt.

"Of course," she replied.

His dark eyes slid over her, seeing all the little signs that she might not even know gave her hunger for him away. He saw many. A slow, sensuous smile bloomed on his hard, swollen mouth.

"We might go skating one weekend at the local rink. Lucy likes that, doesn't she?"

She nodded.

"I'm sorry," he said softly. "I've been so wrapped up in myself and my problems that I haven't wanted people around. Even people I care about."

She shifted in the seat. "Of course. You've got a murder investigation going."

"It has tentacles everywhere," he said, cranking the car as they both put their seat belts back on. "I have suspects living right here in Catelow who may face charges in Denver and even Florida."

"Wow," she said softly.

He glanced at her just before he pulled out into traffic. "You may see and hear things that give you a wrong impression of what I'm actually doing. Try not to prejudge. I'm between a rock and a hard place, trying to put all the pieces together."

She just nodded. "Okay."

"And you may have some extra company on the ranch. Lassiter has a friend who's between jobs. He's asked him to come up here and help out. He's a professional."

She was studying him hungrily, adoring the hard lines of his handsome face. "A professional what?" she asked suddenly.

He grinned. "I don't know. But he'll keep my three girls safe."

"From what?" she wanted to know.

He stopped in the parking lot at her office, cut the engine, and turned to her. "When I start making arrests, and that's going to happen pretty soon, you and Lucy and Hannah may be right on the firing line with me, not to mention my dog." His face was grim. "One of the suspects has a reputation for seeking vengeance on the softest targets." His eyes met hers. "Nobody's hurting my girls."

As he said it, he tugged her face under his and kissed her slowly, with a tenderness that was breathtaking. "And no more Sunday rides with Lassiter, got that?" he whispered against her mouth.

She was struggling to breathe. "Well, what about you and that pretty little blonde?" she blurted out and then flushed.

His eyes looked deep into hers. "I was married for two years. I never cheated on my wife. For six years I've been mourning her. Just a few weeks ago, I discovered that my marriage was a lie. I'm still dealing with that. But I will deal with it," he added solemnly. "I just need a little time. You have to trust me. Things are in motion that are going to look bad to you. I can't tell you what's going on. You have to balance what I'm telling you with what I may have to do in the line of duty while I'm getting evidence."

She thought she understood. Probably he meant he was going to be hanging out with people like Mr. Owens's nephew.

"You're going to be social with some lawbreakers?"

He shook his head. His forefinger traced her pretty mouth, faintly swollen from the pressure of his own. "It's going to look like I've given you up for good. Can you handle that? Because it's a lie. It just may not appear to be one, on the surface."

Her heart was shaking her with its beat.

His big hand went behind her head and pulled it closer. "I've missed you," he whispered, and kissed her again, hungrily, his hands framing her face.

"I've missed you…too," she managed between kisses. "So have Lucy and Hannah."

"It will all be over soon, I promise," he said softly, searching her eyes. "And I have no problem about Lucy, just in case you wondered." He smiled. "But I think several children would be fun," he added involuntarily.

She caught her breath. "I hated being by myself."

"Me, too." His mouth brushed over hers one last time. "I have to go to work. It's not going to look like work. So whatever you see or hear gossiped about, take it with a grain of salt."

"Okay," she replied.

He drew in a long breath and smiled. "It's like coming home from a long journey."

"What is?" she asked as she started to open her door.

"Kissing you, honey," he replied with soft, hungry eyes.

She tried to find words and couldn't. He'd never called her a pet name. Nobody had. At least, no man.

"I'll be in touch. You watch your back," he added quietly. "Don't go anywhere alone. Don't let Lucy go anywhere alone, even on the ranch. That goes for Hannah as well."

"You're scaring me, Cody."

"I don't mean to. I just want you safe."

She drew in a breath. "Okay," she said. "But I want you safe, too. So you be careful."

He smiled slowly. "I've never had more reason for wanting to be careful."

She smiled back, got out and closed the door.

Cody drove down to his office.

The little blonde trooper was sitting in the chair by his desk. "You're late," she chided. "You said ten minutes."

"Some things take longer than we anticipate," he replied, getting out of his shepherd's coat. "What can I do for you?"

"I was thinking a cup of cappuccino would be nice."

He smiled as he sat down. "It would, but I'm expecting a call from the FBI lab. That's why I'm late," he lied. "They'll be phoning me within the hour over some evidence I sent them."

"Oh? Evidence in a case?" she wanted to know.

"Yes. A poisoning case." He leaned back in his chair. "And a murder in Denver," he added.

She didn't react, except that her face tautened a bit. "Isn't that out of your jurisdiction?"

"Well, normally, it would be. However, the poison used on one of my inmates is identical to the poison that was used to kill a woman in Denver." He smiled slowly. "It's derived from a very rare plant found only in South America."

This time she did react. She got up from her chair, still smiling. "Well, it sounds fascinating, but I have to go to work. Maybe we could have a rain check on the coffee?" she added, sounding very cosmopolitan.

"Next time you're in town, call me," he said easily. "I'm here almost every day."

She forced a smile. "Okay, then. See you."

"See you."

When she was out of sight, Cody went back into the detention section where his jailer was sitting, looking frightened and uncertain.

"Problems with the inmates?" Cody asked him.

"No, sir. It's all quiet."

The man looked so anxious that Cody pulled him to one side.

"Okay. What's wrong?" he asked curtly.

"Nothing..."

"Don't lie to me," Cody said shortly. "Tell me what's going on."

"It's that blonde lady," he ground out.

"Which one?" he asked, fearing it might be a threat to Abby.

"That one who says she's a trooper." His eyes met Cody's.

"She's no trooper, sir. I know one of the troopers who works Carne County. I asked him about her. He says they don't have any blonde lady troopers."

Cody wasn't surprised. Small communities thrived on gossip. "What about her?"

He grimaced. "She keeps making me do stuff."

Cody's eyebrows arched. "What sort of stuff?"

"Well, she made me give that soda to Mr. Whatley, and it was already opened. You know, that time he was poisoned. I said something, and she asked me if I..." He broke off.

"If you...?" Cody prompted.

The jailer took a deep breath. "I've got a record," he confessed and flushed. "I hacked the files and changed a felony to a misdemeanor in my record. I'm sorry," he added. "My wife's pregnant and she can't work. I had to get a job and who's going to hire an ex-con?" he asked miserably.

Cody felt bad for him. The man was obviously troubled by the lie he'd told. "What were you in for?" he asked.

"I hit a man who insulted my wife," he said heavily. "He fell onto a pile of wooden pallets and broke his hip. I didn't mean to hurt him that bad, but I hit him with a big piece of lumber instead of my fist. They said it was a weapon and I couldn't afford a lawyer. So I went to jail. I got out in a year on good behavior, but that record will follow me forever." He took a breath. "The little blonde found out. She said if I didn't do what she said, she'd tell you."

"Well, good on you for confessing first," Cody said bluntly. "And just for the record, I don't look at what a man's done, I look at what he's doing. What else did she make you do?"

"She had me try to listen to what you said to Mr. Whatley. And she sent me out to get her some coffee when I was fixing lunch plates to serve to the inmates, when you weren't here. It didn't look like she'd done anything, but that was when Mr. Whatley ate the pie and got so sick."

He looked at the sheriff with dead eyes. "So if you want to go ahead and fire me, it's okay. I deserve it."

Cody put a hand on his shoulder. "You've just become a material witness in a murder investigation, and I have no plans to fire you."

The other man looked stunned. "You mean, I can still work here?"

"Of course you can," he replied. "For God's sake, do you realize how many ex-felons we have in Catelow? And they've all got jobs. We're not a community. We're a big family."

The jailer looked near to tears. "That's what my wife and I are finding out. People have brought her baby blankets and little baby clothes, and even a car seat for when the baby's older. People who don't even know us! It wasn't like this in Phoenix. That's where we're from. I thought when I got out of jail, this would be a good place to live. She and I picked Catelow on the map with a pen. Out of nowhere." He smiled at the sheriff. "Gosh, didn't we do well?"

Cody grinned. "You did, indeed. Now how about seeing to the prisoners while I go talk to Mr. Whatley?"

"Sheriff, it will be my pleasure."

Cody patted him on the back and went on down to Horace Whatley's cell.

"Good to see you, Sheriff," Horace told him, smiling. "How are things going out at my ranch?"

"Fine," Cody said. "I had to interview Julia about the pie. I knew she didn't poison you, though," he added.

Horace blinked. "I know that. But how do you know that?"

Cody chuckled. "Do you know that Julia is in love with you?"

CHAPTER SIXTEEN

Horace Whatley's eyes grew as large as saucers and his breath seemed to sigh out all at once. "Julia...loves me?" he exclaimed. He flushed and smiled.

"Yes, she does," Cody said, chuckling, "and she makes the best coffee I've ever tasted."

"She loves me." Horace wasn't hearing the sheriff. He sat on his bunk and just stared into space, still smiling.

Cody turned to the other cell and opened it to let Lassiter out.

"Things coming to a head?" Lassiter asked.

"Like a whirlwind. The jailer's become a material witness. He can place my little blonde friend right here just before Horace was poisoned, both times. She was playing him. He's got a record."

"No wonder he always looked so harassed. Going to fire him?"

"Hell, no. He can cook." He chuckled. "He's not a bad jailer, either. The inmates like him."

"I noticed. The food here is pretty good."

"Thanks. We do our best."

"Where do we go from here?" Lassiter asked when they were back in Cody's office with the door closed.

"We have enough evidence to get a warrant," he said. "I just want to make sure you've got somebody watching Abby and Lucy and Hannah before I go talk to a circuit judge."

"He got in last night. He's working as a wrangler for Abby's foreman. He applied for the job a few days ago. I understand the foreman was pretty desperate. Fortunately, my friend comes from a ranching background and he can ride anything with four legs."

"Abby doesn't know who he is?" Cody asked.

Lassiter shook his head. "We thought it would work better if she didn't."

"Does he have a concealed carry permit and can he shoot if he has to?" he asked.

"He's a fed," Lassiter confided.

"Good grief!"

"He's on vacation. Sort of. Anyway, his superiors gave him a few weeks off while he's recuperating from a shoot-out, and he's doing me this favor."

"What sort of fed is he?" Cody wanted to know.

Lassiter just grinned. "Not your normal sort, for sure. Need to know. You don't. No offense."

Cody sighed. "As long as he keeps my girls safe, I don't care."

"Finally noticed that Abby was in love with you, I guess?"

Cody's eyebrows arched.

"And I guess you don't know that everybody in town and a dog knew it before you did."

Cody just laughed. "I knew she was fond of me." He drew in a long breath and felt as if he'd just won the lottery. "Well!"

"Don't tell her I told you," Lassiter warned. "She's my friend. I don't have many."

Cody gave him a curious look.

"It was a stage kiss, to throw your deputy off the track. Only that. No bells, no whistles, nothing. Okay?"

Cody relaxed. He smiled. "Okay."

"So, all the players are in place, your girls are safe, you've got an eyewitness. What do you do now?" Lassiter teased.

Cody picked up the phone. "I get a warrant, that's what I do," he replied with twinkling dark eyes.

Fortunately for Cody, the female judge he saw was a law-and-order stickler. When she heard Cody out, and had the facts of the case, she didn't even hesitate to give him an arrest warrant for Jack Owens, along with one for the so-called eyewitness who'd seen Horace Whatley robbing another man, and also an arrest warrant for the blonde so-called trooper who was suspected of poisoning not only Horace Whatley, but Candy Henry in Denver. Of course, the trooper couldn't be charged with a Denver murder in Catelow, where she'd only been charged with attempted murder. But Cody was willing to bet that federal charges would be filed in the Denver murder, in which case they'd ask for extradition and Cody would ask the judge to grant it. Better to have her on trial for murder than attempted murder. Plus, federal charges carried higher penalties.

He took his deputy with him when he went to make the arrests. Jack Owens was on the porch when Cody drove up. He looked half-drunk and surly.

"Well, hello, Sheriff Banks," he said. "What brings you out this way? Want to arrest me for jaywalking?" he added sarcastically.

Cody shook his head as he nodded to the deputy, who swung Jack to his feet and whirled him around to cuff him.

"What in the world are you doing?" Jack demanded.

"Arresting you for conspiracy to commit murder," Cody said. "And this time, your uncle won't be able to pull any strings on your behalf." He turned to the deputy. "Put him in the car and come back quick."

Cody had his pistol out as he heard voices inside. He started in, with the deputy running toward him, his own weapon out.

Cody identified himself as he walked into the house, and before the two people in the living room could react, they were held at gunpoint while the deputy handcuffed them both with the extra sets of cuffs Cody had provided.

"Sheriff, what in the world do you think you're doing?" the little blonde asked plaintively. "I'm an officer of the law!"

"Funny thing, your boss says he doesn't have any blonde troopers," Cody replied. "And we already know that your dad is a botanist in South America. We've traced the poison used in an attempted murder to a plant that's only native to that continent."

The blonde's face turned ugly. "You'll never get me to trial," she said in a soft, menacing tone. "And you'll pay for this outrage, in ways you'll never suspect until it's too late."

"Do your worst," Cody replied. He turned to his deputy. "Read them their rights. We'll do this by the book so there won't be any loopholes."

"You got it," the deputy replied. "I already read Jack his rights."

"Good man."

"You'll all pay for this," the blonde threatened.

"No. You will," Cody replied, and he didn't smile. "You're wanted in Denver in connection with a murder. The feds have evidence and they'll start extradition proceedings as soon as you're booked into custody here."

"Denver?" She faltered just a bit. "There's no way they could get proof of anything! I've never even been to Denver!"

"You can take that up with a jury, in time," he returned coldly.

"There's no evidence!" she persisted.

"They exhumed the victim," Cody said, watching her expression. "She was poisoned. They traced her steps the night she died. They interviewed witnesses at the restaurant." He actually smiled as her expression changed. "There are also charge slips at a local gas station and a credit card was used to make purchases the same day."

She didn't say another word. The deputy took her out to his own patrol car and put his two handcuffed suspects in back.

Cody phoned his investigator and had him get his coworkers on the way to the Owens house to go over it for clues. Before he'd left the judge's chambers, he'd also requested, and been given, a search warrant listing every single piece of potential evidence Cody could concoct, including a warrant to impound and search the blonde's car.

It was going to be the tightest case he'd ever worked. He wanted to make certain that he did everything by the book, so there would be no way for the blonde or Jack Owens to weasel out of the charges on a technicality.

Cody went back in the house, where the nervous so-called eyewitness, Cappy Blarden, was sitting on the sofa with his hands clenched in his lap.

Like most law enforcement officers, Cody was equipped with a camera that recorded his every move. He stood in front of the younger man and just waited, not speaking, with a cold look in his dark eyes.

"She made me do it," he blurted out. "That blonde woman. She made me testify that I'd seen Horace Whatley rob the bank. I never saw him there!"

"How did she make you do it?" he asked.

He swallowed, hard. "She slipped poison into my mother's coffee at the local café," he said huskily. "And told me she had an antidote that she'd give Mom if I agreed to do what she told me. Of course I agreed. I love my mom," he said, averting his face. "She said she had more poison and next time there wouldn't be an antidote if I tried to back out."

"So you never saw Horace Whatley rob anyone?"

"No," he said heavily, looking up at the sheriff. "Will I go to jail?"

"That's not up to me. But you will have to come with me now," he added. "Giving false testimony against an innocent person is a crime."

"I figured that." He stood up. "At least, I won't have to worry about my mom anymore."

He turned around so that Cody could cuff him. "Your mother should be safe. I'm going to ask for a high bond on our blonde so-called trooper, not to mention on Owens. Conspiracy to commit murder is a felony."

"Yeah. I figured that. I hope they never get out of prison," he added coldly. "I never put a foot wrong in my life," he said. "I guess I'll go up for conspiracy, too."

"Get a good lawyer and plead coercion. You've never been convicted of a crime, Cappy," Cody said quietly. "You'll most likely get first offender status, regardless of the charges."

His prisoner had a bad reputation in town for telling lies, but certainly he'd never tried to harm anyone. That would go in his favor. Cody put the younger man in the squad car and drove him to the detention center.

When the blonde was arraigned, it came out that her legal name was Domenica Alvarez, of Manaus, Brazil. She was arrogant, denying any involvement and accusing the sheriff of everything from improper advances to false arrest.

The judge ignored her and continued to explain the charges. She pleaded not guilty and was taken back to her cell. As she passed Cody, she smiled coldly. "Look to your loved ones, Sheriff," she said huskily. "It would be a shame if anything happened to them."

He only smiled.

She averted her face and kept walking.

Jack Owens was a different story. He broke down and cried when he was read the list of charges. Cody felt sorry for him. He'd been hopelessly spoiled by his father, and now there was nobody to stand up with him.

Except there was. James Owens came up to the bench and took his place beside his nephew, who looked first surprised and then grateful. He was still crying. James commented that he'd act as his nephew's attorney for trial. The judge nodded and then smiled sadly. James Owens had never done anything illegal in his life. But his nephew had brought shame onto his family name. In spite of that, blood was blood. Jack was the only relative he had left.

He spoke to Cody after his nephew left the courtroom in custody. "I know it's going to be a rough trial, and I'm certain that he'll have to serve time. But I can't desert him. He's the only family I have left."

Cody patted him on the shoulder. "I know. Family is family. We do what we have to, to keep going."

James cocked his head. "What about you and Abby?" he asked.

Cody chuckled. "If I eat enough crow, I might get invited back over there."

"Just don't turn your back, and watch your surroundings. That Alvarez woman is dangerous. I don't think you have all her accomplices in custody. There was a bank robbery that I'm certain Horace Whatley didn't commit."

"I know that. I have video evidence from the eyewitness that he didn't see Horace rob anyone. He was threatened by the Alvarez woman. She poisoned his mother."

James whistled. "Will they testify?"

"He will. I'll have to talk to his mother. But the Denver charges are the major ones. That's felony murder. This is conspiracy to commit murder."

"I get the picture. You'd rather she faced federal charges in Denver?"

Cody nodded, his face grim. "I want her out of town before she starts looking for ways to revenge herself on me."

"Make sure Abby's men know to watch out for her," James suggested.

Cody smiled. "I'm two steps ahead of you. And I let Lassiter out of jail yesterday. He's sleeping in Abby's bunkhouse," he added in a whisper.

James chuckled. "You'd better watch that young man around Abby. He's considered something of a catch by the women in my office."

"I noticed. But I've got the inside track there," he added smugly and laughed.

James just smiled.

Abby was all thumbs as she put supper on the table. Lassiter had been invited, along with his shadowy friend and Cody Banks.

Hannah saw her nervousness and wondered if it was Lassiter who was causing it. Then she saw the looks that Abby was exchanging with Cody and grinned to herself.

"That looks good," Cody said. "I love beef stew."

"Me, too," Lassiter agreed.

"You don't mind that I brought Alexander with me?" Cody asked, indicating the sweet old malamute who was sharing the fireplace in the living room with Lucy's husky, Snow.

"Not at all. He's so sweet," Abby replied with a smile.

"Snow likes him," Lucy piped in, grinning at Cody.

"I think she does, Lucy," Cody told her.

"You didn't call Bart back about that dance, Abby," Hannah reminded her suddenly.

Cody's eyes glittered. Abby saw that and felt her heart lift. "Yes, I did," she replied without looking at Hannah. "I said no."

Cody relaxed. He smiled slowly, his eyes holding Abby's for so long that she felt as if she was floating.

"Abby, the rolls?" Hannah prompted.

Abby shook herself mentally. "Rolls. Right. Coming up."

She went back into the kitchen, flushed and all thumbs. But she was smiling.

Dinner was fun. Lassiter was recounting past cases that had ironic twists. Cody countered with similar cases he'd worked on. The stranger, Lassiter's friend, said little. He cleaned his plate, sipped coffee, thanked Abby quietly, and went out the back door.

"He doesn't talk much, your friend," Abby said to Lassiter.

"He's a man of few words," Lassiter agreed. "But he's very good at his job."

"He had a pistol in a holster under his flannel shirt," Hannah noted.

"He has a concealed carry permit. Don't worry," Lassiter added. "He won't fire unless he's fired on."

"I don't like guns. Sorry," Hannah apologized.

"No problem." He smiled at her.

"Abby doesn't mind them," Cody said, his eyes meeting Abby's.

"No, I don't," she replied with a long, happy sigh.

"Good thing," Lassiter said.

Cody nodded.

"When are you going deer hunting, Cody?" Hannah asked as they finished the meal and were working through second cups of coffee.

He frowned. "Why do you ask?"

"Venison stew," she said, licking her lips.

"Venison stew?" Lassiter asked, curious.

"When he goes deer hunting, he makes a huge pot of venison stew and invites anyone close to him to share it," Hannah said. She closed her eyes. "I dream about that stew. Nobody can make it like Cody."

He chuckled. "I'm flattered. I'll do my best to get a nice, fat buck. And I'll make a vat of it this time."

"I'll hold you to that," Hannah teased. "Now, I've got to get the dishes done. And Miss Lucy has to have her bath and go to bed."

"Yes, she does," Abby agreed.

"But Cody's here and his dog is, and I don't want to go to bed," Lucy wailed.

"I'll bring Alexander back over soon," Cody promised. "How would you like to go ice-skating Saturday with your aunt and me?" he added.

"Oh, that would be so nice!" Lucy reached up to hug him and kissed his tanned cheek. "We really missed you," she told him with wide, laughing eyes. "Aunt Abby was just so sad all the time…"

"Lucy," Abby interrupted, flushing, "you need to go and have your bath. Okay?"

"Okay, Aunt Abby." She kissed her aunt, and then Hannah. "Can I tell Alexander and Snow good-night?"

"Go ahead," Abby said with resignation and a short laugh. "Oh, procrastination," she said under her breath.

Lucy sat down between the big dogs and hugged them both. Alexander laid his head on her little shoulder and licked her.

"He's a love sponge," Cody remarked, chuckling. "He's turned into a super pet. He's a lot of company." His face softened. "Poor old fellow. He was lying on the side of the road, leg broken, in a horrible condition. The vet asked me if I wanted him put down. I couldn't," he added quietly. "It was the way he looked at me with those soulful eyes. As if he'd given up on people, on life."

"He's beautiful, cast and all," Abby replied. "I'd have done the same thing."

He looked at her. "I know you would."

Lassiter cleared his throat. "I enjoyed supper, thanks very much, but I really need to get back to my motel room and touch base with a few people."

Abby grinned at him. "Okay. You can come back anytime you like."

"Thanks," he said, smiling. "So long, Lucy," he added, as the little girl came running back in. She ran to Lassiter and held out her arms. He picked her up, laughing, and kissed her cheek. She kissed him back.

"Bye," she said. "You come back to see us, okay?"

"Okay, sweetheart," he promised, and put her down.

Abby, watching, was surprised. He liked children. He didn't seem the sort of man who would. Well, actually, Cody didn't, either, but Lucy was already sitting on his lap, telling him about a picture she'd drawn in school.

Abby and Hannah walked Lassiter to the door. He waved as he got into his car and drove away.

"Lucy, bath?" Abby prompted.

"Aw, do I have to, Aunt Abby?" she asked plaintively as Cody put her down.

"Yes, you have to," she said, and she smiled.

"You have to tuck me in."

"I always do that," Abby reminded her.

"Can't Cody come, too?" she added, looking at him.

Abby hesitated.

"I'd like that," Cody said. He smiled at her.

"Okay! I'll go take my bath right now!" Lucy promised.

"I'll run the water," Hannah said when Abby started toward the bathroom.

"Thanks, Hannah," Abby called after her.

"No problem," she called back.

Abby was left alone in the room with Cody. He caught her hand in his and pulled her gently to him. He stood close to her, just looking down at her radiant face, her bright eyes. Yes, he thought solemnly, she did love him. Amazing that he hadn't noticed that. He recalled what Lassiter had said, that if a man she loved lost everything, Abby would stay right there beside him, helping him recover.

He bent and brushed his mouth softly over hers. "You'd never sell a man out," he whispered. "You're too softhearted. I don't know why it took me so long to realize that."

"You were busy with your friend in law enforcement," she murmured sadly.

His lips nibbled at hers, causing delicious shock waves up and down her body. "She's not my friend," he whispered. "I arrested her and she's awaiting extradition to Denver in one of my jail cells."

"Wh-what?" she exclaimed, her eyes widening.

"She poisoned Horace Whatley, but you don't know that," he said firmly.

"Oh, my goodness! But she's in law enforcement…!"

"She's not," he interrupted. "She's involved with Bobby Grant, the man who wants Horace dead so he can bulldoze Nita Whatley into marrying him. After which, she'd have a convenient fatal accident."

"Good heavens!"

His big hands caught her waist and pulled her to him, riveting her to the length of his powerful body. "You smell nice," he whispered as his mouth settled on hers once again, suddenly insistent and devouring.

She moaned huskily as the fever burned high and bright. Her arms went under his and around him and she held on tight.

They didn't hear the first two coughs, so Hannah closed the hall door. Hard.

They jumped apart, breathless, looking like two deer in the headlights at night.

Hannah bit her lip to keep from laughing. "Lucy's had her bath and she's in bed, waiting for both of you," she added.

"Had her bath." Abby was completely out of it. "But she just went into the bathroom."

"Fifteen minutes ago," Hannah drawled, giving them a speaking look. She grinned.

Cody cleared his throat. He was having some discomfort, but multiplication tables saved him before it became visible.

"We should go tuck her in," Abby said.

"We should." Cody linked her fingers into his and smiled down at her.

"Okay," she replied, breathlessly happy.

He grinned. She was pretty when she laughed. She made him feel young, full of hope, she gave him a new lease on life. He'd become very fond of her since she'd returned to Catelow.

They went into Lucy's room and stood beside the bed while she said her prayers. Abby tucked her in and kissed her. So did Cody.

Abby clicked her fingers and Snow jumped onto the foot of the bed. She smiled at Lucy with her whole heart, and her face was radiant with love.

Cody felt the ground shake under his feet as he watched her. She was the kindest woman he'd ever known. She reminded him of his mother; not that he had that sort of feelings for her. She turned and looked at him and his heart jumped up into his throat. He stared at her as if he'd been hit in the stomach with a bat. Why hadn't he realized it before? He... loved her. He really, truly loved her. And he hadn't known it. Not until now, when he saw her so loving with Lucy and thought suddenly of another child, his child, being tucked in at night. His breath caught audibly and there was a faint flush, high on his cheekbones. He looked stunned.

Abby looked up at him worriedly. "Are you all right?" she asked softly.

All right? He was submerged in wonder. Drowning in fantasy. He smiled slowly. "I'm all right. I've never been better in my life."

Abby didn't understand. But she smiled at him and then turned back to Lucy. "Sleep tight," she told the little girl, "and don't let the bedbugs bite!"

Lucy laughed. "Aunt Abby, we don't have any bedbugs."

Abby wrinkled her nose. "Sleep tight anyway," she said, and grinned. She kissed Lucy once more. "I'll see you in the morning."

"Okay. Night!"

"Good night," Cody and Abby both echoed.

Abby turned out the light and closed the door, leaving the two of them alone in the darkened hall.

Cody pulled her close and just held her, rocking her in his strong arms. It was like coming home. He'd never experienced such a feeling of tenderness, not even when he thought he was deeply in love with Debby. That was nothing like this.

Abby didn't say a word. She stood quietly in his embrace, loving the way he smelled, the way he felt against her. She never wanted to move out of his arms.

But after a while, and reluctantly, he let her go, brushing a soft kiss across her mouth.

"We have to exercise a little restraint," he pointed out.

"We do?" she murmured absently, her eyes on his hard mouth.

He cleared his throat. "Abby, men can't really hide their emotions when they're wearing close-fitting trousers," he muttered bluntly.

It took Abby a few seconds to realize what he was saying.

She flushed and then laughed, and then she hit him on his broad chest.

He grinned at her.

"Okay," she said. "How about coffee then?"

"Coffee sounds good." He bent to her ear. "And when we don't have to worry about witnesses, I won't care if my trousers tell on me."

She burst out laughing.

He linked his fingers with hers and led her into the kitchen, where Hannah gave them a knowing smile and poured coffee into two mugs.

Abby had never been so happy in her life. She loved Cody deathlessly, and it looked like he shared those feelings. At least, he wasn't backing away anymore. Perhaps he really was able to deal with Debby's betrayal and go forward.

A happy Horace Whatley was released from jail as the former eyewitness, Cappy Blarden, was processed and placed in detention. Horace went home to a beaming Julia, who met him at the door with a homemade pie and an expression that made him feel as if he could walk on clouds. A number of local people came by in the next few days to wish him well, and one of them noticed that Julia was wearing a brand-new diamond ring on her ring finger.

On the weekend, Cody took Lucy and Abby ice-skating at the local rink.

He was good on skates. Really good. Abby just shook her head as he instructed Lucy on the correct way to get up from a fall, how to fall, how to do a snowplow, and half a dozen other essential pieces of information that even Abby hadn't known.

"How do you know so much about ice-skating?" she wanted to know.

"I took lessons, years ago," he said. "It was a way to get out of the house," he added, and Abby knew he was referring to his brutal, alcoholic father.

"You're really good on skates," she remarked, her eyes on Lucy, who was doing much better as she skated on the edge of the rink.

He moved closer and bent to her ear. "I'm really good at some other things, too," he whispered wickedly. "And very modest about it as well."

She laughed, looking up into his soft eyes. She got lost in them.

He brushed back a loose strand of hair as he searched her face with quiet, inquisitive eyes. "Abby..."

Before he could say anything, Lucy called to them.

"Aunt Abby, look what I can do!" And she demonstrated the snowplow that Cody had taught her, which she'd been painstakingly practicing.

"That looks great, sweetheart!" Abby called back.

Cody laughed at Abby's stricken expression. "We have all the time in the world to talk," he said quietly, searching her eyes. "For now, let's just skate and have a good time together."

She took a deep breath and her eyes twinkled. "Let's do that."

After a long afternoon, Cody drove them home in his truck. He was off duty, and dressed in khaki pants with a soft blue cotton shirt and his shepherd's coat and brown Stetson hat. The truck was a double cab, so Lucy had a place to sit in the back seat, and Abby sat up beside Cody.

Snow was falling. Catelow looked beautiful in the late afternoon, with the lights just coming on inside houses.

"It looks like a miniature village from up here," Abby sighed as they drove down the mountain toward Catelow. "One of those that people put around train sets. My best friend's brother had one of those. We used to turn out the lights in the room and turn on the lights in the little houses and watch the train go around."

"I bought a train set years ago, but I never had a place to run it."

"We got a big playroom in our house, Cody," Lucy told him. "You could put a train set in there and we could all watch it go!"

He laughed. "If Abby doesn't mind, we might...!"

The impact was terrible. The truck went off the road, skidding in the fresh snow. Cody managed to keep it upright, just, but there was broken glass everywhere and Lucy was crying.

Cody muttered some very bad words under his breath as his sharp eyes followed the big truck that had slammed into them. He pulled out his phone and called his deputy, giving a description of the vehicle that had hit them and ordering a BOLO for it. Meanwhile, he phoned the Catelow Police Department, because they were in the city limits and this was their jurisdiction.

The police chief, Bruce Eller, back from time off with his new baby, came himself, along with one of his patrol officers, Emmy Sawyer.

"Do you have any idea who hit you?" Eller asked as Cody helped a stunned and bruised Abby out of the front seat and a weeping Lucy out of the back. He held Lucy in his arms while he turned to the chief.

"I don't know who hit us, but I have a pretty good idea of who ordered it," Cody said. He indicated the sheer drop-off that he'd avoided. If the truck had rolled, all three occupants of the truck would have died instantly from the fall.

"Somebody who meant business," Eller agreed somberly. He winced at little Lucy's tearstained face. He had a little girl about the same age. "Let me run all of you over to the hospital and get you checked out."

"That's a good idea," Cody said, sliding an arm around a

shaken Abby as he cuddled Lucy. "It never hurts to be careful. Thanks."

"All in a day's work. Got a BOLO out?"

Cody nodded. "I phoned my deputy just after it happened and gave him a description of the truck. With any luck, they'll find it before it goes too far."

Just then, as they reached the chief's car, Cody's phone rang. He put Lucy in the back seat of the squad car with Abby and answered it.

"Banks," he said abruptly.

"And guess who we have in custody?" his undersheriff, Jeb, asked in a smug tone.

"I'll bite," Cody replied. "Who?"

"A convicted bank robber with a rap sheet as long as my arm, who told me that a blonde woman promised him two thousand dollars if he'd run you off the road. Paid in advance. With a wire transfer. And guess where the bank transfer came from?"

Cody was feeling better by the minute. "Florida?" he mused aloud.

"There," his deputy chuckled. "I knew you were psychic!"

CHAPTER SEVENTEEN

Cody was delighted at the turn of events. Apparently, his blonde prisoner had lost her temper to such an extent that she'd gotten careless. The wire transfer had been a really bad mistake, so they could now add an additional charge of attempted murder against her, not to mention her boyfriend, Bobby Grant. Within hours, the police chief in Florida had Grant in jail charged with conspiracy to commit murder. That charge would hold him until enough evidence was amassed to send him to Denver to stand trial for felony murder, along with his girlfriend, Domenica Alvarez.

Horace Whatley and Julia announced their engagement in the weekly newspaper, and were seen together frequently around town following Horace's release from jail and being judged innocent of the bank robbery charge. The actual bank robber would have that charge to face, as well as the assault on Cody and his passengers. Considering that he was already on parole for assault, he would go back to prison to serve his full term, plus facing additional time for the new charges.

But none of these things made much difference to Cody

and Abby, except that they'd eventually have to testify when the cases came to trial.

They went walking in the snow, all alone, having left Hannah to babysit Lucy and Snow and Alexander.

It was cold, but they had warm coats on and gloves. They held hands as they walked along a snowy path through the tall pines. Cody stopped and turned Abby to him, his dark eyes soft and hungry on her rosy-cheeked face.

"We get along good together," he began.

She smiled. "We do."

"We like the same things, we're both Methodist, we agree on politics…" He hesitated. It was a big step. In many ways, it was the biggest step he'd taken in his life. It was like walking off a cliff.

She put a gloved hand on his chest, over the shepherd's coat. "We can go along like this for a while," she said. She smiled. "There's no rush. We have all the time in the world."

He drew in a long breath. It was a life-changing event. But he was wary of Lassiter, regardless of the man's assurances that he had no romantic interest in Abby. He was also concerned that his cousin Bart was trying to take Abby on dates. If he hesitated too long, he'd lose her. And there wasn't another woman on earth like Abby. Not a single one.

He framed her face in his gloved hands and looked deeply into her eyes before he bent and touched his mouth to hers in the most tender kiss she'd ever had in her life. It was like a declaration of love in and of itself, even without his whispered "I love you, Abby," just before the kiss became passionate and insistent. He groaned.

She felt the hunger in him and smiled under the crush of his mouth, going on tiptoe to return the kiss.

He wrapped her up tight and just held her, rocked her in his arms. "I'm chock-full of senseless worry and apprehension," he confessed. "But I'm not going to risk losing you to another man! I can't make it without you, Abby," he whispered gruffly. He took a deep breath. "So, will you think about...marrying me?"

She shivered with the delight of her feelings and pressed closer. "How long?"

"Hmmm?"

"How long do you want me to think about it?" she persisted.

"Well...a few days maybe?"

"How about a few seconds?" she whispered and pushed up to rub her lips against his. "I will."

He held her tighter and lifted his head to look into her eyes. His twinkled. "You will, what?" he teased, all his worries about the future suddenly gone, like fog in sunlight.

She laughed. "I'll marry you."

He drew in a long breath and kissed her hungrily. "Say it," he whispered.

"I did..."

"No. Say the other thing."

It took her a minute to realize what he meant. She beamed as she lifted her face. "I love you," she said softly. "I always will. As long as I live. Longer."

He ground down on the pincushion in his throat. He'd never had much from Debby, no words of love, no promises, no tenderness. But this woman in his arms gave him all those things and a promise of happiness that made him soar like a sky bird.

"As long as I live," he echoed the words back to her. "Longer." He found her mouth again and they stood there a long time together in the snow until a loud voice asked them if they were auditioning to be snowpeople.

They lifted their heads and there was Hannah in an old coat and boots, pointing at them and laughing.

Then they realized what she meant. There was half an inch

of snow on Cody's hat and the shoulders of his coat and an equal amount on top of Abby's knitted cap and jacket. They looked at each other and burst out laughing.

"Coffee's hot!" Hannah called, grinning. "Come on inside. You can lock yourselves in the living room and do that in comfort."

"I always knew I loved you, Hannah!" Cody called.

She waved a hand at him and led the way back in.

Abby tried to convince her friends that a nice white suit would be fine for the wedding. Nobody listened. Horace Whatley chartered a plane to fly Abby down to Neiman Marcus in Dallas and brought Julia along to buy her own trousseau at the same time. There was a store in Denver, but Mr. Whatley was fond of a particular store in Dallas, so there they went, by appointment, to buy Abby a designer wedding gown, Mr. Whatley's wedding present to the couple.

Carried away by the selection, Abby finally chose one with mutton sleeves and a keyhole neckline, white satin with an overlay of imported lace, which was echoed in the fingertip veil. The dress had a long train, and it was fit for a princess. Not only was she encouraged to buy the dress, but Julia, at Mr. Whatley's urging, took her to buy fine silk gowns and negligees and delicate slippers, and also undies, hose and satin shoes to go with the dress. And a garter to throw.

"How can I ever thank you both for this?" Abby asked them.

They just smiled.

So Abby walked down the aisle of the local Methodist church with half of Catelow filling the pews and aisles, with Lucy and Hannah and her friend and coworker Marie as flower girl and maid of honor and matron of honor, respectively. Cody chose Horace Whatley as his best man, which flattered the rancher no end.

Cody's cousin, Bart Riddle, was tapped to walk Abby down the aisle, to everyone's amusement—Bart was nowhere near old enough to be anyone's father. But he seemed delighted to be part of the wedding, just the same.

And Lassiter was in the audience, dressed to kill and gathering feminine glances from all the women present.

Their vows spoken, Cody lifted the veil and looked at her for several long seconds before he kissed her tenderly and walked her back down the aisle to congratulations from all present and out the front door into a shower of rose petals.

The reception was held in the fellowship hall, catered by the local café, and Cody and Abby fed each other wedding cake for the photographer and generally had the best day of their lives captured minute by minute.

Lucy hugged them both and declared that now she had an uncle of her very own and she was going to take very good care of him. Which caused Cody to have to swallow down a very big lump in his throat as he hugged the child.

The big step he'd taken—marrying Abby—suddenly seemed like the most natural thing in the world, not worth all the agonizing he'd done over it. One thing stood out above all. They loved one another. That made everything worthwhile.

They spent their honeymoon in Jamaica, at Montego Bay, where they mostly saw the hotel room.

First times were supposed to be unpleasant, but Cody was slow and tender and patient. He built the passion with soft kisses and light brushes of his fingers, encouraging Abby to explore him as he was exploring her. Long before he moved over her, she was hot with such a fever of need that she was almost sobbing.

"Shhhh," he whispered as he moved over her and slowly, tenderly, inside her. "Slow down, honey. It's all right. There's no rush."

"Yes...there...is!" she sobbed, shivering.

He laughed softly. "Slowly, Abby," he whispered as he moved deeper and deeper, and she opened her legs and lifted her hips to encourage him, gasping with each motion of his hips against hers.

And all through it he watched her, ached for her, but paced his passion so that she was ready for him before he took the final step. And when he did, she cried out and shuddered as the pleasure reached a peak, only to reach another and another. She dug her nails into his back and he covered her mouth with his to silence her cries of pleasure. Her passionate response made him bristle with masculine pride. He took her from one plateau to another, from one side of the king-sized bed to the other, in a marathon of lovemaking that only ended when they were too exhausted to do anything more except sleep.

Abby woke to sunlight streaming through the windows and the sound of the waves lapping over the breakers onto the shore outside.

She lifted herself up and looked down at her husband, adoring him with her eyes.

He opened his own eyes and looked up at her with a slow smile. "I hope you want babies right away," he drawled.

She recalled a prophylactic placed on the bedside table, but she'd been so desperate that it was the last thing she'd thought of. She just grinned. "Lucy shouldn't be an only child," she whispered, and brushed her mouth softly over his.

"That's just what I was thinking," he teased, rolling her over to trace her soft, yielding body with his fingers. "I love kids."

"Me, too."

He drew in a long breath. "I'd love to do more of what we did last night. But..."

She linked her arms around his neck. "But...?"

He bent down. "I'm sore."

She caught her breath and burst out laughing. "Now, isn't that a coincidence? Because I'm sore, too," she whispered back.

He kissed her hungrily and wrapped her up tight in his arms. "Oh, God, I love you," he said huskily.

"I love you, too, Cody," she said softly. She searched his eyes. "I'll never cheat on you, and I'll love you forever."

He traced her eyebrows. "I was living in a fool's paradise with Debby," he said. "With my eyes closed. This time, they're wide open, and I love what I see. This is the real paradise," he whispered, and he kissed her again. "I'll take care of you, all my life."

She curled up against him with a soft sigh. "And I'll take care of you, all of mine," she murmured sleepily.

He cuddled her close and pulled the sheet over them with a contented sigh. Outside, the palm trees swayed lazily in the wind, and the sound of children laughing in the swimming pool nearby fell softly on the silence. Inside, two happy people slept in each other's arms, and their dreams were sweet.

★ ★ ★ ★ ★